"I don't want anything from you. I can provide for this baby, take care of her by myself. You needn't feel beholden to me on that account," Isla said.

Evan dipped his chin, acknowledging her pronouncement. "Be that as it may, I refuse to be a negligent father. I had one, but I will *not* be one. I intend to be a part of this child's life. As much as possible."

The dismay that crossed her face clearly said this was not the response she'd been hoping for. Other men might like to be let off the hook, but Evan stayed. Evan cared. Evan wanted this child and wanted this child *to know* he wanted this child.

"Evan..."

"I mean it, Isla," he said, hoping his tone struck the right balance. "I won't let you shut me out. I have rights."

"I know. It's just...after what you did..." She shot him a wounded look. "You deceived me and my family and tried to—"

"I was wrong to do that. I said I was sorry."

She gave a bitter laugh. "I'd be a fool to trust you again."

Dear Reader,

I have loved introducing you to the Cameron family in the Cameron Glen series, and this month the youngest sister, Isla, gets her turn for happily-ever-after! Of course, trouble lurks on the path to that happy ending. This time, trouble for the Camerons comes in the form of a corrupt and vicious businessman who has his sights set on taking possession of the Camerons' family legacy, Cameron Glen.

You met bad guy Gene Gibbs in the first book in the Cameron Glen series, *Mountain Retreat Murder*, and he lingered in the back of my mind through the other stories like a cloud of doom. He needed to be brought to justice! But how and by whom? Surely not Isla, the gentlest and most tenderhearted of the Cameron children. Oh, yes. Isla indeed!

Isla, a woman who loves openly and trusts indiscriminately, finds her world turned upside down when her destiny arrives in town in the form of Evan Murray, a tall, dark and handsome stranger...with a secret agenda. I hope you'll love Isla and Evan and their roller-coaster relationship. Meanwhile, I'm cooking up more stories about the Camerons and their extended family, so stay tuned for more adventures in Cameron Glen!

Happy reading,

Beth Cornelison

PROTECTING HIS CAMERON BABY

Beth Cornelison

HARLEQUIN
ROMANTIC
SUSPENSE

HARLEQUIN®
ROMANTIC SUSPENSE™

Recycling programs for this product may not exist in your area.

ISBN-13: 978-1-335-59368-9

Protecting His Cameron Baby

Copyright © 2023 by Beth Cornelison

For questions and comments about the quality of this book, please contact us at CustomerService@Harlequin.com.

Harlequin Enterprises ULC
22 Adelaide St. West, 41st Floor
Toronto, Ontario M5H 4E3, Canada
www.Harlequin.com

Printed in U.S.A.

Beth Cornelison began working in public relations before pursuing her love of writing romance. She has won numerous honors for her work, including a nomination for the RWA RITA® Award for *The Christmas Stranger*. She enjoys featuring her cats (or friends' pets) in her stories and always has another book in the pipeline! She currently lives in Louisiana with her husband, one son and three spoiled cats. Contact her via her website, bethcornelison.com.

Books by Beth Cornelison

Harlequin Romantic Suspense

Cameron Glen

Mountain Retreat Murder
Kidnapping in Cameron Glen
Cameron Mountain Rescue
Protecting His Cameron Baby

The Coltons of New York

Colton's Undercover Seduction

The McCall Adventure Ranch

Rancher's Deadly Reunion
Rancher's High-Stakes Rescue
Rancher's Covert Christmas
Rancher's Hostage Rescue
In the Rancher's Protection

Visit the Author Profile page at Harlequin.com for more titles.

For Paul—always

Prologue

Seattle, Washington

The doctor's expression was grim as he took a seat in the visitor's chair, a file folder with printouts and X-ray film in his hand.

Seeing the frightened look on his mother's face, Evan Murray reached for her frail hand and clasped it between his own.

"It's bad news. Isn't it?" Tracy Murray asked, her voice hoarse and weak after so many months of fighting this damn disease.

Dr. Pendelton drew a breath, as if for courage. "I'm afraid so. The tumor is still there. It's grown. And…"

His mother's hand squeezed his, and Evan could hear his own heartbeat thudding in his ears during the pregnant pause when the doctor hesitated.

"And?" Evan prompted. "Just tell us."

"Well, we've run out of treatment options. As I said

from the start, this type of cancer is so difficult to treat. We can do another round of the chemo, but that's really only to slow the progression."

Through his grip on his mother's hand, Evan could feel the shudder that rolled through her at the prospect of enduring another course of the debilitating chemotherapy. Therapy? More like poison. His gut churned knowing the physical toll and misery the months of chemo would cost his mother.

"You don't have to take the chemo if you don't want to. We can shift to a pain management strategy with—"

"You mean give up?" his mother asked.

The doctor shifted on his chair. "Well, I wouldn't call it that. But—"

"But that's what you mean." Evan pinned a hard look on the doctor. "By 'pain management strategy' what you're saying is end-of-life care. You're telling us her choice is another round of poison or throwing in the towel?"

Evan actually felt sorry for Dr. Pendelton. He could see the regret and—yes, grief—in the other man's eyes. They'd been working with the doctor for so many months, they'd gotten to know the man as a friend. Evan knew this news was difficult for the man to break to them. A miserable part of his job.

"Like I said, we can do another round of chemo, but your mother will be starting from a much weaker state this time. It will be all the harder on her and might even—"

"I don't care. I'm not a quitter." Tracy divided a look between her only child and doctor. Determination lit her eyes. "I will do the chemo or anything else as often as necessary. I won't give up if there's even a grain of hope that we might find our miracle yet."

"You're sure?" Dr. Pendelton asked.

Evan's throat tightened. He was so damn proud of his mother's fighting spirit. So devastated to know what lay ahead for her. God, if only he could take the treatments for her, endure the pain, the nausea, the weakness, the hair loss, he would in a second. He had to swallow several times before he could speak. "This is really all that's left? Clearly she's willing to try untraditional treatments or experimental medicines or—"

Evan stopped abruptly, narrowing his gaze on the doctor. The change had been subtle and short-lived, but he'd seen something in Dr. Pendelton's face. "What?"

Dr. Pendelton's fingers tightened on the file folder. "Excuse me?"

Evan aimed a finger at the older man. "When I mentioned experimental treatments, your expression changed. You thought of something, didn't you?"

The doctor sat taller and opened his mouth without saying anything. He furrowed his gray eyebrows as if debating what to say.

"Please, Dr. Pendelton, if you know of something that might help, a drug trial I could be part of, tell us. I'll do it! I'm not afraid to try something new and unproven. I mean, what's the worst that could happen? It might kill me?" His mother laughed at the irony.

The doctor's shoulders slumped. "Okay, here's the deal. There is an experimental treatment, but getting approved for the trial at your stage of the disease is only the first battle. Your insurance won't pay for it. I already had my office check. And the cost of this drug therapy is…well, astronomical. Hundreds of thousands of dollars. I read that one family's bill was over one million dollars. I know that you're already strapped, paying for current hospital bills, and I didn't think you wanted to go further into debt trying something that might not work."

"Oh," his mother said, wilting into her pillow. "I understand. Forget it, then."

Evan blinked, rotating on his seat to face his mother and gripping her hand more tightly. "What? No! Don't 'forget it.' Mom, this might be your miracle!"

She used her free hand to pat his clutching ones. "Darling, I can't die and leave you with an unsurmountable bill to pay. It would ruin your life!"

"Mom, you let me worry about that," he said, his tone fierce. "If Doc can get you in the trial, I will get the money to pay for it. Somehow."

Her expression dimmed. "Honey, thank you, but... no." She gave a soft, wry chuckle. "My God. Where would you even get that kind of money? I won't have you robbing a bank!"

"You let me worry about that." He angled his head toward the doctor. "Get her in that trial." His tone was urgent and unyielding. "Pull all the strings you have, call anyone you have to. Please. I'll get the money."

The doctor hesitated. "You're certain you want to go this route? There are no guarantees it will work."

"Evan..."

He met his mother's eyes. "If I get the money to pay for this treatment, will you fight? Will you follow the treatment plan and stay optimistic?"

"You know I will. I'm not ready to die. I will always fight for you, my dearest boy, but the cost—"

"Then it's settled." Evan nodded to the doctor. "We want in that trial. Whatever it takes."

Dr. Pendleton's jaw tightened, and he exhaled heavily. As he stood, he said, "I'll see what I can do."

"Evan, honey, I appreciate the spirit behind your offer,

but I have to reiterate my concern for you taking on so much debt. Where do you even think you'll get that much money?" The dark circles beneath his mother's eyes seemed all the more sunken and ominous as she held his gaze. "As much as I want to fight this illness, I don't want to do it at your expense. Your future."

A rock of dread settled in his gut. What had he set himself up for? Where was he going to find the kind of money he'd need to pay for the medical trial?

"I don't know. But I'll figure something out."

A little voice whispered in his ear, *You* know *who has that kind of wealth.*

He chewed the inside of his cheek and glanced away. "Maybe if I told Gene about your—"

"No!" His mother's tone was as hard and firm as he'd ever heard it.

He shifted his gaze to hers, and fire lit her blue eyes. "No, Evan. Promise me you won't tell him anything about this. Promise me you'll stay far away from him and his money. I swear to you, son, that man is nothing but trouble."

Evan sighed and gritted his back teeth. "Mom, he owes you this. At a minimum. If I promise not to tell him why I need the cash, maybe—"

"Evan!" she said, cutting him off. "No! I want *nothing* from him. *Ever.* I want nothing to *do* with him. Ever. And I beg you to stay far away from him! He is dangerous, Evan. Dangerous! Do you hear me?"

His mother's pleading expression and impassioned tone bore deep inside him, gutting him. His desire to appease her battled with his determination to find the funds to help heal her. She was the only parent he'd ever known and had been so instrumental in his life. She'd sacrificed so much for so many years to feed, clothe and educate him. Since the earliest days of his life, when his father walked out on them, they'd been a team, struggling and taking on life's challenges together.

When she'd been diagnosed with cancer and needed difficult treatments, he'd taken extended personal leave from his position as a mechanical engineer in Portland and moved back to Seattle in a heartbeat to be at her side, to encourage and take care of her. The idea of losing her to this damned disease wrenched inside him, hollowed him, scared him.

He stared at their clasped hands and felt moisture fill his eyes, lead fill his gut and grief fill his heart. He couldn't pass up any chance he had to get her the medicine, the treatment, the miracle she needed. Gene Gibbs had money, and damn it, the man owed them!

His mother jiggled his hand to draw his attention. "Evan? I mean it. Promise me you won't go to Gene about this or anything else."

Evan sat back in his chair, tugging his hands free from his mother's to drag them both down over his face. His palms scraped against his three-day beard as he groaned. He hadn't left the hospital, hadn't shaved or showered or left his mother's side in the three days since she'd collapsed in her kitchen and been rushed to the ER. His shoulders sagged, and he shoved his hands in his pockets. Crossed his fingers.

"I promise."

Chapter 1

"That stuff will kill you, ya know," Isla Cameron told her adopted brother with a grin as he filled a gigantic cup with soda at the fast-food restaurant drink station.

Sixteen-year-old Daryl raised one black eyebrow, the rest of his face stoic as he let the foam settle, then stuck the cup against the fountain lever again to top up his cup. "The sprouts you like are a breeding ground for E. coli and salmonella."

Isla laughed. "Touché, *mon frère.*"

Daryl slurped his drink and headed back to their table, and she collected packets of ketchup for her French fries. *Talk about something that'll kill ya!* She'd long ago sworn off most fried foods but still indulged in French fries now and then.

"Everything in moderation," she said under her breath, quoting her favorite professor.

Turning, she reached for the napkin dispenser just as the man beside her reached for the bin of artificial sweetener packets. Their hands bumped, and Isla snatched hers back, gushing, "Oops. So sorry!"

"No. My fault. Go ahead, please," the guy returned, gesturing for her to get what she needed.

She raised her gaze to meet his eyes with a smile, but when she saw his face, she gasped, and her stomach swooped. Before she could stop her tongue, she blurted, "It's you!"

He gave her a puzzled look. "Um, yeah. It's me. But who do you think I am?"

Her body hummed with surprise…and recognition. The satisfaction and confidence of knowing her instincts, her premonition, her…whatever this sixth sense of hers was…had been right again. She'd known she'd meet him today, and now…here he was. But what did she do about it?

At the moment, he was still staring at her with his soul-awakening dark eyes, waiting for an answer. With a wince, she waved him off. "If I told you, you'd think I was nuts."

"Well," he said and smiled as he took several pink packets and dumped them on his tray, "unless you think I'm a road-weary visitor from out of state, then you've got me confused with someone else."

He had a dimple in his cheek, an adorable dimple that softened the rugged cut of his square jaw and angular cheekbones.

"Mmm, right."

His dark hair was cut in a neat style of a businessman, and although his smile put a certain twinkle in his chocolate gaze, the stress lines around his mouth and eyes spoke of a recent heartache more than simple travel fatigue. In her chest, a twang of sympathy twisted. She longed to offer him some comfort, but again had to bite back the impulse. As far as he knew, she was just a random stranger who'd bumped into him at the local burger joint. "Out of state, huh? Where are you from?"

"Seattle. Well, Portland really, but…long story." He stirred his drink with his straw and turned as if to leave. Then hesitated. "If you're local, maybe you could recommend a place where I could stay for a couple nights while I'm in the area?"

"You don't have a reservation?" Isla asked in dismay. When he shook his head, she cringed. "Oh. That's unfortunate. Being the peak of the fall colors, this is just about the busiest tourist time of the year around here. You'll be lucky to score a room anywhere, short of a last-minute cancellation. My family's cabins have been sold out since this time last year."

He twisted his mouth in consternation. "I was afraid of that."

She thought of the bedroom in her own house that had been vacant since her sister Cait married and moved out. *You can't invite him to stay with you. He's a complete stranger*, her worldly voice said.

But he couldn't be dangerous if he was the man she was meant to be with. And, of that, she was certain. The dream, the hum in her veins as she looked in his eyes, the peace that filled her spirit as she stood here with him. Why not help him out?

Because women in today's world simply didn't invite men they've just met to move into their homes.

Patience, Isla. You've met him. Now fate will take care of the rest.

"But…" she said, stopping him as he nodded his thanks and started to move away, "you could try the

Valley Hideaway Motel. I know it doesn't look like much from the outside, and the rooms are pretty spartan, but the beds are clean and rent is cheap. I know the owner, and she runs a tight ship."

"Valley Hideaway. Good to know. Thanks." Again he turned away, and after glancing out the restaurant's large window toward the street, faced her once more.

"Turn left out of the parking lot," she said, anticipating his question, "then in about half a mile, go right on Haywood. From there it's about a mile. On the right. Green-and-white sign."

The dimple reappeared, and her heart gave a fluttering kick.

"You're a mind reader," he said with a chuckle.

She shrugged. "It was the obvious question."

He thanked her again and went to find a table. With a happy sigh, Isla joined Daryl.

"Who was that guy you were talking to?" Daryl asked, his mouth full of hamburger.

Isla slid into the booth across from her brother, and with a satisfied grin, she let the truth settle over her. "I didn't get his name, but there'll be time for that later."

Daryl wrinkled his nose. "Huh?"

She slipped a French fry from its paper sleeve and munched it, her thoughts spinning. "I had a dream last night that I'd meet him today. And then, poof! There he was, right on schedule."

Now her brother's face grew skeptical, and he furrowed his brow. "Are you talking about your weird woo-woo stuff again?"

"Yep. Weird and woo-woo. But always right."

"So, who is he? Why do you think you dreamed about him?" Daryl's expression had grown uneasy.

She sent her brother a wide smile. "He's my future. That man is my soulmate."

Evan raised his gaze to meet the cold eyes of the man who'd answered his knock on the thick and ornate door. The guy was frowning. No, more like glaring. And he was huge. Probably a good six inches taller than Evan's own six feet two inches and as much as one hundred pounds heavier, most of it muscle. *Day-um!*

Who was this guy? His heart stutter-stepped at the idea he could be a relation. He appeared close to Evan's age, somewhere in his early thirties. Half brother perhaps? Evan studied the man's pale face closer, looking for features similar to his own. Why hadn't he considered the fact that his father could have another family? Of course he could. *Double damn.*

Thirty-three years had passed since his dad had taken off, leaving his mother to raise Evan alone, unsupported. Evan wouldn't be here today, if not for—

"What do you want?" the guy asked in a gruff voice when Evan took too long to recover from the shock of the guy's size and intimidating demeanor.

"Oh, sorry. I'm looking for Gene Gibbs. This is his house, right?"

"And you are?"

Evan stuck out his hand. "Evan Murray."

The proffered hand went ignored. "What do you want?"

"Is Gene Gibbs home?"

"What do you want?" the huge guy snarled, repeating the question more slowly for emphasis.

Okay. Whatever else the mountain-sized guy was, he was a gatekeeper to get past. Evan was pretty sure that at least one of the bulges under the huge guy's jacket was a gun instead of more muscle. An armed guard… *Day-um!* Drawing a deep breath, Evan squared his shoulders and drew himself to his full height. "I have business with Mr. Gibbs. I want to talk to him. Is he home?"

"What business?"

"Personal business…and none of yours."

The gatekeeper narrowed his eyes in displeasure. "Get lost."

When the door started closing, Evan shot his hand out and braced it against the immense walnut panel. "Tell him I'm here with information about Tracy Murray."

One dark eyebrow shot up on the man's stony face. "Who's that?"

"He knows. I'll wait here."

The big man's nostrils flared with irritation, but he jerked a nod before forcing the door closed.

Evan exhaled harshly and wiped his hands on his jeans as he turned his back to the door to look out over the rolling hills of Gene Gibbs's estate. The property extended for many acres, over rolling meadows and a pond, while a thick forest around the perimeter afforded privacy—along with a high gate at the end of the driveway. Getting past that hurdle—the gate swung open when his rental car pulled up to it as if sensed by an electric eye—had lulled him into thinking he'd get in to see the estate owner easily. The gatekeeping goon had quashed that notion soon enough. But why did Gene Gibbs feel he needed the huge man to screen his visitors? Sure, Gibbs was clearly extremely wealthy, as his research had indicated, so he supposed some level of protection was warranted. Still…

His gut seesawed, and he considered leaving, giving

up his quest. Only the image, burned in his mind, of the woman he loved the most in this world—confined to a bed, pale and thin to the point of skeletal—kept him from marching back to his car and abandoning this fool's errand. Evan squeezed his eyes shut and forced down the swell of pain that rose in his chest in unguarded moments. He had to keep his composure until he'd finished his meeting with Gibbs. He knew without testing the theory that showing his grief wouldn't be helpful in winning Gibbs's cooperation.

He let his thoughts drift back to the beautiful woman with strawberry blond hair that he'd met at lunch. Though kind of quirky, she'd been as calming to him as she had been attractive. She had the kind of soothing voice and tinkling laughter that could charm a raging bull. When she'd smiled, a somewhat knowing grin, as if she knew a juicy secret about him, her clear blue eyes had sparked with life and joy. He'd wanted to invite her to sit with him, had wanted to get to know the secret lurking behind her grin. But she'd been with someone, a Black teen whom he thought he'd heard her call her brother in French. But, damn, she been hot. And intriguing. And—

He heard the door open behind him, and he spun back to face the giant guard. The man's hard expression remained stony as he jerked his head toward the inner hall and growled, "This way."

Steeling himself, Evan followed the large man into the dark home, which seemed all the dimmer because his eyes hadn't adjusted after he'd been out in the bright sunlight. The dark wood paneling in the foyer and hallway didn't help alleviate the feeling of walking into an unlit cave. Evan swept his gaze over the decor and glanced into the rooms they passed as they moved deeper into the house. He caught sight of a taxidermy deer head over a fireplace in a den, shelves of books, brass lamps and Persian rugs in tones of red, gray and black. A black leather couch and love seat sat at angles in front of the stone fireplace, and a grandfather clock stood sentinel in the corridor. The clock's chimes sounded as Evan was led past, the hands of the clock showing the time to be 2:00 p.m.

The walls of the hallway were devoid of the framed family photos that, to this day, decorated his mother's walls. Pictures of Evan at all stages of his life, right through his graduation from Oregon State University. Did Gene Gibbs not have family whose photos he wanted to savor or was the man just not the sentimental type?

"In here," his escort said, motioning him in the last room on the right.

Evan moved to the door and hesitated. He leaned in for a look and spotted the barrel-chested man with thinning dark hair sitting behind a wide mahogany desk.

The man spied him, as well, and waved him in. "Come in. Take a seat."

Evan stepped close to the desk and offered his hand. "Mr. Gibbs? I'm Evan Murray."

The older man's graying eyebrow sketched up, and as he grasped Evan's hand, his eyes narrowed and seemed to take the measure of Evan. "Tracy Murray's son?"

Evan swallowed the sharp retort that rose to his tongue and simply jerked a nod. "And before you ask, she has no knowledge I'm here and wouldn't like the idea if she did know. I'm here for my own reasons."

Gene Gibbs continued to stare at Evan with appraising dark eyes. He rested his linked hands on a middle-aged belly paunch. "And those reasons are?"

Evan lowered himself into the chair he'd been offered earlier and squared his shoulders. "Well, I'm thirty-five years old and figured it was about time I got to know my father."

Isla was feeding her goats, Pickles, Petunia and their offspring, Daisy, when a man in a dark suit crossed her yard and called out to her. "Excuse me. I'm looking for Neil and Grace Cameron. Are you Grace?"

Isla smiled and wiped her hands on the seat of her jeans. "I'm her daughter, Isla." She cocked her head to one side. "And you are…?"

"Harvey Mellinger." The man extended a hand for her to shake.

Isla winced and held her dirty hands up palm out. "Ordinarily I'd be happy to shake your hand, but I'm not sure you want me to at the moment. I've been cleaning the goat pen and treating Petunia's ear mites."

The man actually took a step backward, clearly repulsed by the notion of any kind of grime or infectious pest. Isla stifled the laugh that bubbled up but couldn't quite staunch the grin of amusement at the man's stricken expression. Mr. Mellinger recovered his composure and tugged at the sleeves of his dress shirt, which poked from the cuff of his expensive-looking suit. "Right. Well, is your mother or father at home?"

"I'm not certain, since I don't live with them," she said, softening the reply with a pleasant grin. Plenty of people made the mistake of assuming any number of her family members lived in the old, white-clapboard house with her, since it was the first house you reached after entering the property known as Cameron Glen. At least twice a week, she directed or escorted arriving guests, delivery drivers or other visitors to her parents' house. Or her sister Emma's home. Or her sister Cait's cabin. In fact, only her brother Brody and his new wife lived in town, away from the family's 150-acre vacation retreat. "My parents live up the driveway a spell. I can take you there if you'll give me a minute or two to wash up?"

Mr. Mellinger bobbed his head in agreement. "I'd appreciate that."

She strolled across her yard toward her front porch, and her visitor fell in step beside her. "Are my folks expecting you, Mr. Mellinger? Usually if someone is stopping by, Mom will give me a heads-up to watch for their arrival and point them in the right direction. While the road through the property circles around and comes back here to the front entrance, people tend to get confused by the side driveways to all the cabins and my family's homes."

"Uh, no. I don't have an appointment," he said and averted his eyes from her when she glanced up in surprise.

"May I ask the nature of your visit?" If she could spare her parents the interruption of an unwanted solicitation, she would send him away.

Mellinger drew himself more erect. "I'm a lawyer, here on official business."

A prickle of alarm chased through her. "What kind of business?"

The man's expression soured. "I'm not at liberty to disclose that information. If you'll just point me in the right direction, I can find—"

"No, no." Isla held up a finger. "I'll be right back and take you there." With another polite smile, she hurried inside her house, pausing only long enough to toe off her rubber boots and shuck out of the smock she wore over her clothes when she worked outside. Once she'd hastily scrubbed her hands clean, she hustled back to her front yard, half expecting to find her parents' visitor had headed off without her. But Mr. Mellinger was pacing the lawn restlessly and looked up when the screened door on her porch slapped noisily shut.

"This way," she said, hitching her head toward the one-lane paved driveway that meandered through the retreat property.

He trailed behind her, casting his gaze about the landscape, clearly drinking in the vibrant fall foliage that painted the surrounding mountains in shades of red, gold and orange. Closer to home, the family's fir tree crop lined the rolling hills that framed the valley that gave Cameron Glen its name. Several of the Douglas and Fraser firs would soon be harvested and sold as Christmas trees, perfuming the air with the crisp scent of evergreen.

Mellinger seemed to startle when a chipmunk scurried across the road in front of them. The furry resident of the glen darted into its hole under a wooden deck, where a bench swing hung on an A-frame in the shade beside one of the fishing ponds.

"Where do you call home, Mr. Mellinger? Or are you new to Valley Haven?" Her hometown was too small for her to have not known of the man living in the area, but Asheville and a few small towns were within easy driving distance. Local residents often did business in neighboring communities.

"Oh no." He knitted his brow in an expression that said the notion of him living in a small town was preposterous. He gave a dismissive, practically condescending chortle that chafed Isla's love for the hamlet where she'd been raised. "No, I don't live here. I'm based in Charlotte."

"Based in Charlotte?" His wording struck her like a gong, vibrating discordantly in her soul. "Does that mean your roots are elsewhere?"

"My roots?" He took a white handkerchief from an inside pocket of his suit jacket and dabbed his forehead as they walked. "What do you mean?"

"Well, *based* sounds like you're merely there for business purposes. I was just curious where your family was from. Where you call home."

He grunted as he put the handkerchief away, then gave her what seemed an insincere smile. "Home is where the job is, Ms. Cameron."

Not for me. She swallowed the reply, deciding there was no point debating the point with him. For Isla, *home* had been a concept as deep and strong as the roots of the hardwood forest that surrounded Cameron Glen. Family was a cornerstone upon which she'd built her life. This property—the hills and ponds and wildlife and pine-scented air—was her lifeblood. Her legacy. Her true north. She shoved aside the niggle of irritation for the lawyer's earlier answer and knew a moment of sympathy for him. Not everyone was as fortunate as she was to have been born into a big, loving family, live on a slice of heaven, and appreciate the blessings of the sun and land and wind.

She tipped her face toward the afternoon sky and watched a cottony cloud drift over the Smoky Mountain range just beyond her valley. Inhaling deeply, she filled herself with the essence, the energy of her world and exhaled the negative.

"Is it much farther?" her companion asked, running a finger under his collar to tug at his shirt. He did seem to be breathing harder than normal. The incline of the road didn't bother her, but she could see how the angle could be taxing for someone unaccustomed to the climb.

"Just up here." She pointed to the gravel driveway that led up to her parents' house. "I'm afraid it gets a bit steeper now."

Mr. Mellinger considered the steep driveway with a frown, muttering, "I should have driven."

Isla ascended the hill slowly for the lawyer's sake, giving him time to pause and catch his breath once, then a second time at the top of the hill so he could mop sweat from his face and neck. When he composed himself, she showed him inside, giving the front door a quick knock as she cracked it open. "Hello? Mom? Dad? You have company."

"They're out back, *mo ghràdhach,*" her Scottish grandmother called from the living room, using a Gaelic endearment.

She led Mr. Mellinger in to meet Nanna and offered him a seat before she stepped outside to fetch her parents from their garden. Her mother wore a large floppy hat and gardening gloves as she cut flowers and added them to the basket hooked over her arm. Her father appeared to be pulling up the last of the tomato and bean plants from that summer and prepping the ground for an autumn crop of leafy greens, broccoli and shallots.

"Good afternoon," she called, shielding her eyes from the sun. "I hate to drag you away from your gardening, but there's a gentleman in the house who has asked to speak to you two. Can you come in?"

Her mother straightened and put a hand at the small of her back as she stretched. "Who is it?"

She gave her parents the man's name with a shrug.

"I don't know him, but he said he's a lawyer and has business with you."

Her father frowned as he stepped over the chicken-wire fencing intended to keep rabbits and deer from munching the family's vegetables. "Business with us? Grace, what could that be about?"

"Well," her mother replied, "one way to find out." She removed her hat and used the back of her wrist to swipe at the moisture beading on her temple. "Let's go talk to the man."

When they reached the living room, Nanna was entertaining Mr. Mellinger with tales of her medical issues. "—can live with the pain in my knees, but the arthritis in my hands makes it near impossible to crochet anymore." She lifted the pink yarn project in her lap to show him. "I've been working on this doll blanket for my great-granddaughter since July, but I can only do a couple rows at a time. I mean for it to be a Christmas gift."

Mr. Mellinger gave Nanna a polite smile, then rose to his feet, relief crossing his face, when her mother and father entered the room.

Introductions were made, handshakes exchanged and Mr. Mellinger accepted her mother's offer of iced tea, which Isla fetched from the kitchen. When she returned with the cold drink, Mr. Mellinger had already started his spiel.

"—would like to offer you the opportunity to retire a wealthy man, Neil. May I call you Neil?"

"Uh, sure," her father said hesitantly, his baloney radar obviously blinking red, as Isla's was. "What sort of opportunity?"

"Well, I have been authorized by my employer to offer you a substantial—" he paused and raised his eyebrows for emphasis "—very substantial price for the property here at Cameron Glen."

Nanna snorted.

Her father smiled as he glanced at her mother, who was clearly trying to mask her reaction to the lawyer's opening salvo. For her part, Isla bit the inside of her cheek and quashed the flutter that always stirred in her belly whenever even the suggestion of the ownership of Cameron Glen leaving her family came up.

"I'm sorry, Mr. Mellinger," Neil said calmly. "Cameron Glen is not for sale."

"Not even for a *very substantial* price?" the lawyer countered.

"Not even for all the gold in Fort Knox." Her father stood. "It's seems you've wasted your trip out here. I could have told you this in a phone call."

Mellinger turned to face her mother, plastering on a cajoling smile. "Grace, the kind of money my employer is willing to offer would set you and your children up for the rest of your lives. You could buy anything you wanted, travel anywhere you wanted, live anywhere you wanted. Don't you want that for your family?"

Her mother lifted her chin, a gracious expression in place, but Isla knew the spark in her mother's eyes well. Mellinger had ticked her off. "It's *Mrs. Cameron*, if you don't mind. As far as your employer's generous offer... I already live where I wish to. I don't want for anything, and my greatest desire for my family has nothing to do with money and everything to do with love and happiness and the privilege to raise their families on this beautiful property, as the Camerons have for three generations."

"But financial security—" Mellinger started.

"Sir, was something about my son's 'Cameron Glen

is not for sale' unclear to you?" Nanna said, frost in her tone.

Mellinger cut a glance to Nanna over his shoulder and chuckled awkwardly. "Everything is for sale at the right price."

Isla barely contained a groan, and she took a seat on the overstuffed couch next to her mother.

Mellinger glanced from Nanna to Isla and sighed. "Neil, maybe we could finish this conversation in private?"

"No need," her father said. "I have no secrets from my family, and you already have my answer, so…" He spread his hands as if to say "what's the point?"

The lawyer shifted on his chair, took a sip of tea and took out a pen. He scribbled something on a small notepad and tore the sheet off for her father. "This is our offer. That's a lot of zeros, Neil."

Her father glanced at the note, his nostrils flaring. "It is. It is also insulting."

"Insulting?" Mellinger barked a laugh and rubbed his chin. "Wow. You do drive a hard bargain. All right. Double that number. Does that change your mind?"

Isla sighed audibly. She couldn't help it. A glance at her mother, whose lips were pinched in a taut line and whose hands were balled on her lap, confirmed that she too was struggling to bite back a rude response.

"Double?" her father asked, and the intrigue in his tone drew Isla's attention, her pulse scattering.

"Yes. Double." Mellinger leaned forward in his seat.

"Well, that changes everything," her father said, his expression one of awe and excitement.

Isla's eyebrows snapped together in confusion. Her gut bunched in horror. "Dad?"

"Really?" the lawyer said, his tone bright. He rose

to his feet with a smug smile tugging his cheek. "We have a deal?"

As if a light switch had been flipped, her father's awe disappeared. A darkness filled his eyes, and his features grew stony. "No, you vulture!" He took a large step closer to Mellinger and poked a finger in the lawyer's chest. Through gritted teeth, he snarled, "I said my family's land, our home, our heritage is not for sale, and I meant it. You could triple that offer, add as many zeros as you want, and my answer would be the same. Cameron Glen will *never* leave my family. Period."

Mellinger's eyes narrowed, and he drew his shoulders back. "It would not be smart of you to reject this offer. My employer is being more than generous, and your refusal will not sit well with him."

Her father matched the lawyer's glower, not backing down an inch. "Is that a threat?"

The escalating tension rippled through Isla like the first rumbles of thunder ahead of a violent storm. The air in the room crackled with ominous potential, and the negative energy sparked along her nerves, making her tremble from her core.

"Call it what you want, but if I go back to my employer without a deal, he's likely to resort to a different strategy to secure ownership of this property. He doesn't take no for an answer. Ever."

Her father folded his arms over his chest and cocked his head to one side. "And who is your employer?"

"He wishes to remain anonymous for the time being."

"Is it Gene Gibbs?" Isla said, drawing the lawyer's attention. Judging by the flicker of dismay that crossed the man's face, she knew she'd caught him off guard. And that her guess was right. "It is, isn't it?" She scoffed bitterly, "We've told that man to take a flying leap more than once. What is his problem?"

"The problem will be yours if you don't give him what he wants."

Her mother shot to her feet. "That's definitely a threat. And we don't deal with blackmailers or extortionists, Mr. Mellinger."

"Oh, but you will." Mellinger tugged at his tie, straightening it. "One way or another, you'll have to deal with the man and his interest in this property. He aims to have it, and have it he will."

"We're done here," her father said, stepping aside so the lawyer could leave. "I want you out of my house."

"I'll go, but we're not done. Not by a long shot. You'll be hearing from Mr. Gibbs again, one way or another."

Chapter 2

Isla shivered and watched Mellinger stalk past her father to the front hall. After the door slammed and they saw Mellinger cross the front lawn and head back down the driveway, Isla released the breath she'd been holding.

Her father moved to the chair he'd been using earlier and sank down with a weary sigh. The lawyer's threat had rattled him. Proof of that was etched in the lines around his eyes and the furrow of his brow.

Guilt pinched Isla. If she'd pressed the man for more information about his business with her parents, she could have sent him away immediately and spared her family this ugly encounter.

"Crivvens!" Isla said, borrowing one of Nanna's favorite expressions.

"And help ma Boab!" Nanna added, setting her crochet project aside and rubbing her swollen knuckles.

"I'm sorry, Mom, Dad. If I'd realized what he was—"

"No," her father said, his voice dark. He held up a hand and took a breath before smiling an apology for his tone and continuing, "Nothing about this is your fault, love. Don't waste another minute thinking that."

"Do you think this Gene Gibbs could really make trouble for us?" her mother asked in a quiet voice, as if afraid to bring the threats about by speaking of them.

"I've heard some worrying things about him in town," Isla said. "He's known to be a dirty player."

Her mother shot her a worried look. "Dirty how?"

"A brutal loan shark. A ruthless real estate developer. And…more." Isla exhaled a sigh. "Remember my friend Chris from high school? He's an officer with the police department now, and we were catching up at Ma's Mountain Diner the other day. When I mentioned some of the troubles our family has dealt with in the past couple years, he said law enforcement is finding a lot of recent crimes in the area lead back to Gene Gibbs in some fashion. Some directly, some indirectly. Nothing they can pin on him with enough certainty of conviction though. Apparently, if it's profitable, whether it's illegal or not, Gibbs has his fingers in the pie." She fisted her hands in her lap adding, "He may even have had some connection to the human trafficking ring that took Fenn last year."

Even mentioning her niece's kidnapping made Isla sick to her stomach.

Neil jolted upright and scrubbed a hand over his face. "I already knew he had something to do with the debt Cait's ex-boyfriend and his brother got into—the reason behind the thefts from Jake's construction company. He does seem to be involved in a lot of trouble our family incurs."

"What a *jobby*," Nanna grumbled.

Isla sputtered a shocked laugh, hearing her grandmother use the rude Scottish term. "Nanna!"

"Well, it's true! He should be flushed down the loo!"

Neil paced across the room and gazed out the front window before turning to her. "Isla dear, would you mind heading back down to the front of the property to make sure Mr. Mellinger found his way out?"

"Not at all." Isla pushed to her feet and crossed the room to give her father a kiss on the forehead. "Try not to worry, Dad. I'm sure everything will be all right. As long as there is a Cameron with breath in their lungs, Cameron Glen will always belong to our family."

Gene Gibbs continued to stare at Evan with an even, subtly hostile expression. "And you're under the illusion that I am your father. Is that it?"

"It's no illusion. My mother's not a liar. And *she* is faithful in her relationships." The slight quirk of Gene's eyebrow told Evan his father had understood the implication in his tone. "But I'm perfectly willing to take a DNA test if you need proof I am the two-year-old boy you abandoned thirty-three years ago."

Gene chuckled and drummed his fingers on the armrest of his large desk chair. "You certainly have Tracy's sharp tongue, I'll grant you that." He propped his elbows on the arms of the chair now and steepled his fingers. "As far as a DNA test…" He angled his head. "That depends on what you want from me. Why are you here? Because I don't buy for a minute the idea you traveled all the way across the country just to have a few beers with your old man and reminisce."

Across the country…

Evan sat straighter and gritted his back teeth. After Gene had walked out on them, Evan's mother had moved to Seattle to get them as far away from Gene's orbit as she could. That Gene might know where they settled was a bit unnerving. "How long have you known where I live?"

Gene pulled a face as if that should have been obvious. "It's just good business to stay informed on all fronts. Social media and the web have made my job keeping track of business associates a lot easier."

His father's unctuous grin turned Evan's stomach, and he frowned. "Is that what I am? Business?"

"Potentially. You're here now, aren't you? Proof enough that I was right to keep tabs on you and your mother."

Evan pressed his lips into a grim line, and he grated, "And yet you never saw fit to reach out in all these years. Nothing on holidays or birthdays."

He wasn't sure why he'd delivered the condemnation with such scorn and heat. He'd not been given the chance to form a bond with Gene Gibbs, had been perfectly happy growing up with one parent. His mother had given him enough love, support and encouragement for two parents. So why did he feel such resentment toward this man? Certainly getting on Gibbs's wrong side didn't serve him well if he wanted the man to do him any favors. And he needed a huge favor.

Gene appeared to take the chastisement in stride. He waved one hand lackadaisically, as if swatting away an annoying fly. "I don't do family or sentimentality."

Evan took a moment to shove down the tension and bitterness that had roiled to a boil inside him. He held Gene's gaze levelly and exhaled slowly, intentionally relaxing his grip on the armrest of his chair, discreetly stretching the kinks from his neck muscles.

"I'm a busy man, Mr. Murray. If you have something

besides thirty-year-old resentment to discuss with me, I suggest you get to it. Or I'll have Leon see you out." He directed his gaze to the office door.

Evan turned to find Mr. Mountain-sized Gatekeeper standing sentinel just inside the room, blocking the door. He hadn't realized the other man had lingered at the door, eavesdropping, and a stir of rancor tripped through him.

Facing Gibbs again, Evan dug deep for patience and calm. He was here for his mom. She was what mattered. And Gene Gibbs could be her last hope for affording the expensive medical trial.

Mustering his courage and humility, he said, "I need your help."

Chapter 3

His father's eyes narrowed with suspicion. "What kind of help?"

Evan scratched his chin, picturing his mother wasting away in her hospital bed. She'd begged him not to come here, warned him away from Gene Gibbs, but Evan had seen no other option. He *had* to find the money to get his mother the promising experimental treatments. "My mother is dying. She has cancer and has run out of options, other than an experimental treatment that her insurance won't cover. Her doctor recently got her invited to join the trial, but it will cost—" He paused and sighed. "Well, a hell of a lot more than she or I have. I've already sold my house and her car to cover previous bills. We need the first payment by the end of the week or they'll give her spot in the trial to someone else."

Gene scoffed and angled a look toward the door where

his oversize assistant stood. "It's always about money. Am I right, Leon?"

"You are right, boss."

Evan gritted his teeth. "It's about saving my mother's life."

Gibbs shrugged one shoulder. "We all gotta die sometime."

Heat flashed through Evan, and he surged to his feet. "You coldhearted prick!"

Leon took a step forward, and Gibbs waved him off, meeting Evan's eyes levelly. "Sit down."

Still seething, Evan glared at Gibbs for several tense seconds, his body bowed up defensively. His breath sawed roughly from his flared nostrils, and he itched to smash his fist into his father's flat expression. "You have history with my mother. You were intimately involved with her for five years, and she worked her ass off to pay your tuition for your business degree, based on your promise to marry her when you graduated—a promise you didn't keep."

Gibbs looked unconcerned by Evan's mention of the breach of faith. "Like I said—I don't do family."

Evan squeezed his hands into fists as dismay hardened into disgust. "Does her life really mean so little to you? Can you not dig deep enough in that stone heart of yours to muster even a little compassion for her?"

The older man's face darkened, and in a steely voice, he repeated, "Sit down."

Shaking the tension from his hands, Evan gathered the frayed edges of his composure and dropped back into the chair.

"All right then." Gibbs folded his arms over his chest and angled his head. "Now, where were we? Oh yes. You want money from me." He pursed his lips and flapped one hand. "And what is it you intend to offer me in exchange for my money?"

Evan flinched internally. "Uh…in exchange?"

His father shot him a wry grin and barked a dry laugh. "You didn't honestly think I was going to just hand over—how much did you say? 'A hell of a lot?'—of my money to a perfect stranger without getting anything in return. Did you?"

Evan squeezed the chair's armrests, his gut roiling. "I'm your son. We're talking about my mother, someone you once cared about—"

"Allegedly."

"What?"

"Until I see that DNA test, I have no proof you're anyone but a swindler, looking for a payday."

Evan swallowed. Sighed. "I've already said I'd take a DNA test to prove it."

Gibbs grunted as he uncrossed his arms and leaned forward. He pinned a hard look on Evan and curled up his lip. "Yes. But why would *I* bother taking a test that—" The landline phone on the desk beside him rang, and Gibbs fell abruptly silent. He glanced at the display on the phone's small screen, and his expression brightened. He snatched up the receiver. "Tell me you closed the deal. Did you get Cameron to sign?"

Gibbs's face flashed from expectant to irritated, like the flip of a switch. Barking an obscenity, he slammed his fist on his desktop so hard everything sitting on it rattled.

Evan jolted and shifted uneasily in his seat as a flood of adrenaline kicked his pulse up a notch. He gripped the arms of the chair harder as he followed his father's end of the conversation.

"You told them the price I offered, didn't you? I mean,

good God, that's twice what the property is worth. What does that old goat want?" Gibbs's jaw hardened, and his eyes grew colder. "He said what?" The knuckles in his father's hand blanched as he squeezed the receiver, scowling. "Well, maybe that's our play, then. What sort of accident can we arrange that would eliminate an entire family?"

Evan's neck prickled. Holy crap! Was Gibbs planning to murder an entire family to get his way on a land deal? He realized he was gaping at his father with an incredulous look and quickly schooled his face. Stared down at his shoes. Strained to hear the rest of what Gibbs was plotting over the bass drum of his blood in his ears.

"Oh, you don't think I'm serious? If the Camerons aren't swayed by money, then perhaps they'll come to the negotiating table if they know the lives of all those children and grandkids are at stake. If family legacy is what's blocking the deal, then we eliminate the problem."

The man is evil, Evan. He has no soul. I swear he doesn't. Stay away from him. Evan closed his eyes as his mother's warnings echoed in his brain. She'd been right. His father, it seemed, was discussing the slaughter of innocents to advance a business deal. He'd heard of that sort of cold, brutal tactic within drug cartels or the Mafia, but…for God's sake! Did his father fancy himself some sort of don? Were his threats real or just hot air and posturing? He really didn't want to know the truth.

Evan's mouth had gone dry. He tried to swallow, to choke down the rise of bile in his throat. He shouldn't have come. Had he really thought that a man willing to walk out on his two-year-old son and the child's mother and completely ignore their needs for thirty-three years was going to jump at the chance to help them now?

"Because I've already sent everyone in my employ to try to negotiate with them. I'm running out of opt—"

More than Gibbs's abrupt silence, a sense of being skewered by a hard stare brought Evan's head up. His eyes darted to meet his father's piercing glare.

"I have an idea," Gibbs told the person on the phone, "Stay by the phone." With that, he hung up and turned more fully toward Evan.

An uneasy feeling skittered down Evan's back and, resigning himself to the fact that he'd not be getting blood from this turnip, that it had been a mistake to try, he pushed to his feet. "I should go. You're obviously busy."

"Wait." Gibbs stood and walked around his desk to stand in front of Evan.

Well, now he knew from whom he'd inherited his height and wide shoulders. Gibbs was almost as large as his henchman, Leon.

His father gave him an intense up-and-down scrutiny, as if he were sizing up a bull for purchase at the county fair.

"Are you married?" Gibbs asked.

The left-field question threw Evan enough that he could only frown his confusion at his father for a moment. "Um…"

Gibbs waved off his answer. "Never mind. Doesn't matter. What the wife doesn't know doesn't hurt her, huh?"

The man's attitude toward fidelity rankled, and Evan lowered his brow as he growled, "It matters to me. I'm not married, but if I were, I would never cheat, if that's what you are saying."

Gibbs gave him a negligent shrug, then glanced to his henchman. "Leon, would you say Mr. Murray was handsome?"

Once again, the unexpected question puzzled Evan. Clearly Leon had been caught off guard, as well, because the other man blinked and shifted his feet before answering hesitantly, "Well, he's not my type. I don't look at men that way." When Gibbs raised both eyebrows, indicating he wanted a better answer to his question, Leon added, "But Sally would probably say he was. I've heard her call his sort *hot*."

Speaking of hot, heat crept up Evan's neck until even his ears tingled. Bad enough to have his father sizing him up like livestock, but to be graded on his appearance was just…humiliating. Evan huffed his frustration and turned toward the door. "Enough. I'm done here."

"No, you're not," Gibbs returned, and Leon stepped in front of the door to prevent his exit.

Working hard to rein in his anger—he *really* didn't want to rile this dangerous man's temper—Evan faced his father. "I am. If you aren't going to help me get the money I need, then there's no point in my—"

"I've changed my mind."

Evan took a moment to replay what he'd heard so that his stunned brain could catch up with his ears. "What do you mean?"

Gibbs snorted. "Just what I said. I've decided to give you the money. All of it."

Evan gaped at Gibbs as his mind whirled. He scrambled mentally to make calculations, sort out reasons and guess at the man's motives. Clearly something had changed when he got the phone call. A business deal he was willing to kill a family to close had gone sour, and now he was offering Evan hundreds of thousands of dollars for his mother's medical expenses? Evan was highly suspicious, maybe even a bit anxious about what that meant.

The voice that had said his visit today was a mistake shouted at him again. *Get out while you can. Don't get involved with this man.*

"I've changed my mind too. I don't want your money." He faced Leon again—and the quandary as to how to get past the behemoth.

"So then you're choosing to let your mother die?" Gibbs asked.

Ice sluiced to Evan's core. He saw his mother's ravaged face in his mind's eye, thought of the terrible days and excruciating pain she'd endured. He'd sat beside her sickbed feeling bereft and helpless to do anything for her. Could he really walk away from a chance to get her a promising new treatment? To offer her a glimmer of hope? To give her some quality of life for many more years to come?

I'd wanted to hold my grandchildren, she'd told him in tears the night before he left town.

You will, he'd promised her.

Her failing hope and despondency was one of the reasons he'd come on this fool's errand.

Slowly, he faced his father again and took a deep breath. "What's the catch?"

A smug grin spread across Gibbs's face, and he returned to his desk chair. "Sit down. We'll talk."

Talk. Such a mild, harmless-sounding word. But as Evan moved back to the chair across from his father, every fiber of his being screamed that he was, in fact, making a deal with the devil.

Chapter 4

Isla stood by her parents' living room window and stared out at the sprinkle of colorful leaves that drifted like snow to cover the lawn with each rustling breeze. Gibbs's attorney had cast such a shadow over her mood, she found it hard to maintain the optimism she typically offered the family. She saw it as her duty to keep her brothers and sisters focused on the good things in life when times got hard. And good grief, they'd seen a lot of trying times lately.

But they had survived—thrived, even, despite the trials. There. That was the bright side she needed to focus on, she thought, and forced a smile to her lips.

"Isla? Want to share? I could use a grin about now," her oldest sister, Emma, said.

"She's probably thinking about her *soulmate*," Daryl said with a droll timbre.

"Her what?" Nanna asked, perking up.

Isla sent her younger brother a withering glance, but

mentally acknowledged the leap of joy in her core at the mention of the handsome man from the restaurant. Keeping a calm demeanor, she said, "Let's not get sidetracked with that right now. There's not anything to report…yet." She turned to her father. "Did your lawyer have any advice when you spoke to him this afternoon?"

"As long as we don't sign anything, Cameron Glen is safe from Gibbs. But everyone in this family must be vigilant about avoiding legal traps and verbal agreements on the phone, or any other tricks he might employ to squeeze his foot in a legal crack."

All around the room, where her siblings and their spouses had gathered after dinner, heads bobbed in understanding.

"We can file charges of harassment against him if he persists. Or get a restraining order if he proves to be a physical threat, but I'd rather not go that route prematurely." Neil scratched his jaw and shared a look with Grace before adding, "I think any legal move on our part at this time would do more to inflame Gibbs's ego than anything else. Better if we let things lie. We'll let our no be no and move on."

"Of course, if he takes any further provocative measures, we won't sit idly by," Grace assured her children.

Her brother Brody's new wife, Anya, sidled close to Isla and whispered, "Soulmate? Do tell."

Isla couldn't help the grin that sprang to her lips. When Anya saw the smile, her own face brightened, and she nudged Isla with her elbow. "So there is someone!"

Their whispers caught Brody's attention, and he arched a curious eyebrow.

"I can keep a secret," Anya said, her dark eyes twinkling with mischief and intrigue.

Isla snorted a laugh that drew more querying looks

from her family. "In this family? Anya, there is no such thing as a secret in the Cameron family. You should just get used to that fact of life now, my sister."

"Need I remind you how you hounded me for details of my relationship with Brody from the moment we met?" Anya hooked her arm through Isla's. "Turnabout's fair play."

Isla squeezed her sister-in-law's hand. "When there is something to tell, you'll be among the first to know. I promise. I know nothing about him other than a whisper in my soul that our lives will be intertwined. The rest is up to fate."

Evan sat in the small motel room he'd rented, thanks to the tip from the lady at Burger Palace, and stared at the file in his lap. Scanning the pages of information his father had compiled on the Cameron family felt… *skeevy.* Voyeuristic. He hated making himself complicit in Gibbs's scheme to wrest the family's land from them. Having heard Gibbs talk of more violent means to change the landowners' minds about selling, however, he considered the fact that he might be sparing the family from whatever tragedy Gibbs had intended to inflict.

He studied the pictures of the property, Cameron Glen, and could understand both why Gibbs wanted it and why the Camerons would refuse to sell. The place was beautiful. Idyllic even. Well landscaped with trees, ponds, creeks and flowers, surrounded by the mountains, a productive Christmas tree farm, lovely cabins, old-growth forests and wildlife. Evan dragged a hand down his face and heaved a conflicted sigh.

Gibbs had conscripted Evan to the job of changing the Camerons' minds about selling the property. A Herculean task, to be sure, but if he could convince the family to make a deal with Gibbs, his father had agreed to pay his mother's medical debt in full. The businessman had insisted Evan sign a contract with the terms spelled out. The offer had been too tempting to resist. Not because of the money, but because it was a real chance to save his mother. Gibbs had even written Evan a check for the down payment toward the medical trial's costs. He'd gone straight to a bank to wire the cash to his mother so she could start the treatment plan. Gibbs had also forked over a healthy first week's salary for living expenses while Evan was in town, working on his assignment.

His assignment.

Evan scoffed. That was certainly a euphemistic term for what he was doing. And while he'd eased his own conscience by swearing not do anything illegal and reminding himself that the Cameron family would always retain the option to refuse any offers, he still had a queasy feeling in his gut. Gibbs wanted him to worm his way into the family's trust, tactically chip away at the patriarch's stone-wall resistance by whatever means he could, and ultimately convince a majority of the family that it was in their best interest to sell Cameron Glen to him. As a shell for his father. Once in Evan's control, Evan would sell the 150-acre property to Gibbs, collect a small fortune to take back to Seattle and cut ties with Gene Gibbs forever. Blood relation be damned.

He flipped more pages, more pictures in the file Gibbs had created—fodder to manipulate, extort and blackmail the family.

"A good businessman knows everything about the people he's dealing with," Gibbs had repeated when Evan expressed dismay over the stalker-ish file.

When he reached pictures of the family, clearly

taken with a telephoto lens without their knowledge, his misgivings keyed higher. But he dutifully studied the images, reading the tidbits of information about each family member, learning things that might help him discover an "in" with the family.

Neil, age 68, retired. Enjoys golf, fishing, shares responsibilities for Christmas tree crop with son, Brody, age 30. There were pictures of each of the men.

Grace, age 65, retired. Enjoys gardening, tutors reading at elementary school, sells vegetables at local farmers' market in summer with assistance from youngest daughter, Isla, age 28. Evan studied the picture of the attractive older woman, and his chest squeezed. The woman was a mother, a grandmother, by all appearances, a kind woman who gave back to the community. A woman not unlike his own mother, before cancer had drained so much vitality from her.

He flipped to the next picture, and his breath caught. He lifted the picture now on top of the stack and held it closer to the pool of light from the floor lamp behind him. *Isla.*

His heart pounded as he stared at the beautiful woman with sun shining in her strawberry blond hair, caught midlaugh, her face alight with joy.

It's you!

He replayed what details he could remember of the brief exchange he'd had with the woman at the fast-food restaurant earlier today. He was certain this was the same woman. Maybe he shouldn't be too surprised he'd run into Isla Cameron already. Valley Haven was a small town.

Just the same, his pulse was erratic as he read the information below her photo.

Isla Cameron, age 28. Student, master's program at

UNC Asheville studying public health. Teaches yoga. Enjoys gardening, animal rescue, environmental causes. With her mother, raises vegetables for produce stand at local farmers' market.

Evan sat back and studied the photo of Isla another minute or two before flipping through more photos of the family.

The oldest Cameron daughter and her husband, Emma and Jake Turner. Two children—Fenn, age sixteen, and Lexi, age five.

Middle daughter and Cameron Glen rental property manager, Cait and her husband, Matt Harkney. Stepson Eric, age seventeen.

Evan hesitated, furrowing his brow as recognition prickled. He'd just read a military thriller by an author named Matt Harkney. Sliding his finger down the page to read about Cait's husband, he found his work listed as fiction and true crime author.

"Well, I'll be damned."

Next was another photo of Brody Cameron, owner of a landscaping company, and a newspaper clipping of an engagement announcement in which he was posed with a beautiful South Asian woman. Anya Patel. ER nurse.

Flipping the page, Evan found a picture of a light-skinned Black teenager whom Evan recognized as the guy Isla had sat with at the burger joint today. *Daryl, age 16, adopted son of Neil and Grace Cameron. Student at Valley Haven High School. Plays football for school team. Enjoys video games.*

Evan chuckled wryly. What teenage boy these days didn't enjoy video games?

Flora Cameron, age 89, widowed. Lives with son Neil and Grace. Enjoys yarn crafts and baking.

The file went on to include printouts of banking rec-

ords, lists of car models and license plate numbers—
each page more intrusive and creepier than the last.
Gibbs had been thorough. The file had a pretty exhaus-
tive background profile of each member of the Cameron family. At the back were newspaper clippings. He
skimmed the headlines about a serial murderer, human
trafficking arrests, embezzling at a local construction
company. One article was titled "Miracle on the Mountain." He set these aside to go through later, unsure what
the new bits had to do with the Camerons.

How was he supposed to insert himself into the family dynamic? Form a relationship that earned their trust?
Who was the key? The teenage son? Neil? Maybe the
son-in-law whose book he'd read? How far could he
take the reader and fan angle without reminding Matt
Harkney of Stephen King's *Misery*?

Flipping back toward the front of the file, he returned to the photo of Isla Cameron. She was the only
adult child of Neil and Grace who had no mention of a
spouse. He steepled his fingers and touched them to his
lips as he considered this fact. Was she his entrée into
the family? Could he use the fact that they'd already
met to finagle—

He scoffed and dismissed that idea. No way would
she remember him as the random guy she'd said three
words to at a fast-food restaurant. If not for her beautiful red-gold hair and bright, memorable smile, he might
not have recognized her. Which left arranging for them
to "meet" again. But how?

The car came from nowhere.
Crunch!
Isla gasped, then cringed at the idea of her new Prius
getting dented. The fender bender might be minor in the

grand scheme of things, but even minor wrecks could mean a huge headache dealing with insurance and repair shops and... *Crivvens.*

Shoulders sagging, she turned off the engine and shouldered open the driver's door to get out and examine the damage.

"Oh jeez! I'm so sorry!" the driver of the other car, a dark-haired man with trendy sunglasses and a Seahawks T-shirt said as he climbed from his Ford sedan and met Isla at her back bumper. "Are you all right?"

"I, um..." As she stared at her puckered fender, a parade of directions her brother-in-law had given her to follow, things *not* to say if you're in a car accident, marched through Isla's head. Jake had been hoping to protect her from nasty repercussions of living in the highly litigious society the United States had become. "I'm fine. Really. Just...a little shaken." She cast him a fleeting glance. "And you?"

"Just a little shaken. Not stirred."

His James Bond joke startled a chuckle from her, and she turned to face him, regarding him fully for the first time.

He slid off his sunglasses saying, "Hello. I'm Bond. Evan Bond."

And she gasped. It was *him*. Again. Kismet was working its magic, just as she'd expected. She shook the hand he offered, her attention drawn to his stunning dark brown eyes. A tingle raced through her, though she couldn't say whether the source was his sexy eyes, the firm grip of his hand or the devil-may-care smile that lit his face. Or maybe just her soul recognizing his touch. Regardless, her breath backed up in her lungs, and she needed an extra beat to find her voice. "Cameron. Isla Cameron."

He bowed his head as if meeting royalty. "Pleasure to meet you, Ms. Cameron."

She blinked and gave her head a small shake. "Uh, perhaps it is a pleasure, but did you have to hurt Betty in the process?"

His eyes widened a bit with guilt and dismay. "Someone's hurt?"

She pointed to her loose bumper, cracked taillight and dented back quarter panel. "My car, Betty White."

Now he laughed. "You named your car Betty White?"

Isla straightened her shoulders. "I did. As an homage to a woman who did great work advocating for animals. And because the car is white. Well, when I get around to washing her, she is."

Evan—she supposed that was really his name, even if she doubted the Bond part—gave her a funny look. "She? So you're all in. Even with the pronouns?"

Isla angled her head and narrowed her gaze. "Something wrong with that?"

Evan's eyebrows rose, and he held up a hand. "Sorry. Didn't mean to offend. I, uh, admire your commitment to the whole car-naming thing."

She made a sound in her throat she'd learned from her Scottish grandmother that expressed both skepticism and dismissal.

The driver of the car behind Evan's sedan honked.

"We should exchange information, but—" he aimed his thumb over his shoulder to the impatient driver "—I should move out of the lane first."

"Of course." She gave a nod, excusing him.

He raised a hand as if making a vow as he backed toward his vehicle. "I promise I'm not fleeing the scene. I'm just moving—" he glanced down the row of parked cars and pointed to an empty space "—there."

"I trust you," she said with a smile.

Her reassurance seemed to stop him for a moment, and something akin to guilt flickered briefly on his face. She puzzled over his reaction as she located her insurance papers in her glove box, a pen and notepad from her purse to write down his contact information. She took a moment to consider the epochal dimensions of what was happening, telling herself to be fully present, to savor every second of this life-changing event. She was about to find out her soulmate's name, discover the street where he lived, learn how to contact him in the future...

One day she'd be able to tell her children, *their children and grandchildren*, about this moment and the one when they'd met at the condiment counter at Burger Palace. Not the most romantic setting, but who was she to criticize fate? It was what it was. They'd have other romantic moments. Hikes in the mountains. Sunset picnics. Mornings in bed with the rain falling outside.

"Okay." The male voice behind her startled her out of her daydream. "I have the rental car registration and my insurance card. What else do you think you'll need?"

"Um." She pressed a hand over the fluttering of her heart. "Shouldn't we, um, call the police?"

He blinked, and the flash of guilt returned before he shook his head. "Since this is a parking lot, and therefore private property, I don't think the police get involved. At least that's been my experience."

She twitched a grin. "You make a habit of crashing into people in parking lots, do ya?"

He chuckled and pulled a skeptical frown. "Technically, I think you'd be considered at fault since you were backing out and I was already in the lane."

She tipped her head and matched his dubious look.

"Perhaps, technically. But you were coming down the aisle rather fast. I had looked, and the way was clear before you came around the end of the row and…" She aimed a finger toward her dented bumper.

He held up both hands, palms toward her. "Hey, I don't want to fight over fault. Can we say it was mutual and forget filing a claim?"

She twisted her mouth, gave her Prius a pointed look, then walked two parking spaces over to his Ford and examined his nearly pristine front bumper. "Seems you get the best end of that deal."

Evan scratched his chin, then bent to rub his thumb over a thin scratch. "Hmm. Yeah, I see your point." He straightened and met her gaze. "Well, seeing as how I might not have a place to sleep if not for your tip about the Valley Hideaway Motel—"

She sputtered a laugh. "Then you do recognize me!"

He hiked up a corner of his mouth, dimpling his cheek in the process. "How could I forget a face as beautiful as yours?"

She laughed harder and wagged a finger. "Nope. You're not going to charm your way out of this one. You crumpled Betty White's fender. My girl is wounded."

"*We* crumpled Betty White's fender," he amended, waving a finger back and forth between them.

She imitated her grandmother's low rumble of dissatisfaction and doubt in her throat again, but she liked his use of the plural pronoun. As if they were already connected, already a team. A crumpled fender wasn't such a huge price if it brought her closer to her destiny.

Evan felt like the lowest-of-low dirtbags. He watched Isla climb back into her car and drive away from the parking lot before returning to his rented sedan with self-deprecating thoughts and a groan.

Having waited on the side of the highway outside Cameron Glen, then followed her to the grocery store, he'd watched for her to return to her car so he could purposely hit her car as she backed out and stage the meeting with her. He may have accomplished his goal, but the underhanded tactic left him off-kilter and wanting a shower. He'd not be able to wash away the sense of slime and deceit though. His association with Gibbs, his agreement to help fleece Isla and her family made him worse than his father. His father had clearly chosen a path of lawlessness and had no respect for others. Gene Gibbs didn't care who got hurt in his pursuit of wealth and power.

But Evan did. And his betrayal of his values made this mission to get close to the Cameron family under false pretenses all the more loathsome to Evan. Anytime his conscience pricked him, however, he pictured his mother's frail body and gaunt face, the pain that clouded her eyes, the dejection that rattled in her sighs. He had to do this for her. He had to find something to ease his mother's suffering and give her hope. She had to remain in the new drug trial.

At least stage two of his plan helped soothe his conscience a little bit. Now that he'd inserted himself in Isla's path, he had an excuse to seek her out, to appear contrite—not hard since he *was*—and hope that a little charm and goodwill would earn him a chance to enact stage three of his plan—romancing Isla.

Chapter 5

The next evening, Isla was enjoying a bowl of home-made vegetable soup and a grilled cheese sandwich when someone knocked on her front door.

"Come in! It's open!" she called, accustomed to having members of her family drop by unannounced. Instead of one of her nieces or her parents poking their head in the door, the knock sounded again. She put down her spoon, wiped her mouth and headed to her foyer to see who her visitor was.

When she spotted the now-familiar dark hair and broad shoulders through the glass in her door, her pulse gave a giddy leap. She greeted Evan with a smile that spread wider when he extended a large bouquet of flowers toward her. "Wow! Those are lovely. To what do I owe this honor?"

He gave her a boyish grin that made his dimple appear, and warmth pooled in her belly that had nothing to do with soup. "Just wanted to say I'm sorry for the scrape yesterday. Especially since your car took the worst of it."

She sniffed the carnations in the bouquet and savored their sweet scent. While not her favorite flower—blossoms grown wild and free of commercialization would fill that bill—she certainly appreciated his gesture. "Fortunately, Betty will be fine. I have good connections at a body shop, and they've promised to put her back in fine fettle."

He lifted one eyebrow. "Fine fettle?"

She chuckled and accepted the flowers from him. "Sorry. That's an expression my grandmother uses. Probably too old-fashioned for common use anymore." She hitched her head toward her living room. "Will you come in? I want to put these in water, and I'd love to fix you a bowl of soup if you're hungry."

"I was actually intending to ask you out for dinner if you were available and interested."

Her spirits lifted. "Definitely interested, but can we do it tomorrow? I've already got the soup made and my serving half gone."

He spread his hands. "You pick the day. I have no other plans, since my itinerary recently changed."

"Changed? So you're going to be in the area for a few days?" A thread of anticipation spun through her.

"Seems so." He shrugged one shoulder. "Could be a few weeks, even."

Weeks? Her heart did a little happy dance. While her mysterious intuition had assured her Evan was *the one*, she still knew a moment of relief that things were falling into place. Her opportunity to get to know him, fall in love with him—and he with her—was proceeding nicely.

She gave him a lopsided smile and held her screen

door open wider for him. "Come have some soup and tell me more about what it is that's brought you to our little town."

Evan stepped inside the old clapboard house and inhaled the homey scents that older houses exuded whether in North Carolina or Washington. Aged wood, a hint of mildew, the years of living and loving that seeped into the pores of a house. Over these familiar smells, the savory aroma of soup and toasted bread lured him toward the kitchen.

"Would you like a goat cheese sandwich with your soup, Evan?" Isla asked.

"Goat cheese?"

Her lips twitched as if she knew a secret. "I make it myself. With help from Petunia of course." She stepped over to her kitchen window and drew back the curtain. "Did you see them on your way in?"

He crossed the floor to peer out into her yard. A pair of goats, one brown, one white—wait, there was a third smaller one, too—milled about in a pen with a tiny shack-like barn for shelter. Beside it was another small house-like structure with wire fencing and several chickens milling about. He pointed toward the larger pen. "One of the goats is Petunia, I presume?"

"And her husband, Pickles. The baby is Daisy. But she's not old enough to breed or produce milk yet."

He opened his mouth to make a joke about reference to the male goat as Petunia's husband but swallowed the gibe. He was here to win her favor and friendship, and it was far too soon to take the liberty of teasing. "Homemade goat cheese. How can I pass that up?"

"You can't. Not without regret." She let the curtain fall back into place and busied herself with serving soup into a ceramic bowl and spreading a thick swath of creamy white cheese on bread.

He took the chair across from hers at a knotty pine table and watched her work. She had a fluidity of movement, like a ballerina, but unlike most dancers he knew of, she had a slim figure ripe with womanly curves. In fact, he decided, taking in the whole feminine package from her thick strawberry hair to her bare feet, she was simply stunning.

Simply... The word resonated in his brain. Yes, Isla was simplicity...in that she wore her hair in a plain ponytail, had on no makeup, had dressed in basic jeans and a well-loved T-shirt. Her kitchen had ancient appliances, a child's drawings taped on her refrigerator, homespun crafts for decor. He detected no artifice. No glitz. No pretense. The realization made his stomach clench and a guilty prickle chase down his back.

Hearing a sizzle, he refocused on Isla's activity. She'd moved his sandwich to a cast-iron frying pan and adjusted the flame of the gas burner. She opened a drawer to retrieve a spoon, then set his bowl of soup on the table. "So what is it that brings you to Valley Haven, Evan?"

"Well, family business, originally." He stalled, stirring his soup and searching for the most honest answer he could give without exposing his ploy, his underlying motive for stopping by her home.

The fragrant soup looked and smelled nothing like anything he'd ever had from a can. "Would I be right in guessing the soup is homemade as well?"

Her blue eyes lit with pride. "You would. The vegetables are among the last we'll get from our summer garden."

"Wow. I'm impressed. By contrast, I pat myself on

the back for shopping at the whole-and-organic-foods store back home. My default is fast and fried."

"Like the other day when we met at Burger Palace?" she asked, flipping his sandwich to cook the other side.

"Prime example." He glanced across the table to her bowl. "Aw, man. Your soup is getting cold." He rose and tried to take the spatula from her. "I can finish the—"

She lifted an arm to scoot him back. "It's fine. You're the guest, and I can heat my soup up with a fresh scoop from the stove. Sit. Eat. Don't wait for me. This is almost done."

He sat, ladled up a spoonful. And sighed with pleasure. "Oh wow. Isla, this is the best soup I've ever had!" He took another bite, confirming what his taste buds had told him. "You're a genius with garden vegetables and broth, ma'am. This is delicious."

She lifted his sandwich from the pan and slid it on a plate. "Thank you. My mother and grandmother perfected the recipe over the years, so credit goes to them."

"Well, kudos to them."

When she finally joined him at the table, she spooned up a bite and asked, "You have family connections to the area then?"

"Hmm?" he hummed around his first bite of the melty goat cheese and yeasty bread.

"You said you were here on family business."

"Oh, uh, right. I was…tracking down an old friend—well, acquaintance more than friend—of my mother's."

"Oh. And did you find them?"

Unfortunately. He swallowed the honest response, washing it down with another bite of soup and a large dose of compunction. "Yeah. I did."

"And did she remember your mom?"

"*He* did." Evan stirred his soup, staring into the bowl

of carrots, potato, beans and corn with a sense of fore-boding crowding in.

"You're frowning," Isla said, lowering her spoon to regard him with a worried look. "Does that mean your business with your mother's acquaintance didn't go well?"

Evan schooled his face. *Jeez.* He had to be more careful. If he was going to lull Isla, and ultimately her family, into a sense of well-being and community with him, he needed to guard against showing the dark feelings toward Gibbs and ill motives stirring inside him. He forced a smile and took a bite of sandwich to buy time to form a butt-covering response. "It went. While not the way I'd hoped, I still accomplished part of what I'd intended. Along with some surprise twists."

Her reddish eyebrows lifted. "Do tell…if it's not too personal, I mean."

"Well, he gave me a job for starters. That's why I'll be sticking around for the time being."

"What kind of job? Who is this man?"

Evan balked. If Gibbs had been trying, unsuccessfully, to purchase the Camerons' property for several months, he wouldn't have a good reputation with Isla. And tipping his hand that he was working for the shyster wouldn't help his cause. Evan cleared his throat. "Oh, uh, I doubt you'd know him."

She made a contrary sound as she tipped her head. "While I can't claim to know everyone in town, I come close—the town being as small and close-knit as it is and my having lived here all twenty-eight of my years. Try me."

No way in hell he could reveal the truth. That'd be game over before he started. Taking another bite of sandwich to stall again, he scrambled for a name, a lie, an out. He saw the massive henchman in his mind's eye and sputtered, "Uh, L-Leon something. I don't remember his last name."

"Leon, Leon…" she muttered, her expression thoughtful. "Doesn't ring a bell."

Whew! he thought while keeping his expression impassive.

"Is he's local?"

"No," he said, latching on to the excuse she unwittingly offered. "He lives down the way some…outside town. In the…country." *Good grief, Murray. Change the subject!* "Enough about me. Tell me more about you. What do you do for a living?"

She sipped soup from her spoon and sent him a curious look. "Have you ever thought about the way society labels people according to what they do to make money? How they earn—or don't earn—a wage? It's as if we are identified only by our ability to participate in commerce. People are so much more than a job."

"You're right. So then, who are you, Isla Cameron?"

Her mysterious grin returned, and she lifted her sandwich. "That, Evan Murray, is for you to discover, one layer at a time."

"Like an onion?"

She lifted one shoulder as she chewed a bite of sandwich. "I've heard that correlation before, but to me, onions are rather acrid. I'd hope my layers would be sweeter, like a dessert trifle. So far, you've only seen the frothy whipped cream on top."

"I like whipped cream." He sent her a meaningful glance, hoping she read the honesty and deeper meaning behind his profession. He'd only spent a few minutes in the woman's presence, but already he found himself drawn to her, intrigued by her, challenged by her. While it was a good start toward his goal of earning her trust, his attraction to her deepened his dread of what he'd been tasked to do.

The soup and goat cheese in his stomach churned with the nagging reminder that in order to help his mother, he had to betray this kind and innocent woman.

He ruthlessly shoved the doubts and regrets aside. Maybe he could find a way to accomplish what he needed without hurting Isla or her family. He'd keep thinking, keep planning, keep looking for another out. But any plan he made had to balance the real danger of disappointing Gibbs. He didn't need a crystal ball to know how badly it could go for him if he didn't deliver Cameron Glen to his father. Blood relation or not, Gibbs was dangerous man, and Evan had to tread carefully.

Evan was hiding something from her.

She sensed it on a deep level, but even her non-intuitive brothers could have figured that out. His mood was like the dappled sun under a tree that would flicker from bright to shadowed with each stir of breeze. Whatever internal struggle he was fighting, the battle of his emotions played out plainly in his body language, the waxing and waning light in his eyes, and the mood of the room. Did he know with some innate sense who she was? Was his spirit whispering truth while his reasoning mind fought what he didn't understand?

Likely. She'd learned that men were especially stubborn about listening to their intuition or anything that seemed remotely supernatural…especially when it ran counter to what one might call common sense. Even her own family had trouble accepting her rather spooky ability to discern things before they happened. Six years ago, she'd known her sister Emma was pregnant before even Emma had. Nine months later, Lexi had been born, and Emma had learned to trust Isla's instincts.

"What's troubling you, Evan?" she asked as she walked him to the door after dinner.

His eyes widened, and he shoved a falsely carefree grin onto his face. "Nothing. I'm fine, and dinner was delicious. I owe you two meals now."

But the sadness that lurked behind his eyes remained firmly in place, even as he denied it.

"Are you sure? All too often I catch you frowning or with a crease right here," she rubbed her thumb at the furrow between his eyes, "that says your thoughts have taken an unhappy turn."

He caught her hand in his, and she savored the trill of sweet sensation that flowed through her like an electric current. "Sorry if I was inattentive or worried you. I do have a good bit on my mind."

"Not our fender bender, I hope. Cars are just things, and no one was hurt, so...don't let it burden you." She let a teasing grin tug up her cheek. "Although you could slow down a bit in parking lots."

He barked a laugh. "Yes, ma'am." Then, sobering, he added, "It's nothing you need to worry about. A family matter that just...*is*. I promise to be more cheerful tomorrow." He bent to kiss the palm of her hand, and Isla's knees wobbled. "Shall I pick you up here around seven?"

A family matter. She liked the idea that his family was important enough to him that his concern for them showed. Isla decided not to push. She could root out the source of his familial disquiet later. She'd *make* herself be patient, even though a giddy excitement jangled through her veins around Evan. Even knowing he was her destiny, she recognized they had to build their relationship one brick at a time. One conversation, one private joke, one shared day at a time. They were only at the whipped-cream level, but her heart clamored to dig into the rich puddings and jammy fruits that made Evan tick.

"Seven sounds perfect. I'm looking forward to it." She rose on her toes and kissed his cheek. "Good night, Evan. Sweet dreams."

Her dreams that night were restless, full of conflict. And one featured Evan locked in a cage, held prisoner. Isla sat up in her bed and shook her head, trying to clear the unwelcome images. Evan a prisoner? What did that mean?

She tossed back the sheets and padded into her kitchen to make herself a cup of chamomile tea. Maybe her brain was just processing the fact that some family issue weighed on Evan. Certainly she'd felt helpless, tortured, trapped by recent troubling times for her family. Just that spring, she'd had terrible nightmares while Brody had been missing, buried alive in a root cellar after a landslide.

Her rooster, Doodle-doo—she'd let her youngest niece name him when Lexi was three—must have seen her kitchen light come on, because he started crowing despite the too-early hour. She didn't want the crazy rooster to get accustomed to early feedings, so she turned her light back off and sat in the dark sipping the tea until her mind quieted and sleep seemed possible again. She did sleep again, but at sunup, when Doodle-doo crowed her awake again, the unsettled feeling from the night returned.

She hoped that tonight on their date she could get to the root of the ill feeling and put it to rest. She hated having this little rain cloud hanging over what should be one of the happiest and most memorable times in her life. The start of her forever with Evan.

Forever with Evan. The notion brought a smile to her lips as she turned on the gas burner under her kettle to make a cup of tea. Though she didn't drink coffee, she readied the coffee maker with water and ground beans in case one of her java-addicted family members visited later in the morning. Someone usually did.

This morning it was her middle sister, Cait.

Isla hit the start button on the brew cycle when she saw Cait walking up the gravel drive to her house and headed out to the front porch to greet her sister. "Good morning, Mrs. Harkney."

As intended, the formal address won a smile from her sister who, even more than a year later, was still clearly in the honeymoon stage with her husband, Matt. "Good morning to you too. Got a minute?"

"For you? Always. I've already started the coffee for you." Isla held the screen door open for Cait and noticed a peakedness to her sister's complexion as Cait stepped into the house. "What's up?"

"Well, Matt's editor called him yesterday. It seems the sales of his book have been really good, despite supply chain and distribution problems." Cait made a weary sound as she sank into one of the chairs around Isla's kitchen table. The same chair where Evan had sat last night, Isla thought, and a secret grin tickled the corner of her mouth.

"That's great news! Why don't you look happier about it?" After joining Cait at the table, Isla pulled her tea bag from her mug, wrung out the liquid and set it aside.

"Oh, I am happy. I'm thrilled for him," Cait said, and

a genuine smile lit her face, even if fatigue clung to her eyes. As if to echo Isla's impression, Cait yawned and cast a glance toward the slowly brewing coffee. "I've just been so sleepy lately, and somehow, the thought of coffee makes me sick to my stomach. Even the smell makes my gut turn."

"Oh." Isla frowned. "Should I get rid of that?" She nodded toward the gurgling machine.

"No. That'd be wasteful, and you know Mom will probably stop in and have a cup on her way out to the market today. Did you see the pumpkins she picked yesterday?" Cait chuckled and her eyes rounded. "They're huge!"

"I saw them on the vine and watched them grow these past few weeks. She has the magic touch, huh?" Seeing Cait slump a bit in her chair and muffle another yawn, Isla narrowed a keener scrutiny on her sister. "Are you okay? This tiredness and sick stomach…"

Cait waved off her concern. "I'm fine. I think I ate something bad over the weekend, and it's just lingering a bit. And Matt tells me all the time that I work too hard and should slow down." Cait flashed a crooked smile. "Maybe it's just age catching up to me."

Isla snorted and reached across the table to give her sister's arm a squeeze. "Thirty-four is not old, Caitie-roo." A strange tickling in her brain started as she held her sister's arm, and soon a tingling surety swept down Isla's spine and into her consciousness. She gasped and squeezed Cait's arm harder. "You're pregnant!"

Cait pulled a face and chortled. "What? No, I'm not."

Isla scurried around the table and sat in the chair next to Cait, grasping her shoulders and looking deep into her Cameron-blue eyes. "Oh yeah. I'm sure of it. You mean, you didn't know?"

Her sister's brow furrowed, and Cait met Isla's eyes with a wary, skeptical glare. "Oh my God! Are you doing your weird, woo-woo thing right now? Are you honestly telling me your crazy sixth sense is telling you I'm pregnant?"

Isla took a beat to process the odd feeling and nodded slowly. "I think I am. I mean it would explain your sick stomach and fatigue. And you have the same aura about you that Emma did when she was pregnant with Lexi."

Cait arched an eyebrow. "I...won't even ask what that means." Her sister continued staring at her with a stunned, dubious expression until the coffeepot blared a beep at the end of the brew cycle. Giving her head a quick, hard shake, Cait hiccuped a laugh. "Oh my God! I have to take a test. I want to be sure before I say anything to Matt."

"Well, *I'm* sure. My special intuition is what it is." Isla paused, and her smile broadened. "Speaking of which, it told me something else exciting this week."

Cait's head was clearly elsewhere, processing, but after a moment, she glanced at Isla and said, "Oh? About who?"

"Me, this time. Which is a first. Usually I sense things about other people. But this time..."

"Do tell." Cait leaned toward her, a look of intrigue lighting her expression.

"Remember at the family meeting when Daryl spilled that I'd I met my soulmate?" Isla couldn't help the giddy chuckle that bubbled up in her. "We have a date tonight. Oh, Cait, he's so handsome and charming and so..." She squealed quietly and beamed at her sister.

Joy, and a degree of disbelief, radiated from Cait's face. "Your soulmate? You know this about him already? Who is this guy? Where did you meet him?"

Isla related the whole story, from her dream about meeting her future husband to recognizing him in the fast-food joint to the fender bender that inspired Evan's apology visit and invitation to dinner. "I can't wait for you to meet him. He's…fabulous. I know so. Already."

"After two, three…brief encounters with him?"

"It sounds incredible, I know but… Yes. When I'm around him it just feels…right."

"And does he return your feelings?" Cait asked, concern crossing her face.

"He…is interested, at least. And if my instincts are correct, as they so often are, then it's just a matter of time."

"Well, well. Listen to you. So confident in yourself," Cait said with a teasing grin.

"More like confident in fate and the universe," she countered. "Things have a way of working out as they should."

Cait's gaze moved to the window, then back to Isla, and her hand covered her belly. "So, is your woo-woo thing telling you when I'm due? If it's a boy or girl?"

Isla laughed as she rose from her chair and bent to give her sister a hug. "I'm intuitive, not magic. I'll leave those questions to the doctor."

Chapter 6

Evan arrived right on time, catching Isla in a state of last-minute rushing about. "I'm so sorry. I just need to do a quick freshen up," she said as she held her front door to let him inside.

"Don't do any extra work on my account. You look pretty fabulous to me." He punctuated his compliment with his dimpled smile.

Melt!

"Thank you for that," she said, feeling her cheeks heat with pleasure, "but I've been out with the chickens and goats. I definitely need to wash up and change clothes. Give me five minutes."

When she finished tidying up and running a brush through her hair, she returned to find Evan examining the family pictures she had on display around her living room. He glanced up with a guilty look. "Caught me snooping."

"Oh please." She waved him off. "Look all you want. I love showing off the clan."

"You have quite the large family." He replaced the most recent group shot from her brother Brody's wedding on her mantel.

She nodded as she took her purse from a table by the front door. "Large and growing."

"I'm jealous. I'm an only child and grew up without a father."

She heard a definite melancholy in his tone, and an answering pathos grabbed her heart. She wanted to tell him that soon he'd be part of her big, loving family, but she swallowed the words. Introducing him to her mysterious intuition and powers of prediction now might send him screaming into the hills. Once he knew her better and understood she was harmless, she could wow him with her sixth sense.

"So, just you and your mom, then?" she asked as she followed him out to his rental car. "Are the two of you close?"

"Well, yeah." To his credit, Evan clearly tried to school his expression, but Isla saw the flicker of pain her question triggered. And she knew...

"Oh dear. I've struck a raw nerve. Did you recently lose her?"

His gaze darted to hers, as if startled by the question. "I... No. But, well, she's ill."

She touched his hand where it rested on the open passenger door. "I'm so sorry. Do you want to talk about it?"

"It's not cheerful first-date fare."

"You can tell me as we drive to dinner, if you're willing. If it's important to you, then it is of concern to me."

And so he did. He explained that his mother had a

rare form of cancer and was fading quickly. They were hoping a medical trial she'd just started would help, but it was too soon to tell. "That's kinda why I'm here in North Carolina instead of back in Seattle with her."

"The medical trial is out here?"

"No. But I've, um, taken a job that I hope will pay for the expense, if it all pans out."

"Doing what?" she asked, angling her body to watch the evening light flicker on his face as they drove past a stand of trees and a few billboards. The cut of his jaw, the angle of his nose and the fringe of his dark eye-lashes were endlessly fascinating to her. She studied each feature, trying to memorize every nuance of his handsome face.

He took a moment to answer her question, clearly debating his wording. "A…special project for…a busi-nessman in the area."

"What kind of project?" she asked.

He shot her an amused grin. "I guess I should have expected the third degree, being a first date, but I am honestly rather boring. I don't want to put you to sleep before we've even eaten our meal."

She laughed. "You let me be the judge of whether you are boring or not."

"Well, I majored in mechanical engineering in col-lege—" he started, and she let her head loll, pretending to fall instantly to sleep.

He barked a laugh. "I told you!"

Slapping playfully at his arm, she gave him her brightest smile. "I'm teasing. I want to hear more about your studies. Where did you go to college?"

He turned in at the parking lot of a steak house and parked in the first open spot.

She glanced at the restaurant sign and cringed internally. *Be a sport. This will be a story to tell the grandkids.*

Evan cut the engine and gave her a playful wink. "All will be revealed…at dinner." He climbed out and quickly circled the back bumper to open her door for her. She smiled her thanks as he escorted her inside.

The scent of searing meat greeted them as they entered the restaurant, and Isla shoved down her visceral reaction to the odor. She wouldn't say anything. It was fine. In time, he'd know, but she didn't want to embarrass him tonight. They were shown to their table, a cozy corner booth, and she picked up her menu in search of something she could eat.

"So I went to Oregon State University in Corvallis for my undergrad," Evan said as he perused his menu, "and Washington State—"

"Isla, hi!"

Isla glanced up at their waitress to see one of Brody's ex-girlfriends beaming at her. "Hey, Cyndi! How are you?"

"I'm good." Cyndi set glasses of water and napkin-rolled utensils on the table for each of them. "What are *you* doing here?"

Anxious heat prickled the back of Isla's neck. "I'm on a date." She tried to signal Cyndi—*Don't say it! Ix-nay!*—with her eyes, but the waitress had glanced to Evan and smiled.

"Bold move bringing a vegetarian to a steak house," Cyndi said, chuckling.

Evan shot a puzzled look to Isla, and she gave him an awkward smile and nod.

His menu flopped onto the table as he groaned. "Oh man. We can go somewhere else. I'm sorry!"

"You didn't know?" Cyndi pulled an "oops" face.

Isla flapped a hand. "It's fine. They have salads. And

baked potatoes." She poked the menu. "And this pasta dish sounds good."

His brow creased. "You're sure?"

"Absolutely." She folded her menu and angled her body to give him her full attention. "You were saying... Washington State?"

"For graduate school."

The rest of the dinner passed in pleasant conversation, teasing banter and increasingly intimate touches— hands, wrists, face...

So, too, did their conversation grow more intimate as they lowered their inhibitions and warmed to each other's company. She told him about her family, the family's produce stand at the local farmers' market, which she and her mother ran, and her graduate studies at University of North Carolina Asheville in public health.

"My family teases me about being a professional student, because I've been taking classes in dribs and drabs for so many years. I didn't even start college until I was twenty-two, and I changed majors twice, from anthropology to environmental science then to health and wellness." She shrugged. "My interests changed so..." She took a sip of her tea. "I also briefly had a minor in American Indian and Indigenous studies before I took Daryl to a lecture by a visiting professor from Morehouse College in Atlanta. I was hooked on Africana studies then and changed my minor."

Evan's expression was bemused, and she gave him a self-deprecating chuckle. "What can I say? I love learning. I love people. I love knowing about our planet and all the systems of nature and... I just didn't see a need to stress over finishing in a set number of years. I see my fellow classmates giving themselves ulcers over the workload, and I just…" She shook her head and sighed. "I won't do that to myself."

"But what about starting a career? Finding a job?" he asked, then waved his hands. "Forget I asked that. I'm sorry. That was gauche."

Her smile granted him grace. As her future husband, he deserved to know her finances were sound. "I'm honestly quite happy doing what I'm doing now and may never enter the work-a-day grind. My expenses are low, and I earn enough to get by, between my share of the produce stand, my homemade products and teaching both regular and goat yoga classes."

"Goat yoga?" he said, choking on the soda he'd been sipping. "Say what?"

She laughed, used to the reaction. "You heard me. My students love to interact with Pickles and Petunia. And Daisy is a hoot when she's jumping around and climbing on people's backs as they downward dog. It's been proven that interacting with animals lowers your blood pressure, whether cats, dogs…or goats. It's a very popular class."

"I see." He tucked a wisp of her hair behind her ear, and shimmering sensations flowed through her. "Maybe I'll give it a try while I'm in town."

"You should. It's a great stress reliever, and I sense a great deal of stress in you."

His eyes widened as if surprised by her assessment.

"Being so far away from your mom while she's sick can't be easy." She laced her fingers with his and squeezed his hand.

Evan nodded, and his eyes reflected a relief that she understood his worry.

What started as typical first-date fare—movie preferences, books read, travels taken and longed for—soon progressed to more granular topics of seminal moments in their histories and deeply held beliefs. He expanded on his grief over his mother's illness and feelings of helplessness to do anything for her, the position he'd assumed from a young age as the protector in the family and his loneliness growing up. "Mom was great, but I always wanted siblings, a big family…what you have," he said, confirming her earlier suspicions.

Their meals had been eaten and their dishes long ago cleared away before he glanced out the night-darkened window and heaved a sigh of regret. "I think we've monopolized this table as long as we dare. I just hate to end our evening yet. Maybe we can get dessert somewhere?"

She hesitated, hating to burst his bubble twice in one evening, but wanting honesty between them. "I'm not much for refined sugar. If I'm going to indulge in something sweet, it will be my Nanna's sticky toffee pudding every time. Or ice cream. I do love ice cream."

"Then ice cream it is."

"Deal. And then how about a walk beside the river? I can show you where there's a lighted bike path we can use, if you want."

"Lead on."

She did. After a quick stop at her favorite ice cream shop, she directed him to the trailhead at the local park. Their moonlight stroll evoked more fond memories of childhood autumns, leaf forts and Halloween carnivals. Stolen kisses stoked a heat in her core, and the warmth of his hands stroking her fueled a passion she had no interest in denying. He was her destiny after all. Why fight what had become more obvious with every minute of their time together, what her heart and soul were craving so desperately?

"I want to be with you, Evan," she whispered between long, deep kisses in the shadows of the park.

He met her gaze with one muddled by desire. He was obviously trying to read between the lines.

So she clarified. "To make love to you. To wake up with you. To share all of myself with you."

He blinked as if weighing his decision then asked, "Your place?"

She tweaked his chin. "Your motel is closer."

His grin was devilish but warm. "It is."

Laughing and kissing, they all but broke down his motel room door in their haste to get inside and get naked. Evan tumbled her to his bed, stripping her shirt over her head while her hands fought with his belt. Their first coupling was chaotic and clumsy, and Evan barely got a condom on before she straddled him and sated her longing to be part of him.

I'm home, she thought as he brought her to a staggering climax. The thought repeated as they made love again, more slowly, more tenderly, more thoroughly... several times through the night. She closed her eyes, drifting to sleep in the small hours of the night, content in the assurance that beside Evan Murray was where she belonged.

Evan woke before dawn the next morning, feeling happier than he had in months. He recognized that truth even before his languid stretch found the warm presence beside him.

Isla. A smile touched his lips as he thought the lyrical name and reflected on their enthusiastic sex from the night before. And their intriguing conversation over dinner. And her effervescent laugh that left his spirits lighter and a bubble of hope swelling inside him.

On the heels of those bright and welcome thoughts, he remembered why he'd pursued Isla to begin with, how he'd staged their fender bender, danced around the truth when answering her questions, hidden his ulterior motive for their date.

And while she was under all these misconceptions and ignorant of his agenda, he'd slept with her. His gut twisted in self-reproach. Seducing her had never been his plan, but she'd so quickly and so completely mesmerized him and turned him inside out, he'd lost himself in her. He'd been so focused on Isla, he'd almost forgotten the big picture.

Damn. Where did he go from here? How did he right the ship? He draped an arm over his eyes, and a quiet groan escaped his throat.

"Evan?" she murmured and snuggled closer, her gentle hand slipping onto his chest to rest over his heart. "You okay?"

He captured her fingers and squeezed. "Never better."

She kissed his shoulder. "Same."

He reached for his phone on the bedside stand and woke the screen. Four thirty.

"Four thirty?" she said with a little gasp. "Oh brother. I need to get home. I have animals to feed and relatives who will freak out if I'm not there when they stop by."

"You family comes by your house at four thirty in the morning?"

"Maybe not *that* early, but they know I'm usually up before sunrise. The animals get impatient if I'm late with their breakfast, and I've found that meditating at first light gives me the peace and energy I need for the day."

He squelched the impulse to make a teasing comment

about her morning ritual. Instead, he quipped, "I find that about a gallon of coffee and avoiding the national news give me the peace and energy I need for the day."

She chuckled and patted his chest. "Good choice, avoiding the news. We'll discuss your caffeine addiction some other time. There are worse vices."

"Vice?" He angled his head to give her a disgruntled look. "Coffee is the nectar of the gods. How could such liquid gold be a vice?"

"Most of my family would agree with you, so I'll concede the point. I can even brew you a pot, if not a gallon, when we get to my house." She rose on her elbow to kiss his mouth before rolling away and tossing back the covers.

He caught her arm and tugged her back against him. "Hold up, beautiful." He cradled the back of her head with a splayed hand and drew her close. "You need a proper good morning before we go."

Pressing his lips to hers, he slanted a kiss across her lips and inhaled the sweet scent of her. He moved his kisses to nuzzle her neck below her ear and murmured, "You taste good and you smell heavenly, my dear. What is that tantalizing scent?"

"Why, thank you. It's my own blend of patchouli, ylang-ylang and chamomile essential oils."

He raised his head to give her a puzzled look. "Um… what kind of oils?"

"Herbal essential oils. To relax and promote wellness. And it's nice that they smell good too."

He reined in the chuckle that he knew she'd take as dismissive, but the picture he was rapidly forming of Isla Cameron was so much his opposite as to be laughable. An essential-oils-using vegetarian who rose before the sun to feed farm animals and meditate. And while her lifestyle and beliefs were, well, different, he didn't feel out of sync with her. It was as if they were puzzle pieces that, despite their reverse shapes, fit together perfectly. Certainly he'd never enjoyed sex with anyone as much as he had with her last night, and he credited that to the inexplicable pull he felt toward her, the emotional bond, the spiritual—

Whoa! He snorted and shook his head. Good grief, now he was throwing out the same sort of bohemian terminology she used.

"What's funny?" she asked, her nose wrinkling in a way that made him want to kiss it. So he did…

"Us," he said, stroking her cheek with his crooked finger. "We're just so…different. Yet so—" he squeezed her "—good together."

She hooked her leg around his. "So then, you sense it too?"

"Well, yeah. There is something special going on here." He twisted his mouth, befuddled by his admission. "I know it's awfully early to be saying so, but…"

"No. Not really. If the connection is there, why not acknowledge it? I don't want to play stupid society-dictated relationship games. We get to say what is best for us."

Games…

He gave her a smile, hoping to mask the biting guilt that sawed inside him. More than playing games, he was deceiving her outright. While he could do his level best to rectify that situation, find a way to appease Gibbs's demands and protect Isla from the fallout, he was clearly in a sticky position. Tugging her close again, he kissed her hard, then rolled out of bed before she could read his doubts on his face. "All righty then. Let's go feed some goats and chickens."

* * *

The world was still dark as he navigated the roads to Isla's house. For her part, Isla was mostly quiet, appearing reflective as they drove. She sat with her body angled toward him, her attention focused not on the few lights of the sleeping town but on his face. She wore a mysterious smile that brightened every time he glanced at her.

"What?" he asked at last, awkward under the scrutiny.

She gave a small shrug. "Nothing. Just…happy. You have a very handsome profile, Mr. Murray."

"Uh, thanks." After another moment, he mustered the nerve to say, "Tell me more about Cameron Glen." He wondered if she could hear the guilty thumping of his heart. She had an uncanny way of knowing his thoughts and moods, which meant he'd have to do a better job of disguising his motives when with her. But mention of her family's property brought another broad smile to her face.

"Sure. What do you want to know?"

Anything that will help me find a vulnerability to exploit. He shifted in the driver's seat uneasily when the horrid thought whispered in his brain. "How long has it been in your family?"

"I don't know the exact year, but several generations. More than one hundred years." The pride and reverence in her voice reverberated in his marrow like a dissonant gong.

"Wow," he said, squeezing the steering wheel harder and fighting the bile that rose in his throat as he contemplated his odious task. "That long?"

"That long. I grew up there and have explored every nook and creek and tree. I can show you where I had my first kiss, where I broke my arm as a kid and where my parents caught me drinking Boone's Farm with Barry Schuster when I was fifteen."

He shot her what he hoped was an amused glance. "And what happened when they did?"

"I was grounded, warned against drinking again before I was of legal age, and Barry lost interest in hanging out with me the rest of the summer."

He gave her a rueful grin. "His loss."

She pointed to the driveway ahead. "Here's your turn. It's hard to see in the dark since Brody flattened the reflector last month."

"Will you show me the grounds?" he asked, hoping he didn't sound pushy or suspiciously overinterested.

"Sure! And this is a great time of day to see it, with the world just waking up, the birds and critters all stirring and the dew making things sparkle."

Speaking of sparkle, Isla's eyes had a special light in them when she spoke of her family. That shine was there now, as if Cameron Glen were another beloved member of her family.

I grew up there and have explored every nook and creek and tree.

Compunction returned to gnarl his guts and cramp his chest. He shoved his misgivings aside and dragged an image of his ill mother to the fore. *For Mom. Just remember your "why."*

A pickup truck was pulling from the Cameron Glen entrance onto the state highway as Evan slowed to make the turn.

"Wow. So we're not the only people in the state awake after all. Someone you know?" Evan asked.

Isla gave the departing vehicle a cursory glance.

The dark pickup wasn't Brody's truck, so she shook her head. "Could be one of the guests. They've been known to leave at all hours if they have a long drive ahead or are trying to get to a certain mountain lookout for the sunrise."

As Evan pulled up the main drive, nearing her house, Isla pointed through the windshield ahead of them. "The drive makes a loop. Just follow your nose, and you'll come back out here. *Or.*" She gave him a telling look as she paused. "Better yet, park in my yard, and we'll walk."

"Sounds like a winner," he said and pulled onto her gravel driveway.

Isla stepped out of the sedan and took a deep breath, inhaling the sweet fragrance of the fallen leaves and earthy loam, both scents heightened by the morning dew. But a different smell laced the air as well. An acrid smoke. Guests often built fires in the provided firepits in the evening, but those fires should have been extinguished and the accompanying smoke dissipated by morning. An uneasiness rippled down her spine. "Do you smell that?"

Evan raised his nose and took a deep breath. "What am I supposed to smell? I'm getting farm animals, leaves and cut grass. And some pine?"

She headed toward the road and examined the sky with a knit in her brow. While the sort of fog that had given the Smoky Mountains their name hung over the fishing ponds and rolled through the trees, another more ominous haze tinted the air. "Something's burning," she muttered, even as she started jogging up the road.

"Isla?" Evan fell in step behind her.

"Smoke," she called back to him, picking up her pace. The dark scent grew stronger as she reached the far end of the property. Soon the ominous scent was joined by a nerve-shattering cry and the piercing beep of a smoke alarm.

Isla's pulse lurched when she rounded the bend in the road and discovered the source of the commotion. The White Pine cabin was on fire, their rental guests standing on the front lawn in their nightclothes. The mother of the family was in tears, her young son shrieking in fear.

Isla raced to the mother. "Is everyone out?"

She shook her head, her eyes wild with terror. "Our daughter is trapped in the back room. My husband is inside, trying to get her out."

Isla glanced at the cabin where black clouds of smoke billowed out of every window.

Before she could quell her shock enough to respond, Evan darted past her toward the back of the cabin.

Ice sluiced through her. "Evan!"

"Call 9-1-1!" he shouted without breaking stride.

Isla glanced to the woman, who understood the question before it was asked.

"I haven't. My phone's inside. My only thought was my children—"

Isla reached reflexively for her purse, her phone, only to realize she must have dropped her purse without thinking as she rushed in terror toward the fire. Rather than try to search in the thin, predawn light, she ran to the cabin next door and banged on the front window.

Those guests must have already heard the commotion, smelled the smoke because the door was jerked open quickly. Without hesitating, Isla pushed past the older man and grabbed up the cabin's landline.

After dialing the emergency number and sputtering out the address and situation, she shoved the phone toward the man. "Stay on the phone with the operator! Please. I have to go back and help!" To the older man's wife, who watched with worried eyes from the bedroom door, she called, "If you have a cell phone, use it to call the office after-hours number. My sister will answer. Tell her what's happening!"

His heart in his throat, Evan bolted toward the back of the cabin, stumbling in the dark over roots and empty wine bottles in the yard. Through a broken cabin window, he could see flames dancing in the living room, could smell the acrid chemical scent of items in the house burning. He moved farther toward the back, where a newer-looking wing had been built. Could this be the bedroom where the girl was trapped? The window here was black, nothing in the room visible. Judging this window to be his best chance to get inside and find the child, he groped in the pale morning light for a rock or branch or... Bingo!

He snatched up the child-sized baseball bat lying discarded in the grass and hurried back to the window. Standing off to the side of the window—he'd seen enough movies to know about possible back-draft danger—he smashed the glass with the bat. The pane shattered, and heat and smoke billowed out. But not flames. Thank God! Yanking off his jacket and holding his breath, he wrapped the coat around his arm and knocked the rest of the jagged glass from the frame. After stepping away from the clouds of smoke for a deep breath, he removed his T-shirt, tied it around his head so it covered his mouth and nose. Wetting the cloth would have been better, but he went with what he had. Time was critical for the trapped girl.

Hoisting himself onto the windowsill, he wiggled

through the opening he'd made in the glass and fumbled to his feet. Remembering the get-low-and-go rule, he dropped to his hands and knees. The smoke and heat were horrible, but he forged on. Feeling his way in the blinding smoke, he found a dresser, an open suitcase and finally a bed. The little girl was still in the bed, the covers over her head.

"Hey, sweetie…" he rasped, wishing he'd bothered to ask the girl's name before heading off on his rescue mission. He coughed and shook the child's shoulder. "Can you hear me? We have—" cough "—to get out!"

He lifted the girl's floppy arm and knew if she was going to survive, he'd have to carry her out. The popping and roar of the fire filled his ears. Or was that his own adrenaline-fueled pulse? Already his throat and lungs were burning. The heat was intense. He rose high enough on his knees to hook his arms around the child. He managed to get her draped over his back as he hobble-crawled back toward the window. Stinging sweat dripped in his eyes. His chest heaved with effort and the yearning for a deep, clean breath. When he reached the spot where he thought the window was, he bumped into a wall. A chair. Damn! He was turned around, disoriented. Thick black smoke made it impossible to see. Where was the window? If he didn't get out soon, both he and the little girl would asphyxiate.

Chapter 7

Isla sprinted back to White Pine, flashlight in hand, and found the soot-smudged father on the yard, coughing and gasping for air.

"Your daughter?" she asked, casting a frantic glance around for a little girl.

The man's bereaved face crumpled further as he rasped, "I couldn't... The fire..."

The mother was wailing, clutching their son to her side. Suddenly, setting the boy down, the woman took several staggering steps toward the front door. Realizing her intent, Isla grabbed her arm. "No! You can't go in there!"

"My Jenna!" she sobbed. "I have to get my baby!"

Isla absorbed the horror and grief that wrenched the family, their emotions exploding on her like concussive waves that shook her to her core. She battled the empathetic flood in order to stay focused on the emergency, the task at hand.

"Stay with your family," Isla told the woman, gripping her arms and giving her a small shake. "I'll do what I can for Jenna."

The father took his wife's hand and tugged her into an embrace. Tears pricked Isla's eyes, not just from the sting of smoke, but in compassion for the couple, as she rounded the corner of the cabin, searching for Evan.

Smoke billowed through the bedroom window at the back of the cabin, and she hurried to it. Broken glass littered the ground around a discarded child's baseball bat. "Evan!"

Moving closer to the windows edge, she pulled the edge of her shirt over her nose and aiming the flashlight, she peered inside. It was too black with smoke to see anything. She shouted again, and over the ominous roar of the fire and thrum of blood in her ears, she heard a cough. "Evan!"

She barely made out a movement inside, and her heart leaped.

Hearing Isla's shout, Evan turned toward the noise, thankful to have a sound beacon to direct him. He'd passed the window somehow and backtracked now, more sliding on his belly than crawling. The little girl's body felt heavier by the minute. He tried to shout back to Isla but could only cough and rasp.

"Evan!"

He continued scooting on his elbow, slithering across the floor in the direction of her voice. When he reached the wall, he rose to his knees and caught the child as she tumbled off his back. Isla stood silhouetted in the window, the glow of a flashlight below her and a cloud of smoke enveloping her. He'd never been so glad to see someone in his life.

"Take her," he choked out, and Isla reached in the broken window. As he hoisted the girl up, his arms trembled from exertion, from adrenaline, from fear that he was too late for the child.

Once Isla had pulled the girl out the window, Evan struggled to tumble out. He had just enough strength to land on his feet and stagger away from the billowing smoke. Falling to his hands and knees, he gulped fresh air into his lungs, choking and coughing as his lungs expelled the polluted air.

"Come on, sweet girl. Breathe for me," he heard Isla begging the limp girl. Isla laid the girl on her side and pounded her back. Then, laying her flat, she started rescue breaths.

The child's parents saw them in the side yard and ran to hover over Isla and the girl.

"Jenna!" the mother screamed, terror thick in her voice.

Gasping for every raw breath that sawed from his aching lungs and his sore throat, Evan stumbled over to the parents and pushed them back.

"Give…h-her room…" He didn't recognize his own voice, it was so strangled and hoarse. Another fit of coughing gripped him, and he bent to spit out the phlegm that rose from his throat.

He watched Isla work, breathing into Jenna's mouth, his chest aching for more reasons than just smoke inhalation. The girl was far too still.

Between Isla's breaths, a wisp of smoke would drift out of Jenna's mouth. Did this mean the girl was still breathing, however shallow the breaths? Jenna's father sidled close, and pressed fingers to the girl's throat.

"She has a pulse!" he announced with a broken sob of joy.

"Isla!"

Isla and Evan both turned toward the source of the shout to find a woman in a bathrobe and man with a limp hurrying toward them. Seeing Isla's rescue efforts, the man rushed to Isla and nudged her out of the way. "Let me."

Isla moved back, pressing a hand to her mouth as her body convulsed with a sob. The woman in the bathrobe beat Evan to Isla's side to embrace and comfort her.

"An ambulance and the fire department are on the way," he heard the woman tell Isla quietly. "Are you hurt?"

Isla shook her head, then turned, scanning the faces around her until she met Evan's gaze. "Are you okay? Are you burned?"

A fit of coughing racked him at that moment, and he raised a hand and nodded to signal he was okay. Well, okayish. His throat and lungs really hurt, and he was still struggling for breath.

Hearing a whimper and a feminine cough, he glanced past Isla to Jenna. The little girl was moving, and the man with the limp rolled her to her side as she sputtered, coughed and spit out black phlegm.

Jenna's mother gasped in relief and sank to her knees, tearfully repeating, "Thank you, God. Oh, thank you!"

"Oh, Isla!" The woman holding her said, "I think you saved that girl's life. You're a hero!"

Isla shook her head and wiggled free of the woman's embrace. "No. Evan's the hero. He got her out of the house." A giant grin spread across her face, and her blue eyes lit with pride as the first rays of sun peeked over the mountaintops and through the trees. "Cait, this is Evan Murray. Evan, my sister Cait and her husband, Matt."

Cait moved toward Evan, reaching for him. When she gripped his hand, he winced, not having noticed the redness of his skin, singed by the heat. Snatching her hand back, Cait frowned her concern. "I'm sorry. I—"

"Evan?" Isla tipped her head, her brow knitting in query.

He closed the distance between them, ignoring his various pains and lingering cough. He just wanted Isla in his arms. He wrapped her in a hug that she returned with a gentle squeeze. Until he held Isla and allowed himself to release the tension knotted inside him, he hadn't realized how shaken he'd been, how close he'd willingly stepped toward danger. He'd looked the beast, looked death in the eye and said, "Not today. Not for me, not for this child." But now the waves of postadrenaline shock and awe rolled through him, rocked him to his core. And he only wanted, *needed* to sink into Isla's embrace for a few moments to anchor himself, to steady his frayed nerves, to center him.

What might it be like to have her in his life all the time to help him traverse the rocky paths of life? He realized how rash it sounded, even to himself, to be thinking so long-term after one date, one night together. But "oh mother of pearl"! What a night! How was it possible to be so powerfully drawn to her in such a short time? Logic said they were opposites, but some undefinable chemistry drew him inexorably toward her. *Like a tractor beam*, his geek mind added, as if to prove how different they were.

The sound of sirens pulled him from his musings, and Isla stepped back from him, giving his cheek a soft kiss. "I'll be right back."

He nodded and directed his attention to the family huddled around Jenna. Isla joined Cait and Matt, who

were assisting the family as best they could, lending reassurance and moral support. Only then, as the initial
shock of the fire and urgency to save Jenna had passed
did a tickle of suspicion goad Evan to move back toward the burning house, to replay things that he'd seen
and his brain had shoved aside in the midst of the crisis.

He staggered to the first window he'd passed—broken
panes, wine bottles, an acrid scent. At his feet, he found
a scrap of cloth that was damp... He sniffed his fingers
after he touched the fabric. Gasoline. That was the biting
scent he'd smelled. Not the furnishings inside. He snapped
the ugly pieces together, and his gut sawed at the picture
that emerged.

Molotov cocktails. Someone had set the fire. He only
needed one guess to know who.

"Arson?" Isla's father repeated, his face expressing
the same shock and disgust that burrowed into Isla. Neil
stared at the fireman who'd offered this stunning con-
clusion later that morning. "You're sure?"

"We found gasoline-soaked cloth and wine bottles
outside the living room window and broken glass inside on the floor," the fireman said. "And the burn pattern appears to show the fire had several ignition sites."

"But...who would do such an awful thing?" her sister Emma asked.

Her father's face grew stony. "I think we all know
who."

A silent wave of realization passed through the hud-
dle of her family members, all of whom wanted to hear
the fireman's report.

Feeling numb, Isla angled her gaze toward the charred
shell that was all that remained of the White Pine cabin.
Evan and the entire Nash family had been transported

by ambulance to the nearest hospital, where Anya was an ER nurse. Jenna had been alert and communicative when the family left for the ER, but Isla was eager to go check on both Evan and the Nashes. She'd not been allowed to ride with Evan in the ambulance as she'd wanted, but she'd promised him she'd meet him at the hospital as soon as the situation with the fire and her family's reactions to the tragedy had calmed. Her empathic absorption of her family's distress over the fire and the injuries to the Nashes and Evan had worn her down. Her head throbbed, her heart ached and her soul wept.

Knowing that someone—who was she kidding? It had to have been a spiteful Gene Gibbs—had intentionally burned the oldest cabin on the property and put their guests lives at risk lit an anger and hatred inside her. This level of negativity was unusual for her. Unhealthy. A bit frightening in the way it manifest itself with tremors from her core and tensed muscles and heat flashing through her blood. And the potent urges to do something equally evil in return, to seek vengeance, was a foreign feeling for her. An eye for an eye was not her typical path, but the injury and danger to her family, to innocents was too recent, too raw to extend any forgiveness or understanding. She didn't want to believe that Gene Gibbs's dark intent and cruelty could have lasting power to scar her spirit, but at the moment, she had trouble seeing past the blackness that hung over her.

She had her eyes closed, taking slow, cleansing breaths—that weren't helping much—when her mother sat down beside her on the lawn. She knew it was her mother from the scents of lavender lotion her mother applied every night before bed and menthol cream she used to combat the ache in her arthritic knees. Her soft sigh and warm brush of her fingers pushing hair behind Isla's ear confirmed her companion's identity. "You all right, ladybug?"

"No," Isla answered honestly.

Her mother draped an arm around her shoulders and tugged her closer. The comfort from her mother broke the dam of tears that Isla had been valiantly fighting. She wanted to keep it together, needed to find the composure to drive to the hospital and find Evan and the Nashes. But touch had a way of breaking down barriers and exposing raw emotions. And *crivvens*, she was a seething cauldron of emotions today. Hers and everyone else's.

"That gentleman friend of yours certainly saved the day, did he not?" her mother said.

"Evan." She opened her eyes and sent her mother a wobbly smile. "His name's Evan Murray, and yes. He was very brave. He saved that little girl." She hiccuped a half laugh, half sob. "I'm so proud of him."

"Caitie says you had a date with him. Is that right?"

Isla nodded.

"And do you think there'll be another date?"

A ray of sunlight reached her aching soul when she thought about Evan, their passionate lovemaking and her sure sense that he was *the one*. She bobbed another nod to her mother. "I think you should get used to seeing him around here."

Her mother's eyes widened, brightened. "In that case, I think I should invite him to join us for Sunday dinner."

After receiving treatment for smoke inhalation at the hospital and getting discharged later that afternoon, Evan drove directly to his father's estate, bracing himself for the confrontation ahead. Bristling with anger and spoiling for a fight, he stomped down the niggle of doubt that said calling out the smarmy businessman's actions might not be the safest move. He'd defied death once today. Did he really think the grim reaper would look the other way a second time if he angered Gene Gibbs?

Evan needed only to think of Jenna Nash's limp body in his arms to quash those reservations and fuel his righteous anger again.

He banged on the front door, and without a wait— Gibbs must have seen him arriving him on his security cameras—his knock was answered by Gibbs himself.

"What's the matter? Your lackey too tired from his early morning arson run to be your butler today?" The rasp of his smoke-damaged voice earned a startled look from Gibbs before the man's expression flattened again.

Evan fisted his hands at his sides and glared at the man he was growing increasingly dismayed to acknowledge as his father.

Gibbs didn't answer the question. Instead, he shoved his hands in his pockets and stared back with a bland look. "Something I can do for you, Mr. Murray?"

Evan squared his shoulders. "Yeah. You can look me in the eye and admit that you're behind the arson at Cameron Glen this morning!" The force he'd put behind the words made him cough. He'd been warned to rest his voice while his throat healed.

One of Gibbs's eyebrows lifted dismissively. "Why would I do that? I was nowhere near Cameron Glen this morning."

Evan huffed, "Maybe not. But one of your minions was. Black pickup ring a bell? Leon, perhaps? Or do you keep someone else on the payroll to do your dirty deeds?"

His lungs seized, and he battled a coughing fit, having to step to the edge of Gibbs's porch and expel the blackened slime that he'd dislodged from his throat. He hated the coughing, the wheezing that made him appear weakened as he faced down his father's stare. "Call off your dogs. Leave the Camerons alone."

Gibbs narrowed a dark glare on him. "Watch yourself, Murray. I call the shots in our arrangement, and, right now, you're on shaky ground."

"Am I?" Evan returned sourly, taking a step closer to the older man and wishing his voice was stronger. The muted, sandpaper quality limited his ability to shout as loudly and as vehemently as he wanted. He wanted to rage, wanted to tear Gibbs apart, wanted to avenge Jenna, her brother and parents. And Isla's family.

"You are." Gibbs's surly tone matched Evan's. After a tense beat, his father's expression shifted, as if a thought had occurred to him. He cocked his head slightly as he asked, "How did you know there was a fire at the Camerons' property this morning? Were you there?"

Evan scoffed bitterly. "I didn't get this voice, this cough from cigarettes. I went in a burning house to save a little girl who almost died because of you."

Gibbs shook his head again, his expression maddeningly mild. "No. As I said, I was nowhere near Cameron Glen this morning." He folded his arms over his chest and cocked his head to the side. "So does this mean you have made progress ingratiating yourself with the family?"

Evan hiked up his chin and clenched his back teeth, doing quick calculations as to how he should answer that loaded question. Gene Gibbs was such an unknown to him, he couldn't be sure the best way to protect Isla and her family and also find a way to disentangle himself from the morass of evil he'd gotten himself into.

While helping his mother was still his priority, he couldn't do it at the expense of other lives. He didn't want even a tangential association with Gene Gibbs if that association led to another's harm. If he could peel off Gibbs's DNA and walk away from his parentage, he'd do that in a heartbeat. He'd never erase the sight of Jenna Nash's pale, young face, or blot out the cries of grief her mother had wailed before the girl was revived. Evan hadn't started the fire, but being in league with the man who had placed an anvil of self-reproach on his shoulders.

When he hesitated, Gibbs flashed a smug grin. "I see." He stepped back and waved Evan inside. "Come in. I want a full report."

Reluctantly, Evan followed his father into the house. In Gibbs's office, he took his usual seat across the large desk from the other man. Gibbs rocked back in his chair and flapped a hand toward Evan. "So tell me how it was you were at Cameron Glen before sunrise this morning."

While seething over the lurid I-bet-I-know tone and smirk his father employed, Evan almost missed Gibbs's wording. He let the question penetrate his haze of fury, then returned his father's question with, "I never said what time of morning the fire happened. How did you know it was before sunrise?"

"Because Leon is smart enough not to go when the family was awake and could see him."

"Except he was seen," Evan said. Gibbs's admission of guilt barely registered. Evan had known as much, but the man's hubris screamed to be punctured and knocked down. "He was seen leaving the grounds, both by me and Isla as we were arriving at the property at five."

Gibbs's face twitched, his only visible sign of dismay over this news.

"Your flunky also left behind an empty wine bottle and a gasoline-soaked cloth. Even now, the police are checking that bottle for prints, I'm sure."

Gibbs grunted. "Not like Leon to be sloppy." A dismissive shrug. "I'll deal with Leon and any necessary cleanup of that situation later."

"Cleanup?" He gripped the arms of his chair as he leaned toward Gibbs and snarled, "Is that what you do after you nearly kill an innocent little girl and her family? A girl with no connection to the Camerons other than her family rented a cabin from them while on vacation?"

His father seemed surprised by this news and furrowed his brow as he asked, "Which house was burned?"

"I think I heard it called the White Pine cabin…as if that matters. You still endangered that family. A little girl almost died, you prick."

Gibbs glowered and smacked a hand on his armrest. "Leon torched the wrong house. He was supposed to burn the oldest daughter's house."

Evan goggled at the older man. "And how is that any less reprehensible?" He fought for a breath as the enormity of his father's coldness sat on his chest. He recalled both Isla's comments about her family and the file he'd been supplied by Gibbs. "You mean Emma's house? You realize Emma has both a five-year-old girl and a teenage daughter, don't you?" he railed, his voice cracking with smoke damage and emotion. "How can you justify putting children in danger? How can you justify hurting any of them, for that matter?"

His father lunged forward, his eyes angry slits. "They were warned there would be repercussions if they didn't sign my offer! They had to suffer the consequences of their actions or I'd lose all credibility in further negotiations!"

"What negotiations? You're extorting them!" His throat burned as he shouted, and Evan had to pause to gasp for a breath.

His face still hard and angry, Gibbs flipped up a hand. "Whatever works."

Evan flopped back in his chair, his guts churning with disgust and horror. He couldn't even form a coherent response to such vile dispassion.

Gibbs turned to gaze out his office window a moment before shooting a stern glance toward Evan. "Enough. Just give me your report. Where do you stand with the Cameron family? Have you made inroads with this *Isla*, beyond her bed?"

Heat rose in his blood as his fury was rekindled. "None of your business."

"Oh, it's absolutely my business. You were hired to get close to the Camerons, win their trust and get them to sign over the property at Cameron Glen. What has my money bought so far?"

Evan exhaled harshly, his nostrils flaring as he met his father's glare. No way would he give the repugnant man the satisfaction of knowing Isla had slept with him last night. Not that Gibbs hadn't guessed, but Evan would not share anything that would further soil the precious time he'd spent with Isla. Instead, he focused his mind on getting free of this devil's pact. Surely he could give Gibbs the impression he'd done his best to fulfill their deal and still protect the Camerons in the process. But how?

Taking a slow breath to calm his pulse, quiet the roaring anger in his blood, a question rose to the surface, needling him. "Why is the Camerons' property so important to you?" he asked. "Can't you just shift your development plans to another part of the county or even another part of the state? Surely there are other tracts of land for sale that would meet the criteria for whatever building development you have in mind."

Gibbs pursed his lips and twisted his mouth as he studied Evan. "A reasonable question." He sat forward and dug a key out of a tray on his desk before rising from his chair and crossing the floor to a wood-paneled wall. Gibbs inserted the key in a discreet lock and with a tug, a large section of paneling swung down on hidden hinges to reveal a map, covered with ink markings and pierced by numerous tiny pins. Turning back to Evan, Gibbs motioned for him to come closer to take a look.

Evan rose and stood next to Gibbs as he pointed at the map. "This is Valley Haven and the surrounding area. This—" he tapped an area in the northern part of the map that had no markings or pins "—is Cameron Glen. This—" he moved his finger to indicate an area adjacent to the Camerons' family land "—is considered by every economic indicator, geographic study and business model to be the best place to build the ski resort—" he tapped another spot "—shopping center—" *tap* "—and manufacturing complex in a four-county region. I have plans for an airstrip to go in here." His finger indicated an area close to Cameron Glen and next to the planned ski resort. "What do you notice about the locations I'm trying to develop? The areas I've already sunk millions of dollars into purchasing and battling city hall to have rezoned for my purposes?"

Evan's shoulders sagged. "Cameron Glen is right in the middle."

"Exactly." Gibbs's hands fisted at his sides. "If I don't get Cameron Glen, all my efforts, all my investments, all my plans go down the crapper." His jaw tightened, and his eyes blazed. "I refuse to lose everything I've been building these past few years because one stubborn family refuses to sell their land. My offers have been fair, generous even, but I'm tired of negotiating with that hillbilly. I will take that land any way I can. And you are going to help me do it."

No, I'm not, he thought, but rather than share that truth with Gibbs at the moment, he asked, "And how am I supposed to do something you've not been able to accomplish in all the months you've been trying? Clearly they have emotional ties to the land that aren't breakable."

"Then break those ties, damn it! I don't care how. But if you fail to deliver, I can make your life…and your dear old mom's…hell on earth."

Evan felt the blood drain from his face. He even swayed with the shock of Gibbs's threat. Why hadn't he realized that this man, who cared nothing about endangering a family with children, could also turn his evil on Evan's mother? He couldn't be in two places at once, couldn't protect both his mother and the Camerons at the same time. And if he refused to do Gibbs's bidding, how much worse could things get for himself and the people he cared about?

He stumbled back to his chair before his knees could buckle and muttered one terse, earthy curse word.

Gibbs, too, returned to his seat and leveled an icy stare on him. "I expect to see results from you, Mr. Murray. Soon. Now get out of my house and do your job."

Chapter 8

Over the next several days, Isla spent many hours each day visiting Evan at his motel room. She wanted to make sure he was following his doctor's instructions to rest, do his breathing exercises and use the antibiotics and inhalers as prescribed. Each time she visited, Evan said the same thing. "You don't have to do this. I'm getting better every hour."

To which she'd reply, "Hush. You're not supposed to talk. Rest your voice." And then she'd pour him a cup of homemade vegetable broth or herbal tea she'd brought in a thermos. She kept him company, read aloud to him from one of her brother-in-law's novels and reported to him on Jenna's condition.

The little girl continued to improve, though she stayed in the hospital where she could be monitored and receive hyperbaric oxygen therapy. With the rest of the Cameron Glen cabins full of other guests and Jenna's parents needing to be close to the hospital where Jenna was staying, Isla and her parents had moved the Nash family into Isla's house. She, meantime, had moved in temporarily with her parents, sleeping in the bedroom she'd once shared with Emma as teenagers.

During her visits with Evan, she learned new snippets of information about him, asking questions about favorites—movie, food, bucket-list travel, books— which he answered in short phrases he scribbled on a whiteboard she'd bought him. (*Shawshank Redemption*, peanut butter cookies, Iceland and anything by James Michener.)

In turn, she regaled him with stories about her family, life in their small hometown and her corresponding favorites. (*Ever After*, her Nanna's sticky toffee pudding, also Iceland—or New Zealand—and *Anne of Green Gables*.)

She was telling him how she'd come to own her goats when he wrote something on his whiteboard and turned it to face her.

He'd written *"You're beautiful. Inside and out."*

The compliment and the warmth that glowed in his eyes as he smiled at her were such a sweet surprise to her that she lost track of where she was in her tale. "I, uh…" She felt the heat of embarrassment and pleasure sting her cheeks, and thanks to her redhead tendencies, she knew her neck and face had flushed bright red. "Thank you. That's kind."

"It's the truth," he rasped.

Grinning like a kid at the start of summer break, she pressed a finger to his lips. "No talking."

He caught her hand and kissed her palm before he was gripped by another coughing fit.

She handed him the mug of herbal tea she'd made with a generous dollop of local honey and waited for him to regain his breath before finishing. "Anyway, the guy said I could have them free if I promised to give them a good home. He just couldn't take care of them properly anymore and hated to see them put down."

"Huh?" He grunted as he settled back on the stack of pillows she propped behind him on the motel bed. "Who?"

"Pickles and Petunia. My goats."

He nodded and gave a thumbs-up.

She studied his face as he closed his eyes with a weary sigh. He was beautiful too. And she was learning that despite some surface differences—West Coast vs. East Coast, meat eater vs. vegetarian, technically inclined left brain vs. free-spirited right brain—at their core, they shared more traits than separated them. They both prioritized their family, valued honesty, defended the weak, loved being outdoors, reading and wry humor. Her chest was so full of joy and optimism about their future that she blurted, "I love you, Evan."

His eyebrows shot up, and he inhaled so sharply, he started coughing again.

Isla chuckled and rubbed his back. "I'm sorry. I didn't mean to send you into a panic attack."

"I'm...not..." he rasped, "I just—"

She held up a hand. "Don't say it back if you don't mean it. I know it's early." She shrugged. "Maybe too early. I don't mean to scare you. But it's how I've been feeling. It happens quickly sometimes. My brother and his new wife, Anya, knew within a few days they loved each other."

Again he made a strangled attempt to speak, and she shushed him. "Really, Evan. I'm not trying to rush you. We've got time."

He wrote something on the board and turned it for her to read.

You take my breath away. <3

She laughed and kissed his cheek. "Thank you? I think."

With a sparkle in his eyes, he tugged her closer and stole *her* breath with a deep kiss.

I love you, Evan.

Alone that night, lying on his motel room bed, Evan replayed Isla's startling profession, turning it over in his mind and sorting out his tumble of feelings. Isla was special. As different as they were, he really enjoyed her company, and he'd certainly been shaken by how deeply he'd been moved when he made love to her. Under other circumstances, he could see himself sticking around and exploring this relationship further. He could even see himself falling in love with her.

Under other circumstances. And there it was...the bite of acid in his gut, the flood of guilt that soured what should be sweet. He still had his father's odious demands and threats hanging over him, the huge expense of his mother's medical treatment, his intention to return to Seattle to be with his mother in her time of need as soon as he could.

As soon as he conned Isla and her family.

He gritted his teeth and battled down a surge of self-loathing, because he couldn't escape the truth. He was conning Isla, one of the kindest, most loving free spirits he'd ever known.

You're beautiful. Inside and out. He hadn't lied about that. She was the real deal, and she'd opened herself to him, body and soul. Too fast? Maybe. But he got the sense that Isla was not the sort to do things halfway. She loved fully. Gave fully. Trusted fully.

Ouch. The viselike pinch of his deception twisted harder.

And her mother had invited him to meet the rest of her family, share Sunday lunch with them at her parents' home tomorrow. He should be celebrating the fact that, by all appearances, his efforts to get close to the family were moving along so swimmingly and so quickly. But was he getting in too deep? The better he got to know Isla, the more he hated the idea of hurting her for his own or Gibbs's gain.

So why did you sleep with her? His conscience chafed like a too-tight collar. Sure, at the time he'd thought they were just having mutually agreed-upon fun. She knew he lived out of state, that his mother needed him. She had to have gone into their night of passion with her eyes open. But any perception that Isla had ever intended their lovemaking to be a one-night fling had crumbled the moment she'd used the *L* word with him.

So now what did he do? He couldn't take back the night they'd spent together. Accomplishing his mission for Gibbs required he spend more time with her, give her more false hope about their relationship. He couldn't tell her he'd made a mistake sleeping with her and then expect her to be happy about any further business propositions he might bring to the family. He'd have to walk the fine line between keeping her happy and not leading her to believe his feelings were anything but casual attraction and passing companionship. Except…

He scrubbed his hands over his face and groaned. He did feel more for her than casual attraction. Not love, but more than just a fling too. Maybe it was *his own* feelings for her that needed to be reined in so that he could do what he had to. If he felt too much for Isla, he'd never have the nerve to follow through on Gibbs's orders. The Camerons might lose Cameron Glen, but Evan justified his course of action by telling himself his intentions were the best option the Camerons had at this point. If he could save them from any further violence or danger, assure they were paid handsomely for the property, ensure they were able to make a fresh start together somewhere else, he figured he'd have served the best interests of everyone involved. Right?

A gnawing guilt ate at his gut.

You're just doing a job. Don't dwell on anything else.

His hands balled at his sides, and he firmed his resolve. By shutting down his emotions, numbing himself to the repercussions of what he'd been asked to do, he could get through the guilt, get paid and get out of town. The sooner he completed his task for Gibbs, the sooner he could get back to Seattle. He was his mother's only family, and she needed him, especially if the coming months proved to be her last.

The wash of grief that thought brought buoyed his determination to get the financing he needed from Gibbs. Gibbs had known he had a son, had abandoned his responsibility to his son's mother as she raised Evan. As far as Evan was concerned, the man owed his mother something for all the years she'd worked multiple jobs to put Gibbs through business school and then provide for the child he abandoned.

After hours of tossing and turning, Evan finally got a few hours of nightmare-riddled sleep. He woke the next morning plagued by images of his dying mother begging him for help, of Isla being tortured by Gibbs—only to have Gibbs's face morph into his own—then of terrifying fiery creatures chasing him, cackling gleefully.

He did everything he could to clear his mind of the disturbing dreams, even heading down to the riverside trail in town to let the sound of babbling water and scent of autumn leaves refresh his soul. But he'd walked this trail with Isla on the night of their date, and every step of his walk reminded him of her. The gurgle of the river brought Isla's bubbly laugh to mind. The fresh, earthy scents of fall reminded him of the herbal aroma that was uniquely Isla's. *Ylang-ylang? Patchouli?* Some aspects of Isla Cameron were truly baffling to his engineer's mind, but her passion for the things that made her stand apart was endearing as well. Damn, but he'd entered some foreign territory here in North Carolina…and he didn't mean the geography.

When the time came to drive over to the elder Camerons' home for lunch, Evan hadn't quieted the riot of unrest following his turbulent night. Instead, his walk, his memories of their date and lovemaking had stoked a stronger affinity for the quirky, beautiful and warm woman he'd found in Isla. Exactly the opposite of what he needed to do. He pinched the bridge of his nose as he sat in his rented sedan and braced himself for the onerous task ahead. Not that dining with the kind, welcoming family would be difficult, but keeping his heart, his feelings disengaged would be.

You're doing this for Mom. Keep the endgame in mind. For everyone involved, he had to find the cleanest and most precise surgical method to do his job. Get in and get out with as little collateral bleeding as possible.

The driver's door opened, jolting him out of his deliberations.

"Hey, you," Isla said, bending to kiss his cheek. "Are

you praying?" Her tone and her twinkling blue eyes teased him. "Working up the courage to meet the family?"

Evan shoved aside his anxiety and gave her a brave smile. "Not at all. I'm not bothered by meeting your parents," he said, his voice carrying only a hint of rasp now that he'd rested it all week. He climbed out of the car and wrapped her in a hug as he glanced toward the front entrance where a few curious faces peeked out the storm door. "Hmm, maybe a little intimidated."

She laughed, and with her arm around his waist, Isla tugged him toward the porch. "Come on. They don't bite."

He followed her inside, where the mouthwatering scents of yeast and garlic and some spice that reminded him of Thanksgiving perfumed the air. His stomach rumbled in anticipation of the savory meal.

A small crowd waited for him in the living room. The home's decor harkened to the 1990s, with shades of gray blue, burgundy and navy, and floral-print upholstery. *Like Mom's house.* He battled down the twist of pain that thought stirred and aimed his smile at Isla's family.

"Everyone, may I present—" Isla said, her face beaming. She motioned to him with a flourish, as if a game-show beauty revealing a jaw-dropping prize. "The hero of the day, Evan Murray."

His gut flip-flopped hearing her refer to him in such grandiose terms. Far from a hero, he felt like the worst of villains, invading their home under false pretenses to dupe them out of their cherished heritage. He had to struggle to keep the smile on his face, and he prayed they excused the fine sheen of sweat on his brow as general nerves.

"He saved Jenna Nash's life and—" Isla continued,

her blue eyes bright as she grinned at him "—has brought a renewed joy to mine."

His heart bumped uncomfortably. Although he cared for Isla, seeing the sparkle in her gaze and hearing her speak of him in glowing words to her family left him off balance.

He gave the family an awkward smile as they all called out greetings and welcomes and praised his heroism with Jenna.

"How is Jenna?" he asked, redirecting the conversation from himself. "Have you heard?"

"She'll probably be discharged from the hospital today," Brody's wife, Anya, the ER nurse, said. "She's going to be fine. No lasting damage, thanks to you."

"We put her family in Isla's house until it is safe for them to travel home with Jenna, which they think will be Wednesday morning. Isla is in her old bedroom here with us," Neil said. "I must admit, it's been nice seeing her sunny face in the mornings, like old times."

Brody grunted. "Ugh. Morning people." He nudged his teenage brother, Daryl. "Am I right?"

Daryl shrugged. "Wouldn't know. I'm not up then."

"I rest my case." Brody hooked his arm around Daryl's neck and gave him a noogie...which led to playful jabs and mock wrestling.

"Boys, please!" Grace scolded. "Use that energy to get the food to the table, eh?"

"Anything I can do to help?" Evan scanned the women's faces, his hands splayed in query.

"Come keep me company until we're called to the table," Isla's grandmother said, her thin hand held out to him.

He crossed the floor and took the hand she offered as he sat on the couch beside her wheelchair. As he faced the older woman with a smile, she sandwiched his hand between hers with a surprisingly strong grip.

"Mr. Murray, is it?" she asked, her blue eyes bright and alert. They had a spark that reminded him of Isla's.

Isla snuggled close beside him on the sofa as he replied, "Yes, but please call me Evan."

"Murray is a good Scottish name, sir. Did you know?" her grandmother asked.

"Is it?" he glanced at Isla and back.

"Oh, aye." He couldn't tell if Isla's grandmother added the Scottish burr on purpose or if it came naturally, but she wiggled her eyebrows flirtatiously as she answered, "Indeed it is."

"I didn't know that. I hate to admit I know very little about my family tree."

The old woman seemed disappointed with his answer. "Oh. That's a pity. Everyone should know where they came from, *who* they came from. Do you know, I can trace my family all the way back to Robert the Bruce!"

"Um…" He must have had a blank look on his face, because her eyes widened with dismay and she released her grip on his hands.

"You know who Robert the Bruce is, aye?"

"Nanna," Isla cut in with a chuckle. "Not everyone had you for Scottish history lessons growing up. Don't put him on the spot!" Then leaning close to his ear, Isla whispered, "King of Scotland in the early 1300s that won Scottish independence from England."

Isla's brother-in-law and sister, both of whom he'd met the morning of the fire, joined them in adjacent seating.

Matt gave Evan a sympathetic look. "Uh-oh. Are you getting the third degree?"

"Because the truth of it is, you're not allowed to date Isla until you get Nanna's approval," Cait said with a teasing grin.

"Dating?" Matt divided a curious look between Cait and Evan. "You and Isla are dating? When did this happen?"

"We've had one date," Isla said and tucked her arm in his. "But it went very well, I think."

Evan smiled at Isla, his body vibrating with the same electricity she always roused in him. "I agree. I hope you'll honor me with another soon."

Cait jabbed Matt's ribs. "I told you about their date. The guy who hit her car?"

Evan cringed. "Ouch. That doesn't paint me in a good light. And I still contend she didn't look before she backed."

He gave Isla a playful wink, and she laughed. "I did too!"

Evan turned back to Matt. "You're the author, right?"

Matt seemed startled to have been recognized. "Yeah."

"I thought I knew the name when Isla told me about her family," Evan said, quashing the uneasy niggle that crept through him telling this white lie. He'd first learned Matt was Cait's husband from Gibbs's infernal file. "I've read your books. Love 'em."

"Thanks," Matt said with a self-conscious grin. "So you're the one who bought my book."

Cait elbowed her husband. "Stop. You've had good sales. And your publisher was happy enough to sign you for a new contract, so there's that."

"Congratulations! I'll look forward to reading it. I read *Operation Cover-up* while my mom was in the hospital last spring. It was just the escape and distraction I needed."

After several more minutes of small talk and enjoying the teasing banter of the family, Isla's mother poked her head into the living room. "Come to the table, clan. Dinner is served."

"You mean *tables*, don't you?" Daryl asked. "I mean, look at this." He motioned to the arrangement that had a smaller table shoved next to the already leaf-extended dining room table and sixteen place settings. "This is crazy!"

"Hush," Nanna said, with a flick of her hand. "It's fabulous! The family is growing, and I love it."

Isla directed Evan to the chair next to hers as the family gathered. Neil said a blessing, and the surprisingly ordered process of passing plates and serving dishes commenced. Evan savored the meal with the distinctly Southern flair—fried chicken, corn bread, sweet tea and a variety of vegetables from Grace's garden—and he contributed to the breezy repartee.

"Matt, will Eric be able to visit during his fall break?" Isla asked, passing the chicken without taking any.

"For a couple days," Matt said, then turned to Evan adding, "Eric is my son from my first marriage, and he's a freshman this fall at UNC."

Evan nodded as if hearing this for the first time, although this too had been in his father's file on the family. "Great. How does he like it?"

"He loves it. The reason he'll arrive late is because he's doing an overnight hike on the AT with his roommates Friday into Saturday."

"The AT?" Evan asked, then took a big bite of his corn bread.

"Appalachian Trail. It runs from Georgia to Maine and roughly follows the Tennessee–North Carolina border."

"Oh, that's right." Evan helped himself to another chicken leg. "Corvallis is close to some great hiking trails. I spent a lot of time on bike trails when I was at Oregon State."

Evan fell into a deeper discussion with Matt, Brody and Emma's husband, Jake, about hiking, PAC 10 football and specifically the merits of a playoff system in college sports, but he stayed keenly in tune with Isla and her conversation with her parents and grandmother. When he heard his father's name mentioned, though, he yanked his full attention to what Neil was saying.

"I don't need the police to confirm anything. I know in my gut Gene Gibbs is responsible for starting the fire! He's been threatening this kind of vindictive intimidation tactic for months. Who else has a reason to torch our cabin?"

"I agree," Isla said. "My gut says the same, but what do we do?"

"Of course we all know who's responsible. I'm just saying I wish we could *prove* it was Gibbs who set the fire. Maybe if he went to prison for one of his crimes, he'd finally leave us alone!" Grace said, shaking her head with dismay and frustration.

"Give the police a chance to do their thing. Proper procedure takes time," Cait said.

"True. But in the meantime, there has to be *something* you can do to stop his harassment and intimidation campaign," Anya said.

"If you have a suggestion, Anya love, I'm all ears," Grace said.

Anya shrugged. "Maybe you should rethink a restraining order? I know you were resistant earlier, not wanting to rile Gibbs, but the situation has changed. He upped the ante."

"I think you need proof of physical threat to get one of those," Cait said.

Evan set down his fork, his mind spinning as he followed the exchange. He was as eager as any of the Camerons to end Gibbs's menacing of Isla's family.

"His lawyer made veiled threats when he was here. Isn't that enough?" Grace asked.

Evan's heart thudded heavily against his ribs. He'd come with the intention of doing Gibbs's despicable bidding, but what if there was another way? If he could do something, anything to shield this family that had so graciously welcomed him to their table, to protect Isla, with whom he'd formed an emotional bond, and to show Gibbs he wouldn't be controlled by blackmail, he had to do it. His conscience wouldn't allow him to make any other choice. But what? How did he satisfy Gibbs's greed for the Camerons' land and still protect the property and the safety of the Cameron family? And if he did find a work-around, would his mother somehow suffer the repercussions of his actions? Gibbs certainly had implied as much.

He realized he was staring at Isla's mother when Grace glanced up and met his gaze. The older woman flushed and flapped a hand at her husband. "We should save this conversation for later. We're making Evan uneasy."

"Hmm? Oh, uh, no. I'm fine. Discuss whatever you want. It's your house, your table." He shoved his smile back in place, although the corners of his mouth felt stiff with the effort.

Was this the opening he needed to make his next move? Maybe if the Camerons knew the truth about who he was, they could help him work out a strategy to counter his father's plans. He hadn't wanted to break the news of his parentage to Isla in quite such a public forum. But if it served the common good…

He balled his hand in his lap as his brain ping-ponged through his choices.

Keep silent and try to work behind the scenes to help the Camerons or confess the truth and pray the family would see his connection to Gibbs as an opportunity to find some resolution?

Resolution? a skeptical voice in his mind whispered. *There'll be no resolution with your vengeful, self-centered father until the Camerons sell…or Gibbs is dead.*

Like a premonition of evil, a chill ran down Evan's spine.

Isla stiffened as an odd, icy sensation swept through her. As an empath, she was no stranger to occasionally experiencing others' emotions, as if their feelings were radio waves that she picked up and broadcasted to her brain. Certainly her parents were upset by the current conversation, as she was, but the new wash of anxiety and unrest came from Evan. She was sure of it when she glanced at him and found him glaring at his plate, his brow deeply furrowed and his jaw like granite.

She placed her hand gently on his leg, and he flinched as if she'd burned him. "Evan, honey, what is it?" she whispered for his ears only. "What's wrong?"

He blinked a couple times and raised a fake smile. "Nothing. Just…" He shook his head and wrapped his fingers around her hand on his lap. "I heard you discussing the fire, and I…"

She nodded. "Of course." She squeezed tighter and gave him a sympathetic smile. "You of all people have a reason to get upset. You must have nightmares about going into the burning bedroom."

"Well, sort of. Not so much the fire but…"

"He has to be stopped!" her mother said with particular vehemence, drawing Isla's attention.

"He's been getting away with God-knows-what for years," Emma added hotly, "and nothing sticks! I've heard he has people planted in the sheriff's department, has bribed them to look the other way."

"Then we'll go to the state level if we must," Neil said. "Gibbs is a cancer in our community and he must be stopped!"

She felt Evan shudder at her father's use of the *C* word. Knowing what she did about his mother's illness, she winced internally. As she leaned toward him to offer words that might soothe his aching soul, Evan sat taller in his chair and announced in a voice still gravelly from smoke damage. "I may have a way to help."

Chapter 9

Isla angled her body toward Evan. "We're open to any suggestions you may have."

Evan shifted on his chair and pushed his plate away, even though he'd not finished by half what he'd served himself. He cleared his throat and glanced from her father to her, the corners of his mouth bracketed by tension as he compressed his lips. "The thing is… I know Gene Gibbs. I, well…"

His throat convulsed as he swallowed, and Isla felt a sick dread in her gut. But was it her own premonition of what was coming or was she picking up on Evan's obvious discomfort?

"In fact, he is…my father."

A collective gasp and a few muttered invectives sounded around the table as all other conversation fell silent.

Isla wrenched her hand from his, icy cold penetrating to her bones. "You're what?"

He met her eyes and nodded. "He abandoned my mother and me when I was two." He cast his gaze around the other faces gaping at him in horror, explaining, "I hadn't had any contact with him in all the years since, until a few days ago when I went to his house to try to strike a deal with him."

"What sort of deal?" her father asked, his voice low and taut.

"I needed money, a lot of it, to pay for my mother's cancer treatment. I was desperate to save her and didn't know where else to—"

"What sort of deal?" her father repeated. Louder. More angry. His voice vibrating with venom.

Evan lifted a wary, shamed look Isla. "He hired me to…find an 'in' with your family. To earn your trust and…convince you to sell Cameron Glen to—"

"Get out!" Her father stood, knocking his chair over, as he roared his command and aimed a finger toward the front of the house.

Shock and dismay froze Isla. Her pulse throbbed in her ears and a surge of the full spectrum of emotions flooded her senses. She was drowning. Smothering. Caught in a tornado of one staggering thought and heartbreaking realization after another. Evan had lied to her. Evan had used her. Evan had deceived, manipulated and betrayed her.

"But if you give me a chance to—"

"You heard him," Brody said, shoving his chair back, his fists balled at his sides. "Do you need help out the door?"

"Evan?" Isla finally managed to rasp, searching his face for some hint that this wasn't happening. He was going to laugh awkwardly and say it had been a bad joke. Wasn't he?

But he turned guiltily from her gaze, raising a defensive hand as he said, "If you sell your property to me, Gibbs can't—"

"No!" her mother's voice was as strong and unyielding as Isla had ever heard it.

"I understand you want to protect it, but your family—"

"We will never sell this land!" her mother said over Evan. "It stays in our family. Period!"

"—is in danger. If you don't sell to Gibbs," Evan said, leveling a hard look on her father, "he will keep coming after you. He won't stop at burning down houses either. He will hurt someone. Kill them."

"How dare you threaten us!" Her father quivered with rage, his face growing red, and Isla worried for his health.

"They're not threats. They're a warning!"

Now Matt and Jake rose from their chairs, as well, and with Brody, seized Evan by the arms and dragged him from his chair.

Isla choked on a sob as she buried her face in her hands. Shattered. Confused. And sick with guilt, knowing she'd brought this viper into their presence.

"Isla, please," Evan called to her as the men shoved him toward the exit. "Let me explain!"

She wouldn't look at him. Couldn't. But when she heard the front door open, her brother's growled warning to stay away, she rose and darted to the foyer to follow Evan outside. "Brody, wait!"

Her brother paused and looked over his shoulder to her. "I won't hurt him, Isla. Not if he leaves without any further scene."

She jogged down her grandmother's wheelchair ramp until she could look Evan in the eye. "I need an answer first."

Matt and Brody exchanged a skeptical look, while Jake glowered darkly at their hostage.

Isla could feel waves of guilt shimmering off Evan, like heat rising from sunbaked asphalt. She had to choke back the lump in her throat to speak. "When you hit my car in that parking lot...was it really an accident or was it all part of a big setup to get to my family?"

The shadow that crossed his face answered her question, before he could stammer, "Isla, I know how it looks, but I never meant to—"

She spun away as claws of pain raked through her.

"Isla, wait! I'm sorry!"

She ran for the house but didn't return to the dining room. How could she face her family? She'd been a gullible fool who'd led Evan to them. Her naivete had put the people she loved most at risk.

Dear God, she'd shared meals with this man, made love to him, opened her heart to him! Because her stupid dream had made her think he was *the one*. Her soulmate? Ha! She nearly threw up as self-reproach churned acid in her belly. How horribly careless, flaky and deluded she must seem to the people who loved and trusted her. She'd let her family down and didn't know how she could ever make it up to them. She couldn't believe how terribly wrong she'd been in interpreting what her gut instincts were telling her about Evan. Had she let his handsome face persuade her? Her physical attraction to him?

As she stood in her parents' foyer, listening to the men's angry voices outside, the disgruntled muttering from the dining room, she shivered, trying find her equilibrium, when her world had been turned upside down. She walked numbly to the back door and out to her parents' yard. The garden, where her parents grew and nurtured plants and flowers all summer, usually gave her comfort. She savored being among the plants, the source of life, and feeling a connection to the life cycle of the planet. But now, after being plowed under for winter, the fallow earth looked as bleak and empty as she felt. She strolled to the middle of the patch of dirt and sank to her knees, letting her tears fall.

"Isla?"

Hearing Emma's voice behind her, she wiped her cheeks and angled a look of remorse to her sister. "Oh, Emma, I'm so sorry. I promise you I didn't know his connection to Gibbs or his hideous secret agenda."

"No one thinks you did. You have nothing to apologize for," Emma said with a tone of conviction. Her sister squatted beside her and rubbed a hand on Isla's back. "I just want to check on you. I'll understand if you want to be alone right now, but if you want to talk, I'm all yours."

"I…" Isla was about to ask for privacy, still ashamed of having brought Evan to her family, so blind to the truth, but Emma's comforting caress was a sisterly connection she craved. "Stay. You can help me beat myself up for my stupidity."

"Hey," Emma said as she gripped Isla's wrist firmly. "No beating yourself up allowed. Everyone makes mistakes. We were all charmed by him and swooning over his heroics saving that little girl from the fire. How could we have known he was hiding things?"

"But that's just it. I should have known! I can usually read people better than this." She waved her hand vaguely toward the house, where the devastating scene had unfolded. "And with Evan, it's even worse! I—"

She slammed her eyes shut and turned away from Emma with a sigh of disgust.

"You what?"

Isla shook her head. "It's so awful and humiliating and…"

"What? Isla…?" Emma grunted and stood, tugging on Isla's arm as she did. "Can we maybe get out of the dirt? My old knees aren't what they used to be."

Isla hesitated only a moment before climbing to her feet and dusting the dry soil and clinging leaves from her clothes.

Emma cut a glance to the back door, then in the direction of her own house. "Come on. Let's walk."

As her sister hooked arms with her, Isla fell in step beside Emma, her shoulders limp, her chin down, her heart aching.

"Now, what's eat you? What so awful and humiliating?"

"I slept with him, Em. I thought… I was so sure he was…" She sighed. "You'll laugh."

"I won't." Emma made an *X* over her heart with her finger. "Promise."

So Isla told her the whole sorry story about her dream, about seeing Evan for the first time the very next day at Burger Palace, about the car "accident," his visit to her house with flowers, their date…the whole embarrassing series of events. And her complete faith and surety that she and Evan were fated to be together, happily ever after.

"I let him in my life, my soul so easily, Emma. I trusted the sense I had that he was my destiny, and just…dived in heart first."

Emma's face crumpled in a sympathetic frown. "Oh, Isla, I'm so sorry. I may not be an expert on broken hearts, but I can imagine how deeply you must be hurting."

They'd reached Emma's house now and made their way to the two-person bench swing on an A-frame that sat in a corner of her yard. As they sat down and set the swing in motion, her sister asked, "Do you want to talk about it or do you want me to leave you alone to process?"

Her sister knew her so well, and she squeezed Emma's hand. "Normally I'd want to be alone, but…" She cast her gaze around the yard where the trees boasted shades of gold and red and flaming orange. "Maybe just sit silently with me and keep me company? Today is too pretty not to share it with someone you love."

Her voice cracked on the last word, and Emma tugged Isla's head down to rest on her shoulder. Even before Emma had had her first child at age eighteen and married her high school sweetheart, her oldest sister had always been the maternal sort, looking out for her younger siblings. Especially tenderhearted and highly sensitive Isla.

Now, with her head on Emma's shoulder and her sister's arm around her shoulders, they sat in the peaceful backyard, serenaded by the creak of the swing and the sough of the breeze in the dry leaves. Emma's comforting embrace opened the floodgates of turbulent and tangled emotion, and Isla wept quietly. Before long, despite claiming to want silence for her grief, Isla asked, "How could I have been so wrong about him? The feeling, the dream, it was all so clear and sure."

Emma chuckled warmly. "You're asking me how your woo-woo works?"

Isla snorted. "Woo-woo. More like poo-poo. I trusted a stupid dream and look where it got me. Worse, look what I did to the family!"

"You did nothing wrong!"

"I brought a poisonous snake to dinner! I wouldn't blame you all for hating me."

"Hating you?" Emma's tone was incredulous. She pushed Isla away so she could face her sister and meet her gaze. "See here, Isla Cameron. We love you. Nothing you could ever do would make us hate you! Certainly not this."

"But you must be disappointed in me, at least. The screwball, ditzy sister with kooky ideas and—"

"Stop!" Emma said, a note of motherly sternness behind the command. "I will not listen to you denigrate yourself like that when it is so untrue! You are kind and open and passionate about your well-meant beliefs, and we love your unique and compassionate approach to life."

"But if I hadn't—"

"Stop!" Emma gripped her shoulders and gave her a small shake. "None of this is your fault. You did everything in good faith, and Evan deceived you. He's the one at fault. He lied to you, manipulated you and—"

Her sister swallowed the end of her sentence, clearly not wanting to remind Isla of the most painful part of this fiasco.

He used me, slept with me under false pretenses.

Fresh pain slashed through her, and Isla covered her face with her hands. Hot tears rolled down her cheeks and she let them flow, hoping they'd wash away the sting of betrayal. She couldn't remember a time when she'd ever felt so raw, so bereft and confused.

Lowering her hands to her lap, she raised her wet eyes to Emma. "How do I ever trust my instincts about anything ever again? I was so wrong about Evan. How do I know what's true anymore?"

Emma thumbed away a fat tear from Isla's cheek,

even as moisture leaked from her own eyes. "You still have truth and love on your side. Your instincts and good heart have brought you this far in life. Evan tricked you, yes. But don't give up or start doubting yourself now, or the pain he brought you wins."

Isla meditated on that wisdom, nodding as she let her attention drift to her sister's back porch. The family's orange tabby, Pumpkin, sat blinking in the sunshine next to the feral black cat that Emma and their mother had been feeding for many years.

"Magic and Pumpkin get along?" Isla said, not sure how she'd missed that detail in past family conversations.

Emma gave a short laugh. "Yeah. Go figure. Magic still won't let *us* touch her, but she and Pumpkin are like best buddies. I think Magic had been lonely and was really psyched to finally have a friend."

Isla's heart wrenched. "I can understand that. I thought I'd found someone to end my lonely days too."

Emma's arm instantly went back around Isla and rubbed her shoulder.

"Sorry. That was melodramatic and maudlin, wasn't it?" Isla flashed a sheepish grin.

"Tell you what," Emma said, leaning her head to rest against Isla's. "You be as melodramatic and maudlin as you want for twenty-four to forty-eight hours. You've earned the right, and people need time to mourn a heartache. But then you dust that man from your hands and get back to living the positive, beautiful way you always have. The right man for you is still out there, sis. I know he is."

Isla nodded her agreement, but in her soul, she mourned the loss of *this man*. Because no matter how much his betrayal had hurt her, she couldn't forget the marrow-deep connection she'd made with Evan. Making love to him had been like a homecoming. His touch, his smile and a warmth that *couldn't* have been faked had reached into her very core with both hands. And he still had a tight grip on her, despite his treachery. Isla sighed and nestled closer to her sister's comforting embrace.

How did she expel a man who'd already rooted himself so firmly in her soul? She didn't know how. But today's debacle of a meal proved she had to find a way.

"Well, that went about as horribly as humanly possible," Evan grumbled to himself as he sat alone in his rental car at the exit from Cameron Glen. The highway was clear of traffic, but rather than head back to the motel, he sat debating whether or not to turn around and drive back up to the hill to Isla's parents and make an attempt to repair the damage he'd done. The entire family was outraged, hostile even. And the heartbreak and confusion, the pain and betrayal in Isla's eyes ripped him apart. He squeezed the steering wheel, realizing, now that he'd blown his chances with her, how much he cared about her. She was more than a beautiful woman. She was a warm, one-of-a-kind soul who'd touched him, challenged him, amused him, aroused him and welcomed him into her close-knit family. And he'd thrown away everything she'd offered him.

In his zeal to find an expedient solution to his predicament and get back to Seattle, he'd bungled everything. Had he really thought today, when the family barely knew him, was a good time to bring up anything as delicate as his unfortunate relationship to Gibbs or the hot-button issue of selling Cameron Glen? Never mind that his plan had been to work with the Camerons to find a legal way to turn his father's scheme around.

He scoffed his frustration. What were the chances he could have found a way to fulfill the terms of his agreement with Gibbs and get the money for his mom's treatment, while still protecting Cameron Glen for Isla's family? Slim to none. He knew his father well enough in three short meetings to be sure Gene Gibbs didn't compromise.

The slippery businessman would have inserted a hidden contract clause or had his lawyer include a loophole that would ensure he got his way. And Gibbs played dirty. The cabin fire was proof of that.

Fire…

Evan stiffened, his grip tightening on the steering wheel. *Fight fire with fire.*

Could he beat his father at his own game? Was there a Hail Mary option that could salvage the disaster he'd wrought by acting prematurely?

There had to be.

And Evan was determined to find that option.

Chapter 10

Evan delayed the inevitable meeting with Gibbs as long as he could. He kept praying he could make amends with Isla—or *some* member of the Cameron family who would act as a go-between—so that he could salvage their relationship and at the same time find some hope the family would negotiate a compromise with Gibbs. But every attempt to contact her or the family had met with a stone wall. She neglected his texts, refused to answer his phone calls and ignored his lengthy voice mails in which he tried to explain himself. When he'd shown up at her front door unannounced, he'd been swiftly and firmly escorted off the property by Matt and Daryl, with the assurance the police would be summoned if he set foot on Cameron Glen again. Restraining orders were threatened when he finally got through to Emma and Jake at their construction company office.

Two things kept him in Valley Haven instead of returning to Seattle. First, he refused to leave things with Isla on such a sour note. Even if she wanted nothing to do with him again, he wanted to do something, say something that would ease their breakup for her. He hated that he'd hurt her.

Second, he'd accepted Gibbs's money. He'd spent Gibbs's money. He'd sent the cash to his mother for the clinical trial down payment the same day he got the check from Gibbs. And he had no way to repay the huge sum he now owed the man if he failed to keep their arrangement. He didn't even want to think how his father would deal with his defection.

When Gibbs called, asking for updates, he stalled and hedged for twelve days, until his father demanded an in-person meeting. The older man's tone left no question that Gibbs would not be put off any longer.

Evan drove to Gibbs's large estate outside town, mentally psyching himself for the meeting. Leon showed him in, as he had in the past, and Evan entered his father's home office with the bitter taste of dread in his throat. How did one tell a mob-boss-wannabe that you'd failed to accomplish his goal? That you had, in fact, royally messed up the entire situation beyond repair? Would Gibbs demand the money he'd already paid Evan be returned?

Gibbs was clipping his fingernails as Evan took his seat, and without looking up from his task, his father asked, "So how did it go? Did you win the Cameron woman over?"

Pain squeezed Evan's chest, thinking of the intimate moments he'd spent with Isla, the scent of her hair, the texture of her skin, the soft fan of her breath tickling his ear. Her laugh. Her smile. Her quirky way of expressing ideas. Her genuine warmth and honest passion for life.

He genuinely cared for her, was powerfully attracted to her, had even imagined a real, lasting relationship with her—before he'd blown that hope to smithereens with his ill-timed revelation of his parentage and poorly expressed interest in buying her family property.

He'd not only failed Gibbs, he'd failed his mother. Failed Isla. And he missed her, more than he would have expected.

When Evan didn't answer immediately, Gibbs paused in his grooming to cast a side-glance at him. "Well?"

"Um, yes and no." Evan rubbed his hands on his jeans and gritted his back teeth.

Gibbs's expression hardened. "Don't play word games with me. Did you or did you not make any progress getting the sale of Cameron Glen to move forward?"

"I did, initially. But I, well, I pushed too hard, too soon and, um…they turned me down."

Gibbs cocked his head, his eyes round with shock. "You already mentioned the sale of the property to her?"

Evan clenched his hand in a fist on his knee and gathered his courage. "I already brought it up to her parents. To the, uh, whole family in fact. I kinda blew it."

Gibbs hand smacked on his desktop with a thud that made Evan jump. "You what?"

Evan took a beat to calm the effects of the adrenaline that had lurched in his bloodstream. Clearing his throat he said, "I was having dinner with the family, and the conversation reached a natural segue to the topic—"

"You freaking idiot," Gibbs growled and sat back with such force that his chair rocked into the wall behind him.

Evan remained silent while Gibbs stared out the large window beside his desk, clearly brooding. His father's nostrils flared as he took one heavy, angry breath followed by another. Finally, after what felt like hours, but was in reality only a minute or two, Gibbs muttered quietly. "Fix it."

Evan leaned forward, not sure he'd heard correctly. "What?"

Gibbs whipped his head around toward Evan, his eyes blazing. *"Fix it!"*

The man's roar kicked Evan's heart into a wild, strident cadence. "I don't think I—"

"I'm not paying you to think. I'm paying for results!"

"I know, but—"

"You said you'd made some initial progress. You got yourself invited to dinner with the family, for God's sake. Do it again!"

"I don't think I can. I hurt Isla. I betrayed her trust, and she's not even answering my calls or texts now."

"Well, then, you have a problem." Gibbs leaned forward, his glare menacing. "We have an arrangement."

"I'll pay back the money you've given me." Evan's gut clenched. He didn't know how or when he'd be able to get the cash to repay his father, but if it meant untangling himself from this mess, he would find a way.

One dark eyebrow flicked up on Gibbs's jowly face. "Yes, you will, but I still want your end of the bargain upheld. I want Cameron Glen."

"I don't see how that's possible." Evan sighed and glanced away from the man's steely stare. "The family knows my connection to you now. They don't trust me. They don't want anything to do with me. Especially Isla."

"You're not using the full scope of your imagination, then. Trust isn't required. Results are."

Evan snapped his gaze back to Gibbs. "What are you suggesting?"

"I'm not *suggesting* anything, boy!" his father replied hotly. "I'm telling you to grow a pair, and do what is required to get results! Get Neil and Grace Cameron to sign a sales agreement by any means necessary. I'm sick of waiting. Every day they don't sign, I lose more money and more patience. Do your job and get them to sign, by whatever means it takes!"

Evan squeezed the armrest of his chair, stunned speechless. The man wasn't reasonable, so how did Evan reason with him?

"Mr. Gibbs…" He paused and started again, trying another tack. "*Dad*, I'm sorry that—"

"Do you need a demonstration of the kind of persuasion that yields results?" the older man interrupted, clearly immune to the sentiment Evan had hoped would make a difference. He jerked a nod to Leon, and the goon crossed the office in three long strides. Viselike fingers clamped on to Evan's shoulder, and with his other hand, Leon reached inside his jacket.

A chill slithered through Evan as the business end of a handgun was jammed in his ear.

"I can hardly do your bidding if you have your man shoot me in the head," he said, managing to keep his voice flat and steady, despite the maelstrom of hatred and anxiety swirling through him.

"Oh, he doesn't need to kill you to make my point."

The smack of the gun's butt blindsided him and left his temple throbbing, his ears ringing. Evan reacted as quickly as his pain-rattled brain allowed. Surging to his feet, he swung at Leon…who easily blocked the move and landed a second jab in Evan's gut.

The blow stole his breath, and he crumpled forward,

barely staying on his feet. He angled a glance at his opponent and braced for the next hit. He remembered what his mother had told him when he'd been in elementary school and related events of bullying in his class.

Defend the weak. Stand your ground, but don't return evil for evil. Bullies are seeking power. Don't give them yours.

Evan grimaced. Good advice for an eight-year-old. Not as easy to manage when your bully has a gun and seventy pounds of muscle on you.

He ducked the next swing, but the pistol still clipped his chin. He bit his tongue. As the coppery taste of blood filled his mouth, so did rage. With a feral growl, he lowered a shoulder and charged at Leon. His momentum was enough to knock the larger man back a few steps, but Leon soon had his arm around Evan's throat, choking him with one thick arm.

Evan used what he could to strike back—elbows, feet, teeth. Finally he managed to inflict enough pain that Leon flung him away. Evan stumbled but stayed on his feet…barely. He had just enough time to gasp a lungful of oxygen before Leon was coming at him, hands balled. Bracing his feet, knowing he had the disadvantage, Evan raised his fists, prepared to defend himself. He even got in the first swipe, a solid shot that caught Leon in the chin.

For his efforts, Leon returned a bruising blow to Evan's right eye. Then his jaw.

Ears ringing, Evan surprised his opponent with a roundhouse kick to Leon's kidney. When the big man bent forward, clutching his side, Evan lobbed an uppercut to Leon's nose, hard enough that it sent pain juddering up his arm.

Leon answered with a snarl and punch to the gut that

knocked the wind from Evan. Leon had started batter-ing Evan's face when Gibbs roared, "That's enough! Leon, get him back in the chair."

Rough hands lifted Evan from the floor where he'd crumpled and dragged him unceremoniously back to his seat.

Evan raised his chin, his breathing ragged as he nar-rowed his swelling eyes on his father. "If you think you can beat me into submission—" he paused to draw a shallow, painful breath "—you'd be wrong. I won't hurt Isla…or any of her family…for you." He inhaled a ragged pant and gritted his back teeth. "And I won't stand by…and watch you or your ape—" he jerked his head toward Leon "—hurt the Camerons either. Deal's off. I'm done."

Gibbs flashed a sardonic grin. "Is that so?"

Steeling his resolve, Evan firmed his mouth and nod-ded. "It is."

His father—God, how he hated to acknowledge that relationship to this horrid man now—folded his arms over his chest and gave Evan a blithe look. "If you're thinking of going to the sheriff, you should know I have cultivated a special relationship with the men in that department."

"You bribe them."

"Call it what you want, but they allow me to operate in this county as I see fit." He straightened his spine and stuck his hands deep in his pockets. "I have been part of this community for many years, Murray. I have eyes and ears all over that Podunk town. Something to think about if you decide to try to double-cross me."

Not surprising. Money like Gibbs had bought al-legiance.

Gibbs pinned Evan with an exceptionally cold stare

then, adding, "You know, it occurs to me that your money problems would be solved if something were to happen to your mother. If she met with an unfortunate accident, she wouldn't need cancer treatments."

Ice filled Evan's veins. His heart stopped for a shattering moment before fire blazed through him, and he lunged toward Gibbs, raging, "You stay the hell away from my mother, you son of a bitch!"

"I will. But only until the end of the month. The clock is ticking, Murray." Gibbs matched his feral snarl as he leaned closer. "Now get me Cameron Glen!"

Chapter 11

The weeks that followed the disastrous dinner where Evan had revealed his betrayal passed in a blur for Isla. Somehow she managed to keep her routine, rising early to feed her animals, having coffee ready for whichever member of her family dropped by—they seemed to be tag-teaming to check up on her—and going through the motions of attending class, working the vegetable stand at the farmers' market with her mother, teaching yoga.

One morning, twenty-two days after the disastrous dinner—not that she was counting, but, well, okay, she was—Cait stopped by the house on her way to the rental office.

"Tag. You're it today?" Isla asked as she stepped aside to admit her sister.

"It?" Cait feigned innocence.

"Checking up on me for the family." Isla shuffled toward her kitchen. "I made coffee, but since you're off caffeine during your pregnancy, how about some herbal tea?" She reached into her cabinet and took down the oak box that held her selection of loose teas. She leaned heavily on braced arms as she glanced back at Cait, waiting for an answer.

"Are you all right? You seem...droopy." Cait moved closer, giving her a narrow-eyed look.

Isla shrugged. "I'm okay. Just...tired."

Cait tugged her arm, turning Isla to face her and giving her a look she'd learned from their mother that said "Try again. You're not fooling me."

After three weeks of pretending to her family that she was fine, a sob tripped from her throat. "And h-heartsick."

Cait wrapped her in a hug. "I know, honey."

Her instincts had never before been so far off base about someone, and it shook her beliefs about herself, her confidence in her judgment, her whole perception of who and what she was. "And...my disappointment in Evan, in myself has m-manifest itself in physical ways."

Cait pressed her hand to Isla's forehead. "I don't think you have fever."

Isla sighed and pushed her sister's hand away. "I know I don't. I'm not *sick*, just heartbroken. And mad at myself for jumping to conclusions because I had one stupid dream about meeting Evan and..." She slumped onto a ladder-back chair and groaned. "All the emotion and anger is sitting here." She rubbed her midriff lightly. "I've been sick to my stomach all week."

Cait chuckled wryly and took the chair beside Isla's. "Same. But for wholly different reasons. Whoever named 'morning sickness' really missed the boat. It's all-day nausea and fatigue."

"At least you'll have something beautiful to cherish at the end of your illness. When Evan betrayed me, I lost what I'd hoped was my future. He was so…" She let her sentence trail off, pushing aside the renewed pang of regret and loss.

Cait covered Isla's hand with hers and squeezed. "Is it possible you confused lust for destiny? I admit he was quite good-looking."

Isla lifted one shoulder. "Maybe. We certainly had chemistry to spare. The sex was…incredible. But knowing that just makes the sting of his deception cut deeper!"

Cait made a sympathetic hum in her throat, then blinked and gripped Isla's hand tighter. "Hang on…" Sitting taller in her chair, Cait drilled her with wide eyes. "You're tired and sick to your stomach?"

"Yeah. Why?"

Her sister turned both palms up on the table as if the answer should be obvious. "Like I am?"

An icy feeling washed through Isla, followed immediately by heat as her pulse picked up speed.

"Nooo…" she moaned. She shook her head in denial, as if doing so could add credence to her assertion.

Cait clutched Isla's forearm, her eyes bright with anticipation. "I have a test left from the two-pack I used to confirm my pregnancy. We could know for sure in a few minutes."

Isla swallowed hard and continued shaking her head. "No. No! I would know if I were pregnant! For cripes sake, I knew you were pregnant before you did. Why wouldn't I know it for myself?"

"Your instincts about Evan being your soulmate were off. Maybe your magic-feelings radar is broken?" Cait stood and hitched a thumb over her shoulder toward the front door. "You can know for sure either way if you take the test. What have you got to lose?"

Chewing her bottom lip, Isla sent Cait a panicked

look. "The luxury of ignorance. Taking the test makes it real, and… What am I supposed to do if I'm pregnant? And with the child of a man who betrayed me and tried to take Cameron Glen from us!"

Cait raised both hands in a calming gesture. "Take a breath. We don't know anything for sure. But even if you are pregnant, you have our entire family around you to help you. You'll be okay."

Spiked by the acid of dread, the nausea swirling in her gut ramped higher, and Isla surged off the chair. She rushed down the hall to the bathroom and lost her breakfast in the commode.

After Cait caught up to her, her sister found a washrag. She ran cold water on the rag, then handed the cloth to Isla to wipe her mouth, cool her cheeks.

"Thanks." Isla closed her eyes and focused on slowing her breaths, calming her heartbeat, finding her center. But when she opened her eyes, Cait held her gaze with a look of calm practicality.

With a whimper of reluctance and dread, she gave her sister a nod. "You're right. I'll do the test. I need to know."

"Evan has a right to know." Isla sat huddled on her sister's couch, Cait's arms around her and one of Nanna's crocheted afghans on her lap. But she was still cold. She struggled to wrap her mind around the notion that she was carrying another human being inside her. A baby. *Her* baby.

Evan's baby.

And each time that realization settled over her, a fresh wave of cold dismay sank to her core.

"I admire your consideration of his rights, but remember…he betrayed you. He's…" Cait shuddered and screwed up her face with her own revulsion. "He's Gene Gibbs's son!"

The chill in her bones deepened. "*Crivvens*. That makes this baby Gibbs's grandchild!"

Isla's voice broke, and the tears she'd fought to hold at bay—would her crying upset the baby?—pooled in her eyes. "Cait, what am I supposed to do?"

Her sister tightened her hold on her. "Well, for starters, take a deep breath. Let's look at the bright side of this." Cait's tone was chipper, clearly trying to bolster the mood, but Isla heard the quaver of tension and uncertainty in her sister's voice.

"The bright side." Isla furrowed her brow and tried to shove aside the dark thoughts that crowded her head.

"Inhale for four," Cait instructed, the way Isla usually did when teaching her yoga class or encouraging her family to remain calm.

Isla did as instructed, then held the breath for seven seconds, anticipating the rest of the technique. *Clear your mind. Focus on your breathing.*

"That's it." Cait patted Isla's arm and exhaled through eight beats with her. "Hey! Here's a bright side!" Cait angled her body more directly toward Isla, a smile lighting her face. "We'll be pregnant together! We can help each other, commiserate with each other, celebrate the milestones together." She jostled Isla and searched her face with an obviously forced excitement and glee. "Baby buddies! And our kids will be close in age and grow up together. That's cool, huh?"

"Baby buddies." Isla gave her sister a tremulous smile. "Yeah. Except you're married, and I'm alone."

Cait's expression grew fierce. "You are *not* alone. Do you hear me Isla Grace Cameron?"

A hiccuping chuckle escaped Isla's throat. "You sound like Mom."

"Well…I have to practice. Right?"

Tucking her head onto Cait's shoulder, Isla groaned. "Oh God. I have to break this news to Mom and Dad. They're going to be so upset."

"What? No!" Cait rubbed Isla shoulder. "They were supportive with Emma when she got pregnant in high school. And this is their grandchild too. They're going to be happy for you. I think they'll be more understanding and supportive than you're giving them credit for."

"Two big differences between Emma's situation and mine. She had Jake. They got married right away."

"That's true. But—"

"But nothing. Emma wasn't having a baby with a man who'd tried to cheat their family, the son of a man known for lethal and illicit business practices, thereby linking our families forever."

Cait moaned softly. "Well, yeah. There's that."

"It's entirely that, Cait," Isla said, her voice rasping as her tears leaked. "I've brought a permanent and dangerous threat into all our lives with my recklessness. How can I ever forgive myself? How can all of you?"

From his seat on a public bench, Evan watched a young family with small children feeding corn and peas to the ducks at the pond in the Valley Haven town park. The children's happy squeals and parents' laughter were bittersweet for him. He'd fed ducks with his mother so many times as a boy, and he treasured those memories. But tension coiled in his gut whenever he focused on the attentive father and considered the stark contrast between this loving man with his family and the cold dispassion and brutal tendencies of the man who'd fathered him.

Like the clouds scuttling across the sky, impeding the sunlight before moving on and revealing the bright rays again, his thoughts would shift from dark to light again when he thought of Isla, her tenderness, her family's joy and love for each other, so evident at the dinner table. God, he'd wanted that growing up. A large family, siblings, cousins, multiple generations sharing traditions and culture and teasing. Mom had done her best, and he wouldn't trade his relationship with her for anything.

The cool autumn wind stirred the hickory tree beside his bench, and another cloud drifted across the sky to block the sun. Evan sighed. He missed Isla. He mused a bit on how he could miss her so much when he'd known her so few days, had spent limited hours with her. Sure, the hours they'd had were quality. Meaningful. Paradigm-shifting. But...

Evan scrubbed his face with his hands, regretting it when he encountered his bruises. But nothing. October was drawing to a close, and Gibbs's threats toward his mother were looming larger. He'd run out of time to heal the rift between himself and the Camerons or find a solution that would appease his father. All he wanted now was to get out of Valley Haven, away from his horrid father and memories of all he'd lost with Isla. His job now was to protect his mother, to find another way to finance his mother's treatments.

Gibbs's threats replayed in his head, and a shiver chased through him. Gibbs wasn't going to let him walk away from their deal. The man still clung to his obsession with getting control over the Camerons' property. Evan still owed the man the thousands of dollars Gibbs had advanced him. He couldn't outrun his debt, his broken contract with Gibbs by returning to Seattle. One of his father's henchmen could hop a plane and be on the West Coast in a matter of hours to drag him back to North Carolina or…worse. But if he stayed, if he continued trying to satisfy the devil's pact he'd made, he couldn't protect his mother. If he stayed, what hope did he really have of changing Gibbs's mind about anything?

Evan bit out a low curse and pinched the bridge of his nose. He had no good exit ramp from this that he could see. Bad enough that he'd met a beautiful, interesting, warm woman and blown it all in the space of a few days.

Because of Gibbs. Because of his ill-advised deal with his maniacal father. Because—

In his pocket, his phone vibrated, cutting into his morose reverie. He hesitated, not wanting to answer it…in case it was Gibbs, demanding an update. In case it was the hospital in Seattle telling him his mother had taken a turn for the worse. In case it was his boss at the paper mill back home telling him he couldn't extend Evan's family leave any longer, that Evan had to come back to work or be permanently laid off.

Damn it, he was so tired of bad news and complications. Sighing, he pulled out his cell phone and glanced at the screen. And his heart bumped.

Isla was finally calling him back. He answered quickly, not even bothering to pretend he wasn't ecstatic to hear from her. "Isla! Oh man, I'm so glad to hear from you!" He was greeted with silence for so long that he checked his display to make sure he wasn't muted. "Isla?"

"I just… I'm not sure how happy you'll be after I tell you what I have to."

He furrowed his brow, not liking the uneasy tone of her voice. "Listen, if this is about that stupid way I handled things at your parents' house," he said quickly, trying to get the apology out before she could hang up again, "then let me repeat how very sorry I am—"

"No, it's…"

"And please know I never wanted to hurt you or—"

"Evan, don't."

"But, Isla, I—"

"I need to see you. Talk to you. In person. This—this should be said in person."

His mood lifted. "Um, sure! Yeah! Let me take you to dinner. No steak house this time. I promise. You pick the restaurant."

"No. Not dinner. I—I can say what I have to in just a minute or two. I'll come to your motel room, or… No." She gave a broken-sounding sigh. "Not there."

Not the place where they'd made love and shared confidences all night. She didn't say it, but she didn't need to.

"I could come out to your—"

"No!"

"—house."

"Stay away from Cameron Glen. You and your crook of a father!" The anger and hurt in her tone spoke for itself. She sounded like a protective mother warning a predator to keep far away from her child. *A predator.* No doubt that's how she saw him—a wolf on the hunt who'd attacked her flock. Her family. Her home.

"Neutral ground, then," he said, hating the sound of the term, as if they were warring nations. He didn't want to be at war with Isla or her family. He *liked* the Camerons. He especially liked Isla, but…

"There's a doughnut shop on Main Street called

Sweet Cravings. I never go there, because doughnuts aren't my thing."

If I'm going to indulge in something sweet, it will be my Nanna's sticky toffee pudding every time. Or ice cream. I do love ice cream.

"So you're not tainting a favorite haunt with bad memories?" he asked.

She hesitated a beat, and he could imagine the surprise flickering over her face that he'd understood her reasoning. Maybe it was hubris on his part, but he swore, after just the short time he'd known Isla, he felt he *knew* her.

Her huff of resignation filtered through the phone connection. "Something like that. Yes."

"All right. Sweet Cravings, then. I know the place. When?" he asked.

"Well…"

"I'm free now."

The silent pause told him he'd startled her with his response again. "O-okay. I can be there in ten minutes."

"Then I'll see you in ten minutes." As they disconnected, Evan realized how eager he was to see her again. And how desperately he wanted to seize this opportunity to reconnect with Isla, to fix what he'd broken. In his heart, he knew this might be his last chance to salvage a relationship that had, for a few days, burned so bright and promised such happiness.

Rising from the park bench, Evan headed toward the doughnut shop, his mind already working on a plan to recapture what he'd lost.

Isla lost no time getting to the doughnut bakery in town. The sooner she said her piece, laying out her terms of visitation with the baby, refusing any financial lures, providing Evan a guilt-free out should he choose it, the sooner she could be done with the unpleasant task and focus her energy on the baby. On savoring the pregnancy. On feeding the growing life in her a steady diet of love and music and peacefulness. The flood of stress hormones currently keeping her on edge had to be bad for the fetus.

She stood on the sidewalk outside the bakery, surrounded by the scent of vanilla and yeast that hung in the air, even outside the shop, and her heart raced as if on a sugar high. She put a hand on her belly and rubbed with small, soothing circles. "It's going to be okay, sweetie. I've got this."

But was she saying so for the baby's benefit or her own?

She spied Evan at the counter immediately, her eye drawn to his tall, masculine form like a homing beacon. He either heard her come in or sensed her presence, because he turned and met her gaze within a couple seconds of her arrival. A bright grin lit his face, and she had to fight back the instinctive leap of joy in her core, the answering smile that quivered on her lips and the painful tug of yearning in her heart.

His dark hair was wind rumpled, and his cheeks had a glow that hinted he'd been in the sun recently. Damn his handsome hide! Did he have to be so alluring? His smile so charming? His dimple so endearing?

Would her baby inherit his dimple? She hoped so. Or not. Seeing that captivating reminder of the baby's father every time she saw her child's face would be agony.

She tore her gaze from his and jerked her head toward an empty table, showing him where she'd be waiting. He gave a nod of understanding, then faced the older man behind the counter again.

At the table, Isla closed her eyes and took a few slow, centering breaths.

Calm. Still. Quiet, she told her spirit.

Ha! her jangling thoughts replied.

The table jostled beneath her hands, and she opened her eyes to find Evan sliding an insulated cup toward her—and a greenish bruise darkening his right eye.

"What happened to you?" she asked, pointing toward his eye.

He shrugged it off as if unimportant. "I'm fine." Nodding toward the drink he'd put in front of her he asked, "Chai with a splash of oat milk, right?"

She glanced at the cup and squashed the sentimental twinge over his remembering her hot drink of choice. She started to reach for the tea but stopped herself. "I… No. Chai has caffeine."

"Well, yeah. I guess. But I thought you said—"

"I did. But…" She waved away her plan to explain. Better to get to the root of the matter instead of performing a word ballet. She pushed the tea aside and folded her hands on the tabletop. "Evan, forget the chai. This isn't a social visit."

He sipped from his own steaming cup that smelled strongly of coffee and gave a small nod of concession. "All right. You had something to tell me. So…" He pressed his lips together and nodded to her. "What's on your mind?"

Isla swallowed hard, fighting to squelch the tremble in her soul. Stalling wouldn't change the truth or her need to deliver it. So she raised her chin and looked him in the eye. "I'm pregnant, Evan. I'm going to have your baby."

Chapter 12

The sip of coffee he'd been swallowing went down the wrong pipe, and he sputtered and choked on the inhaled liquid. He snatched up a napkin to cover his mouth so that he didn't spray Isla as he coughed. When he could find a wisp of breath, he wheezed, "Sorry."

"Are you all right?" She left her chair and came around the table to pound his back.

He waved her off. "Fine… I—" He dragged in a wheezing breath and narrowed a stunned look on her. "Are you sure?"

One of her delicate eyebrows hitched up.

Shaking his head, he rasped, "No, forget I asked that. Of course you're sure. You wouldn't have come to me with this if you weren't." He coughed again and drew a slow careful breath as he gazed at her intently, sorting through his mixed feelings.

A baby. With Isla. *His baby.*

A father. Holy. Cow.

Her blue gaze narrowed on him as she returned to her chair. "Before you say anything—not that you were saying anything—" her expression darkened to something of a scowl at this "—I've only told you, because it was your right to know. I want nothing from you and would truly prefer you had nothing to do with me or the baby going forward."

He opened his mouth to protest, and she shot a hand up to silence him. "But." She paused to take a slow breath. "I know I have no right to keep you away from the child, short of taking you to court, and that just seems so…petty. So…" Her cheeks puffed out as she exhaled her frustration. "I guess we have to come to some sort of understanding. I prefer something on paper, something legal and binding. I don't cotton to having my child ripped away from me down the road because your future bride decides she wants your child to be hers."

"What?"

"I've heard of it happening." Her expression grew hard. "But I won't let that happen to my baby."

"I…" He held his hands to make a *T*. "Whoa, whoa, time-out. Let's, um… Jeez. I'm still processing the whole you're-pregnant-with-my-baby part. Can we put a pin in custody battles for a moment?"

She turned to stare out the front window, tears sparkling in her eyes. "This isn't easy for me, Evan. I want to settle what we need to and move on. I want to be free of thoughts of you and worries over what you or your father might do in regard to the baby."

His chest quickened. "My father?"

She swung a sharp look at him. "I can't *stand* the idea that my baby is connected to that man. He's a thief and a con artist and…worse."

Evan nodded. "And worse," he acknowledged in a grave tone.

Isla's face paled a shade whiter, her blue eyes full of alarm.

"I feel the same way, love." He reached for her hand, covering hers as he sent her a sympathizing gaze. "I hate my own connection to him, but I can't change my biology any more than I can change our baby's."

Her throat worked as she swallowed, and Isla slipped her hand away from his, rubbing the spot where he'd touched her, as if burned.

"Well, maybe I can't change my child's paternity, but I will not—*will not*—allow you to use this situation or my baby's life to manipulate me or my family." Her tone was cold, her eyes like ice. This flinty, stark side of Isla surprised him. She'd been so warm and open and full of good humor before...

Before she'd discovered that he'd lied to her, betrayed her.

"I would never do that," he said, meaning it.

She sneered at him. "No? You used *me* easily enough. Took me to bed knowing full well you were only after my family's land!"

"Isla, no. It's not like that." He tried to reach for her again, and she jerked her arm from his reach, her glare icy.

"Don't!"

"I slept with you because I had feelings for you," he said pitching his voice low when he caught the side-glances of the patrons two tables over. He hated doing this in public, but Isla hadn't given him a choice. "Because I was, and still am, powerfully attracted to you and fascinated by you. I longed for a deeper connection with you. And because you wanted the same connection. You said as much. You—"

She stood abruptly and made to leave but stopped at the shop door. She hesitated there a beat before returning to their table. Her beaten expression surprised him…and broke his heart.

Isla sat with her shoulders slumped forward, her arms wrapped around her middle, holding her purse in her lap like a shield. Her body language screamed protectiveness, defeat, dejection. His chest ached knowing he was largely to blame for her mood, for having stolen her joie de vivre, for having extinguished the light that had glowed from within her.

"I asked to meet with you so we could reach an understanding, so…let's do that." Her quiet, reasonable timbre resonated inside him like a low gong, a sense that this could be his last chance to get things right between them.

Evan took a moment, scrubbing both hands on his face as he replayed her announcement in his head. He was a father. She was having his baby!

"I want to be—" he started at the same time she said, "I don't want or need—"

They both broke off and locked eyes.

"Go ahead," he said. "Finish what you were saying."

"I don't want anything from you. I can provide for this baby. My insurance will pay for prenatal care. I can take care of her by myself. You needn't feel beholden to me on that account."

He dipped his chin, acknowledging her pronouncement. "Just the same, I refuse to be a negligent father. I had one, but I will *not* be one. I intend to be a part of this child's life in some manner. As much as possible."

The dismay that crossed her face clearly said this was not the response she'd been hoping for. Too bad. Other men might like to be let off the hook or given permission to ride off into the sunset, but Evan Murray stayed. Evan Murray cared. Evan Murray wanted this child and wanted this child *to know* he wanted this child.

She closed her eyes, then inhaled and exhaled as if fighting for patience. "Evan…"

"I mean it, Isla," he said, hoping his tone struck the right balance between firm resolve and tact. "I won't let you shut me out. I have rights."

"I know. It's just…after what you did…" She rubbed her temple and shot him a wounded look. "You deceived me and my family and tried to—"

"I was wrong to do that. I said I was sorry."

She gave a bitter laugh. "I'd be a fool to trust you again. How can I co-parent with a man who's shown himself to be manipulative and disloyal and selfish?"

Evan dragged both hands over his face and growled his frustration. "God, I hate that you think that of me. That's not who I am!"

She scoffed again and shook her head. "Actions speak louder than words. It's trite but true."

"I did a terrible thing, I admit. But I had the best motivation. I didn't lie about my mother's condition, her desperate need to be part of a medical trial that could save her life."

Her brow furrowed in sympathy, and she glanced out the front window again. "I'm sorry about your mother, but your actions were—"

"Wrong. I get that. It made me sick to my stomach to lie to you and your family. My arrangement with my father was a pact with the devil, that I regret. But I was desperate, and I thought I could minimize the damage to you and your family if—"

She waved a hand to stop him. "Don't. Just…don't.

Because no matter your reasons or excuses, the fact remains that you are Gene Gibbs's son. I know what Gibbs is capable of, how low he's willing to sink to get his way, to make money, to bully people. That alone is enough to terrify me, even before you factor in the part where you betrayed me."

He reached for her hand again, and when she struggled to withdraw it, he clung tight. "Isla, knowing Gene Gibbs is my father terrifies me too. But I swear this to you—I will do whatever it takes to protect you and our baby from him. Always and in every way."

She met his gaze with sad eyes and said softly, "The best way to do that is to stay far away from me and my child." She wrenched her hand free and stood. "Goodbye, Evan."

Chapter 13

Evan sat in the driver's seat of his rental car in stunned silence, replaying his conversation with Isla over and again. *I'm going to have your baby... Stay far away from me and my child.*

He was elated with the idea he was going to be a father. Children had always been a part of his hope for the future. And while these circumstances—the mother of his child hating him was hardly ideal—had not been in his plan, he got a thrill at the notion of being able to fulfill his mother's wish to be a grandmother.

I'd wanted to hold my grandchildren before I died.

A bittersweet pang wrenched inside him. A baby, his mother, Isla's anger. The news was a lot to process. So much so that he almost missed seeing Leon walking into the doughnut shop he and Isla had just been sitting in.

He slumped a little lower in the driver's seat, praying Leon didn't see him and sighing with relief that he and Isla had left the shop before Leon arrived.

Unless…

A chill chased down his spine. Had Leon followed him here? Followed Isla? Could his father's henchman have planted a tracker on his rental car or the Camerons' vehicles?

Of course he could have. And he had no doubt Gibbs *had* tracked him. Or Isla. Or both of them. His father had kept files on the family, he knew details of their life only a stalker, a madman obsessed with getting his way, could have known.

He shouldered open the car door, and crouching by each tire, he checked the wheel wells, removed the hubcaps, then moved on to search the trunk, the bumpers. Nothing.

Then, before climbing back behind the steering wheel, he checked under the dashboard at the electronics panel. There, plugged into the on-board diagnostic panel, was not one but two small devices with blinking lights and the names of two different GPS companies imprinted on the side. *Two?* Okay, one was likely put there for practical reasons by the car rental company. The other…

He muttered a curse word and tossed both GPS devices in a trash can just down the street. His father was tracking him. Damn it! Evan was digesting this revelation when Leon emerged again and turned to stalk down the street, away from where Evan was still parked. He had no coffee in hand or food in a bag. He'd only been in the store a few minutes. Not long enough to order and eat a snack, but…long enough to talk to the guy behind the counter. Who easily could have overheard his impassioned discussion with Isla.

I have eyes and ears all over that Podunk town.

Double damn it! The last thing he wanted was for

his father to know about the baby. If Leon had learned what Isla had told him…

I know what Gibbs is capable of.

Cold settled over him, a frost that permeated to his bones. If Gibbs learned about the baby, Isla could be in very real danger.

Evan spent two restless, angst-filled days desperately trying to reach Isla, to warn her their conversation had likely reached Gibbs. He knew she was upset, hurt, reeling from the unexpected pregnancy and his deception, but given Gibbs's volatility and single-minded obsession with gaining Cameron Glen, he worried how news of Isla's pregnancy would land with Gibbs.

I don't do family.

Evan prayed that would extend to Isla's baby, that the child would be of no import to Gibbs, but Evan had a sinking feeling that Isla being a Cameron meant Gibbs would find a way to manipulate this twist of fate to the detriment of Isla's well-being.

But for two days, Isla had ignored his calls and left text messages unanswered. Who was he kidding? She'd probably blocked him. When he'd stopped by her house, praying she'd answer his knock, she'd summoned the police to escort him from Cameron Glen. The fact that he'd been trying to shout warnings to her—"You're in danger! My father might come after you!"—despite her closed door, only made him look all the more guilty of harassment when the cops showed up.

Isla simply refused to have further discussions with him.

Stay far away from me and my child.

Except it was *their child*, he thought now as he sat on the bed in his pajama pants next to the detritus of his fast-food dinner. Jeez! The notion blew his mind every time he stopped to consider the reality. He was going to be a father. He had a permanent link to Isla… forever. And perhaps most important, Isla and the baby were his family. They might not be married, but in his mind, the moment they'd created a new life together, they became a familial team. He liked that idea, even if Isla refused to consider it, rejecting him and his offers of a truce. But on the heels of his joy came the pain of her rejecting him…and the bone-chilling fear of something happening to them…because of him, because of his link to Gibbs.

Turning off the light, he climbed in bed and prepared for another sleepless night, racking his brain for a plan to soothe Isla's raw wounds and her family's. Could he reach Isla through one of her siblings?

Maybe if he went by her brother-in-law's construction office again and reasoned with—

A pounding on his motel room door cut into his reverie, and he shot a startled look toward the door. It was too late in the day for it to be housekeeping, so who—

Isla? He launched off the bed, his heart thumping a hopeful cadence, and yanked open the door. Leon stood on the sidewalk, wearing a scowl, as if he was the one being disturbed rather than Evan.

Matching the other man's glower, Evan asked, "What do you want?"

"Boss wants to see you."

Evan scoffed. "Well, I have nothing to say to him, so I respectfully decline."

His tone was anything than respectful, though, and Leon's expression darkened. "It wasn't a suggestion. I'm here to drive you."

"What? Now?" Evan checked his watch. 11:24 p.m. "No."

When he tried to close the door, Leon's hand shot up to block it. "The boss doesn't accept no for an answer. Come with me." Leon hitched his head toward a dark SUV. When Evan didn't move, Leon seized him by the arm.

Evan's frown deepened. He waved a hand to his sleep pants and T-shirt, indicating his dishabille. "Hey! I'm not dressed. I don't have shoes or my phone…"

Leon growled, baring his teeth, and marched inside the motel room, grabbed the athletic shoes by the bed. After shoving Evan inside the SUV, he threw the shoes in Evan's lap. "The meeting is come-as-you-are. No phone needed."

Evan jammed his feet into the sneakers and sat in tense silence as Leon drove him to Gibbs's estate outside the city. He spent the time mulling what could be so urgent that he'd be summoned late at night like this. Or did Gibbs just get a power trip from snapping his fingers at odd hours and having his minions jump at his command? Regardless of the reason, Evan knew this audience with Gibbs boded ill. How could it not?

Even if this summons had nothing to do with Isla's baby, Gibbs was unlikely to have had a complete change of heart about Cameron Glen, Evan's financial debt or the regrettable contract Evan had signed. More likely, his father had devised a new threat, had carried out another act of terror he'd use to spook Evan into obedience. A sour roiling settled in his gut as his thoughts went immediately to his mother. Gibbs had promised him the rest of the month to make progress with the Camerons, but what if the hateful man had grown impatient and had hurt his mom?

His hand twitched with the impulse to call her, to make sure she was all right. But his phone was plugged in, charging on the bedside table in his motel room.

Okay, I'm officially spooked. He inhaled deeply, wanting to squash the uneasy churning inside him that would only hamper his focus and reaction speed. He was determined to hold the line. He refused to harm the Camerons in any way. And now he had his own child to consider...and to protect.

Leon parked at a lower-level, rear entrance to Gibbs's huge home and strong-armed Evan out of the SUV.

Evan raised both hands as he scowled at the thug. "Take it easy! I'm coming."

Leon said nothing, only shoved him toward the back door. As they marched down the basement corridor, Evan glanced into the rooms he passed, curious about this part of the house. When Leon paused long enough to toss his jacket into a room with an unmade bed and the general clutter of a messy occupant, Evan wondered again about Leon's relationship to Gibbs, the large man's living arrangement and loyalties.

"You live here?" Evan asked, nodding his head toward the messy room.

"What of it?" Leon groused.

"Just...curious."

Leon answered with a firm hand between Evan's shoulder blades, propelling him farther down the hall. Instead of Gibbs's office, where Evan had always met with his father before, Leon led him to a game room, where Gibbs was playing billiards and swilling a golden liquid from a highball glass.

"You woke me up and dragged me here at this hour to play eight ball with you?" Evan asked, his tone sarcastic.

Gibbs only glared and shoved his glass toward Leon. "Top me up."

Leon moved to the wet bar, with its impressive walnut, marble and leather construction, and unstoppered the glass decanter of liquor. When he'd splashed a generous amount into the glass, he handed it to Gibbs and poured a second glass.

"Thanks, but I—" Evan had started when Leon tipped the glass up and downed the drink in two gulps. Evan grunted. "Right. Never mind."

Gibbs waved a hand toward Leon and the liquor. In a boisterous, overloud voice, he said, "Of course you should have a drink! A toast to fatherhood!"

A chill crept through Evan. So Leon *had* reported back whatever conversation he'd had with the doughnut shop worker. Naturally. Just in case, though, Evan feigned ignorance. "I'm sorry. What?"

Gibbs took a big sip from his glass and eyed Evan over the rim. He smacked his lips as he lowered the glass and wiped his mouth on the back of his hand. "A little bird tells me I'm going to be a grandfather. You knocked up that Cameron woman, didn't you?" he said, slurring his words. "Wha's her name...? Ida, Ira?"

Evan gritted his teeth, unwilling to give Gibbs the satisfaction of Isla's correct name.

Behind him, Leon supplied, "Isla," incorrectly pronouncing it Iz-la.

Clenching his jaw tighter, Evan raised his chin and admitted nothing. He leveled a hard glare on his father, who was clearly well past inebriated and headed for sloshed.

Gibbs frowned when Evan didn't speak and glanced at Leon. "He seems to be tongue-tied. Maybe you could loos'n his tongue for me?"

"One Minute" Survey

You get up to **FOUR** books <u>and</u> a Mystery Gift...

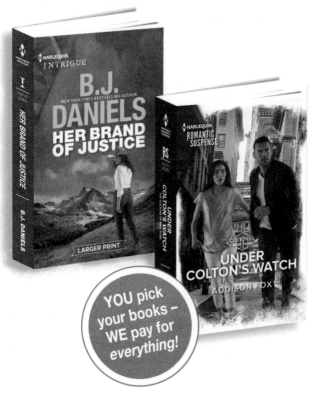

YOU pick your books – WE pay for everything!

See inside for details.

Dear Reader,

Your opinions are important to us. So if you'll participate in our fast and free "One Minute" Survey, YOU can pick up to four wonderful books that WE pay for when you try the Harlequin Reader Service!

As a leading publisher of women's fiction, we'd love to hear from you. That's why we promise to reward you for completing our survey.

IMPORTANT: Please complete the survey and return it. We'll send your Free Books and a Free Mystery Gift right away. And we pay for shipping and handling too! ← *We pay for EVERYTHING!*

Try **Harlequin® Romantic Suspense** and get 2 books featuring heart-racing page-turners with unexpected plot twists and irresistible chemistry that will keep you guessing to the very end.

Try **Harlequin Intrigue® Larger-Print** and get 2 books featuring action-packed stories that will keep you on the edge of your seat. Solve the crime and deliver justice at all costs.

Or TRY BOTH!

Thank you again for participating in our "One Minute" Survey. It really takes just a minute (or less) to complete the survey... and your free books and gift will be well worth it!

If you continue with your subscription, you can look forward to curated monthly shipments of brand-new books from your selected series, always at a discount off the cover price! Plus you can cancel any time. So don't miss out, return your One Minute Survey today to get your Free books.

Pam Powers

"One Minute" Survey

GET YOUR FREE BOOKS AND A FREE GIFT!

✓ Complete this Survey ✓ Return this survey

▼ DETACH AND MAIL CARD TODAY! ▼

1 Do you try to find time to read every day?
☐ YES ☐ NO

2 Do you prefer stories with suspenseful storylines?
☐ YES ☐ NO

3 Do you enjoy having books delivered to your home?
☐ YES ☐ NO

4 Do you find a Larger Print size easier on your eyes?
☐ YES ☐ NO

YES! I have completed the above "One Minute" Survey. Please send me my Free Books and a Free Mystery Gift (worth over $20 retail). I understand that I am under no obligation to buy anything, as explained on the back of this card.

☐ **Harlequin®**
Romantic
Suspense
240/340 CTI GRSD

☐ **Harlequin**
Intrigue®
Larger-Print
199/399 CTI GRSD

☐ **BOTH**
240/340 & 199/399
CTI GRSZ

FIRST NAME _____ LAST NAME _____

ADDRESS _____

APT.# ____ CITY _____

STATE/PROV. ____ ZIP/POSTAL CODE _____

EMAIL ☐ Please check this box if you would like to receive newsletters and promotional emails from Harlequin Enterprises ULC and its affiliates. You can unsubscribe anytime.

BUSINESS REPLY MAIL
FIRST-CLASS MAIL   PERMIT NO. 717   BUFFALO, NY

POSTAGE WILL BE PAID BY ADDRESSEE

HARLEQUIN READER SERVICE
PO BOX 1341
BUFFALO NY 14240-8571

NO POSTAGE
NECESSARY
IF MAILED
IN THE
UNITED STATES

Leon set his glass down hard and took one long step toward Evan. He swung a fist at Evan's chin, the blow coming so quickly, Evan had no chance to duck or dodge. Pain streaked from his mouth to his ears and ping-ponged in his head. Testing his jaw, he opened his mouth slowly and rubbed his sore face. He returned his glare to Gibbs. "Was that really necessary?"

Gibbs shrugged, sipped. "I guess we'll see. You ready to tell me what's goin' on with the Camr'n bitch?"

Evan bristled at the crude term. Heat climbed his neck, and he squared his shoulders as he stepped toward Gibbs. "Watch your mouth!"

Leon grabbed a fistful of Evan's T-shirt and forcefully dragged him back a stumbling step. Evan tensed, bracing for another blow, dividing his attention between Leon and Gibbs.

"You know, I could have Leon beat the truth out of you, if that's the way you want to play this." Gibbs drained the rest of his drink and belched as he set his highball glass aside. He swayed a bit on his feet and blinked hard as if having trouble focusing. "My sources tell me you and Ida, Izla—wha'ever her name is—are havin' a baby. Which makes me Grampa Gene." Gibbs's grin was smug rather than happy.

Still Evan said nothing. He pressed his lips in a taut line, and his nose flared as he tried to squelch the heavy, hostile breaths that gave witness to his fury.

Gibbs lifted his empty glass, realized his mistake and slammed it down again. "Say something!"

Evan did. A terse, vile directive that expressed his antipathy but only enraged Gibbs further.

Leon didn't wait for permission. He slammed Evan from behind, shoving his face into the pool table and wrenching his arm behind him to a painful angle. Grabbing a handful of Evan's hair, he lifted Evan's head and smashed it against the felt surface of the pool table. Twice.

Evan bit his tongue, tasted blood. His nose throbbed and may have been broken. When Leon released him, he straightened slowly and regarded Gibbs through narrowed eyes. "What do you want from me that your henchman and paid informants haven't already given you?"

Gibbs took his pool cue in hand and bent to line up a shot. He missed. Badly. Scowling over the flubbed aim, Gibbs met Evan's gaze. "Access."

Evan's mouth dried. This was what Isla had feared. He shook his head slowly. "I can't..."

Gibbs slammed a fist on the pool table. "You can! That baby's my blood. And I intend to use that blood t' get legal access to the child's share of Cameron Glen." Gibbs's mouth twisted in a cruel grin. "Congratulations, son. Despite your inept handling of our agreement, you have provided me a much more interesting avenue to pursue. I can sue for custody." He paused, then his face brightened as if a better idea had occurred to him. "A grandchild makes a most promising bargaining chip for wh'mever has control."

Evan flinched as if physically struck. "What the hell does that mean?"

"What do you think? If I have cust'dy of the kid, the Camerons will be at my mercy if they ever want to see him."

Evan snorted and shook his head. "You're drunker than I thought if you actually think you're ever going to get that baby away from Isla and her family. They'll fight you tooth and nail to keep you away from him."

Gibbs planted the pool cue on the floor and braced

his weight on it, leaning toward Evan. "Let them try." He pushed off the cue and raised it for another horribly aimed shot. Gibbs cussed at his miss, then glanced at Evan. "What choice will they have if I make a preemptive move? Possession is nine tenths of the law, don't they say?"

"Not with children!"

Gibbs shrugged, glanced to Leon. "See to it Ms. Cameron doesn't leave town before the baby comes." He frowned, twisting his lips. "In fact, let's take measures to see that she doesn't." Gibbs arched one eyebrow as he lifted the corner of his mouth in a gloating grin.

Evan bristled. "Stay the hell away from Isla!" He strode around the pool table to confront Gibbs, his shoulders back. "Whatever sick scheme your pickled brain is concocting, just…forget it! Leave her alone!"

Gibbs shot a meaningful glance to Leon, jerking his head toward Evan. The giant man advanced on Evan, his jaw tight and his eyes hard with purpose.

Evan's stomach sank, loaded with knots of dread. But with a last spurt of defiance, he pivoted toward Gibbs again and grated, "You're a coward, you know that? Hiding behind Leon's brawn, behind the walls of your fortress out here in the boonies. You intimidate people with lawyers and lawsuits and muscle, but you don't ever get your own hands dirty. You're a pathetic excuse for—"

That was as far as he got before Leon grabbed him by the back of the neck and shoved him against the nearest wall, hard enough that Evan's vision blurred. For the next several minutes, Evan did his best to return blow for blow, to dodge kicks and avoid the worst of the beating Leon doled out.

Finally, Gibbs shouted, "Enough. Get him up."

He was dragged to his wobbly legs, his nose leaking blood and his left eye swelling shut. He tasted bile and blood in his throat, and when he tried to spit out the bitter taste, discovered one back tooth was loose. His entire body ached, especially his ribs, and the pulsing in his head kept time with his adrenaline-charged heartbeat.

Gibbs stepped closer to Evan, and alcohol fumes fanned Evan's face as his father snarled, "Remember this, boy. You're expend'ble. Now that you've gotten the Cameron woman pregnant, I don't need your worthless services anymore. You've been a disappointment. Unreliable. Unloyal. Unuseful."

"Well..." Evan rasped, careful to take shallow breaths in order to avoid the worst of the pain in his ribs. "Then I have something to be proud of."

Gibbs's expression darkened. "Get out of my house. Stay out of my business and keep your mouth shut about our dealings, or I won't call Leon off next time."

Evan struggled for a breath. "Gladly. So long as you stay away from my family. That includes my baby and Isla."

Gibbs scoffed a laugh. "Oh no. No deal there. Your mother's life is clearly an incentive to keep you in line. And Isla and that baby are newly useful to me. She's key to my plans moving forward. Thanks to you."

The roil of bile increased in his gut and surged up his throat. "Stay the hell away from her!"

"Take him back where you found him," Gibbs told Leon. Then grabbing Evan's chin roughly, Gibbs kissed Evan's forehead. "A word of fatherly advice as a parting gift to you." With his nose almost touching Evan's, Gibbs growled. "If you value your life, your mother's, don't ever go against me again."

Chapter 14

A frantic pounding noise woke Isla. Her house, her windows were still dark as she shook off the fog of sleep. Had she overslept? What—

The pounding came again. Urgent. Unrelenting. She bolted upright in her bed and checked her phone for the time. 1:52 a.m. Immediately her stomach swooped.

An emergency. Danger. Her family!

Fearing some new disaster like the cabin fire, an illness or accident, she scurried from her bedroom, flipped on her porch light and threw open the door. But instead of one of her siblings or the police, she found Evan pacing in tight circles, his mouth pressed in a grim line.

Anger flashed through her, and she shouted, "Go! Away!"

She had the door half-closed when he spun toward her. "Wait!"

She saw his face, bruised and swollen, and gasped. "*Crivvens*, Evan! What happened to you?"

"Gibbs's thug happened. My father was unhappy that I wouldn't play his games anymore." Stepping closer, he yanked her screen door open. "Are *you* all right?"

His obvious distress sent a quiver of concern through her before her brain told her his problems were not hers. She tried to close herself off to the ripples of agitation and worry she picked up from him. "I'm fine. And you need to leave."

"I will. But you need to come with me."

In the yellow glow of the porch light, his eyes flashed with alarm, and she hesitated. While her head warned her to ignore his pleas, shut him out, the anxious energy he radiated seeped to her core and set her on edge. She gave him a measuring scrutiny. "Why? What's happened? Besides your—" she waved a hand toward his battered face "—makeover, I mean."

He pinched the bridge of his nose, his expression rife with disgust. "My fath—Gibbs knows about the baby."

Icy fingers scraped down her spine, and she wrapped her arms around her middle, as if she could ward off the chill. Protect her baby. Guard herself from the unspoken threat of evil that hung in the air between them.

With a cross scowl, she said, "Gee, I wonder how that happened. Who could have told him?"

He was shaking his head before she could finish. "Not me. His hired muscle has been trailing me. Or you. Maybe he has men following both of us. But after you left the doughnut place the other day, I sat in my rental car for a moment, and I saw him go in the shop where we'd just been. He talked to someone, presumably the employee, who'd clearly eavesdropped on every word we said, and Leon reported it all back to Gibbs."

Isla trembled but took a few deep breaths, fighting to stay calm. "Well, I guess it was inevitable in a small town. Thank you for letting me know," she said, her tone clipped. "But now you should leave. You are still unwelcome here." She tried to shut the door, but he shot a hand up to block it.

"Isla, wait! You're missing the point." He pushed hard against her door, wedging his body in the space he'd forced. "He hasn't missed the fact that he is our baby's grandfather."

The cold that had gripped her earlier intensified, burrowing to her core.

"He intends to use that information as a weapon in his fight to acquire your family's land by hook or by crook." Evan pressed the side of his fist to his mouth as he paused to frame his next words. "He wants custody of our baby, and I think he is forming a plan to come after you."

Her knees buckled, and if she hadn't been holding the doorknob, she might have crumpled. "Wh-what do you mean? Come after me how? He can't kill me without killing the baby too. If that's—"

Her weakened grip, thanks to his frightening news, gave him the advantage he needed to bulldoze his way into her foyer. "I don't know. I only know he dragged me from my motel room tonight to confirm what was reported to him. He made veiled threats, demanding I cooperate with his plans and threatening me and my mother and your family and... Hell! I told him no, and he had his heavy do this." He pointed at his face.

She winced, not wanting to feel any sympathy, but unable to block the surge of compassion for his pain.

"Isla, I don't want anything to do with that man ever again. It was a mistake for me to have entered a bargain with him to begin with. My only excuse is that I was

desperate to help my mother and thought it patently un-
fair that he was sitting on millions of dollars—"

"Stop! Just… Stop!" She waved her hands and covered her ears as she backpedaled from him. "I don't
want to hear your excuses!"

"Fine. But hear me when I say you—and our baby—
are in danger from him." The hard edge to his tone, the
fervor that made his dark eyes spark, stole her breath. "I
don't know what form that danger will take, but you've
already seen his handiwork with the cabin fire. He's
not above inflicting collateral damage to get what he
wants. And he made it quite clear tonight that he wants
our baby. Not because he loves it but to use it as a tool.
A bargaining chip."

She swallowed hard, searching for her voice. "Evan,
I don't know what to— What am I supposed to do?"

"That's why I'm here. Come with me. We'll go somewhere together, lay low—"

She barked a stunned, bitter laugh. "What? No! I'm
not going anywhere with *you*!"

"Isla, the man's dangerous!"

"Clearly! But you are untrustworthy, and a liar, and
disloyal, and—"

He growled his frustration and jammed his hand
through his hair. Then winced in pain. "I'm sorry for
hurting you! I know I broke your trust, but—" He
reached for her hands, and she snatched them away
from him.

"Get out!" She aimed a trembling finger at her door.
"You've brought all of this down on me and my family!
If you'd been honest with me to start with, told me who
you were, I'd have *never* spent even five minutes in your
company, much less slept with you!" Her voice broke
as she raged at him, and tears spilled on her cheeks.

"I understand that, but for better or worse, you're stuck with me now."

A ripple of recognition, of altered perception swept through her, tingling. *Stuck with him?*

Maybe her dream had been telling her—warning her—that Evan would become a fixture in her life because of the baby. Not her soulmate. Her child's father. He was part of her future, not because of a great love story, but because she'd foolishly slept with him based on her first impressions, her impulsiveness and the initial attraction she'd felt toward him. Although, to be honest, she was still physically drawn to him in a frustratingly powerful way, darn it. How did she trust her instincts now? She'd been so wrong with Evan. He threw her intuition in such disarray.

She placed a hand on her belly and took a calming breath. "Evan, please, just go. It's late. This baby is wearing me out, and I don't have the energy or desire to fight with you."

His shoulders squared. "Good, because I have no desire to fight with you either. I'm here because I intend to protect you and our baby from Gibbs."

Isla tipped her head. "Protect me? How?"

"The smartest thing, best I can calculate, is to get you out of town. If he can't find you, he can't hurt you."

She snorted. "No."

"Excuse me?"

"I'm not going anywhere," she said. Firmly and unequivocally.

"Isla, listen to me—"

"No, you listen! My family is here. My home is here. My life is here in Valley Haven. At Cameron Glen. Why would I leave all that?"

"Because Gibbs will—"

"And my obstetrician!" she added, cutting him off when the addendum popped in her head. "I have to be close to my doctor, now that I'm pregnant. Right?"

Evan balled his hands in fists as he paced a few steps, paused to grab his side as he winced, then returned to face her with a taut jaw. "Of course you need to keep up with prenatal care, but—"

"No buts." Her mantel clock chimed 2:00 a.m., rousing her from the sidetrack argument. "It's all a moot point for you, because I don't trust you, don't want anything to do with your schemes and want you out of my house now."

Evan sighed and tapped his balled fist to his mouth, clearly waging a battle between urgency and frustration while keeping his tone reasonable. "Isla, you need to come with me."

"No."

"I can wait while you pack a bag, but we need to get moving."

"No!"

"For all I know, Leon could be headed here as we speak!" His rising sharpness to his tone elevated her adrenaline. He was really scared. And was scaring her…

"Leon?"

"Gibbs's henchman."

She waved a hand, trying to affect a nonchalance at odds with the quiver in her soul. "Whatever. Forget I asked. Just—go!" She aimed her finger at the door again. "You know I'll call the police. I did it before."

"Are you going to pack a bag?"

"What? No!"

"All right." He turned and opened the front door. "If that's the way you want to play this…"

"I—" She never finished the assertion on her lips, because Evan bent and, with a groan of pain, scooped her into his arms, cradling her against him like a child.

She gasped and struggled to get free as he marched out the front door and down her porch steps. "Stop this, Evan! Put me down!"

"Soon... Ow!" He leaned his head back, scowling. "Watch it. My ribs are sore enough without you adding blows."

Compunction stung her briefly, until he opened the door of his rented car and put her on the front passenger seat. He closed the door, his arm wrapping around his middle as he grimaced again. Holding his ribs, he headed around the front fender toward the driver's side. Isla pursed her lips, opened the passenger door and climbed out, shaking her head. "Goodbye, Evan."

He reversed directions, catching her before she went ten steps. "Don't make this difficult, Isla. I'm trying to protect you!"

She snorted, the sound getting cut off with a gasp as he hoisted her over his shoulder. This time, he carried her to the driver's side, set her on the floor of the back seat and closed the door. In the time it took her to scramble up from the floor and fumble with the door latch, he'd hit the childproof door lock that prevented her from opening the back door.

"Evan, let me out! This is kidnapping, you know!"

"For a good cause. You'll thank me later." With that, he jammed the car into gear and wheeled from her driveway. The acceleration threw her back, and before she could right herself, he'd sped down the road and left Cameron Glen in the dust.

Chapter 15

"I'm doing this for your own good," Evan said, casting a glance toward the back seat as he headed down the highway away from town.

"Unlikely." She tried to climb into the front seat, a task made more difficult when he stuck his arm up to block her progress.

"Sit down and buckle up." With his free hand, he steered his rental car onto the night-shrouded highway.

"Turn around now and take me home, or I swear I'll call the police!" she said through gritted teeth.

"Go ahead," he said over his shoulder.

And…she realized her phone was in her house, charging as it was every night. She was in pajamas, barefoot and without any way to tell her family what had happened to her. "I…can't. Give me your phone."

He chuckled. "Nope."

"Evan!" she growled, her hands fisting in frustration. She should have felt more panicked. Evan, Gibbs's son, had kidnapped her from her home in the middle of the night, after all. Yet she was more irritated than scared. Evan wouldn't hurt her. Would he? Her gut said no, but…she'd been wrong about him before. Maybe this apple didn't fall far from the Gibbs tree.

Taking a cleansing breath, she said, "It's not too late to do the right thing, you know. If you take me home, right now, I'll forget about this sorry incident, and we can go back to plan A—avoiding each other except where the baby is concerned."

"What if getting you out of town to keep you safe is the right thing?" he countered.

"I don't need your brand of protection! I have a large family, including a brother-in-law who was with the military police at one time. And, thanks to my family's turbulent last two years or so, we have connections to members of the local and state police departments if more protection is needed."

Evan didn't respond. He did, however, look rather pale. His face pinched again as he held his abdomen.

"Are you…all right? I mean you look a bit like you might pass out."

He shot her a guilty look via the rearview mirror. "I don't have time to pass out. We need miles between us and Gibbs."

"But if you're hurt—"

"Oh, I am that." he shifted slightly, pressing an arm against his ribs again. "Leon saw to that. But I can deal with the pain until we get out of town. Out of state. Until we disappear on the vast US highway system."

"You should see a doctor."

"No time."

"But—"

"No, Isla! Not until you and the baby are hidden."

An odd mix of frustration, gratitude and resentment swirled through her. Knowing how worried her family would be when they discovered her missing, Isla battled down a swell of desperation as well. Surely she could reason with Evan. She could make him see the folly of his plan, and he'd have her home by first light. Right?

Wrong.

Five hours later, as the sun was coming up over an unfamiliar city skyline, Isla rubbed sleep from her eyes and tried to orient herself. She was still in the back seat of Evan's rental car. He was still driving. Her family was likely discovering her gone about now. "Where are we?"

"Nashville."

She huffed her irritation. "And why Nashville?"

"Because that's where Interstate 40 goes after Asheville and Knoxville."

"I meant, does Nashville play a part in your plan to hide me?"

"You're assuming there's a plan beyond just…drive," Evan said through a yawn.

Isla stretched her back and rubbed the kink in her neck. She hadn't meant to fall asleep, but pregnancy made her more tired than she'd ever imagined she could be. "Well, can we stop? I need a bathroom. And food. The baby needs nourishment, and I need something in my stomach or I'll get nauseated."

Evan met her gaze via the rearview mirror. "I'm kinda hungry too. And we need gas. So…yeah. I'll stop at the next good exit."

"Thank you," she said, sounding only mildly peeved. She folded her arms over her chest to pout over her predicament, then she realized the opportunity about to present itself.

They were stopping. She could tell someone what

was happening. Borrow a phone to call the police. Call her family. Heck, she could cause a public scene and refuse to get back in the car until Evan was in police custody, and she had a safe ride back to Valley Haven. She brightened, sat taller and began plotting her escape.

"I know what you're thinking," Evan said, and she lifted her eyes to meet his in the mirror again.

"Oh? You're a mind reader now?"

He scoffed. "I don't have to be. You're thinking what anyone in your situation would. And your face confirmed it. But before you try to ditch me or call the police or get a stranger involved in this, remember why I'm doing this."

She grunted.

"I'm trying to keep you and our baby safe from Gibbs. You've seen his handiwork. He didn't care who got hurt when he had Leon torch your family's cabin. He's got you and our child in his crosshairs now. If you go home, how long do you think it will be before Gibbs has one of his hired guns snatching you off the street?"

She shivered, imagining that scenario.

"Or hurting someone in your family to get what he wants? He'd do it, and make it look like an accident."

The dread he intended hit home, burrowing to her core. "Stop! Your melodramatics, your upsetting me can't be good for the baby."

"Okay." He turned up a palm on the steering wheel. "Sorry. But tell me you're hearing me. Promise me you won't do something rash that will put both of us—all *three* of us—in jeopardy."

She put her hand flat on her belly. She'd never put her baby in danger. But could she believe Evan's assessment of where the greater danger lay? Was she safer here with him than in Valley Haven? At home with her family in Cameron Glen? A thread of doubt wove its way through her.

"If Gibbs is planning some new attack on my family because of this baby—" her fingers curled over her womb as a chill washed through her "—I need to warn them."

His gaze darted back to the rearview mirror, his mouth pinched. "You're right. They need to be alert, but—"

"*But* nothing! Either you let me use your phone to call them, let them know I'm safe and alert them to whatever scheme Gibbs is working on, or I'll—" She fumbled for her plan, scrambling mentally for a strategy to get what she needed. What was she willing to risk? Did she really want Evan arrested? He hadn't physically hurt her. He claimed his motive for this kidnapping was to protect her. He seemed to want what was best for her fam—

She shook her head, scowling. Why was she defending his actions? He'd kidnapped her! He'd lied to her and betrayed her! She wouldn't be in this predicament, wouldn't be pregnant with *Gene Gibbs's grandchild* if Evan had been honest with her, played straight with her from the beginning.

Evan drove past an exit advertising both gas and multiple food options. She waved her hand toward the window. "Hey! You missed your exit."

"I'm not stopping until I have your word that you understand what's at stake. I need to know you'll cooperate."

"I know what's at stake. But how do I know you're my best option for staying safe? What's your plan beyond *driving*? Where are we going? What will you do if Gibbs or this Leon person catches up to us?"

"I—"

"Why am I better off on the road with *you* than with, say…my brother Brody and Anya? Or Emma and Jake? If leaving town is my best option—not saying it is, but—why wouldn't I go somewhere of my own choosing with a friend or my parents or—"

"Okay! I get it. Those are all good questions. But…" He scowled and squeezed the steering wheel as he huffed a sigh. "Honestly, I don't know. I don't have any answers yet, but I had to do something. No delays. No time to overthink things or wait for Leon to show up before I did." He tapped a thumb restlessly, and his gaze flicked from the road to the rearview mirror and back to the road. "But there's another exit coming up, and if you want me to take it, give me your word you won't do anything rash."

She glanced through the windshield to the highway sign advertising her favorite country-style restaurant along with several brands of gasoline. Her stomach growled. "All right. But no junk food. I want eggs and fruit and biscuits with honey. The baby needs a good breakfast, not some processed and preserved something from a gas station."

Evan nodded. "Whatever baby wants." He took the exit and drove to the country-style restaurant first. "Order whatever you want, but let's get it to go. Okay? I'm antsy to put as much distance between us and Gibbs as possible."

As they walked toward the restaurant together, Evan held his side, wincing, and she remembered how much pain he'd clearly been in last night.

"Are you feeling any better this morning?" she asked. His face was less swollen, but the bruises had darkened.

"Some," he said, his voice winded, raspy. "I'm sure I

look worse than I—" He coughed, then groaned. "Correction. I feel like crap. But I don't care. In the big picture, my aching ribs and splitting headache aren't important."

She sighed, concern for him twisting her gut. "Evan…"

He held the door for her, then directed a nod toward the back of the restaurant's gift shop, where the bathrooms were. "Try to be quick about it, huh? I feel like a sitting duck if we're not moving."

She cast a glance to the other patrons, many of whom stared openly at them. Isla, still barefoot and in her nightgown, felt especially conspicuous and awkward. She made a beeline for the restroom. When she'd said she needed a bathroom break, she hadn't been kidding. But she also saw the women's restroom as her best chance to get word to her family or the police without Evan knowing. She took her time in the stall, listening for someone else to come into the bathroom. When she heard the squeak of the swinging door and female voices, she emerged from her stall and signaled the women who'd entered. "Excuse me, but do either of you have a phone with you that I can borrow? It's an emergency!"

The older woman looked her up and down, frowning at her state of undress, and shook her head. "Sorry, darlin'. My phone's in my purse back at our table with my husband. Janie, you have yours?"

The younger of the two women dug in her shoulder bag. "Yeah." She gave Isla a leery look as she passed the phone to her. "What's the emergency?"

Isla opened her mouth to spill the whole, ugly story, but the words stuck in her throat. Did she really want to get Evan in trouble with the police? She believed his story about Gibbs having threatened her and the baby. The bruises on his face were evidence enough that he'd displeased his brutish father. "I…need to let my family know where I am. I left home quite abruptly last night—" she chuckled wryly "—obviously—and left my phone behind."

Isla woke the screen on the cell phone and brought up the keypad to dial… Who? Her parents? Emma? Shoot! What was her sister's number? She didn't actually have the number memorized. Her sister's number, all of her family's cell numbers for that matter, were just saved in her contacts and one button press away in her favorites contacts list. She racked her brain. Didn't Daryl's have a pattern to it? She was painfully aware of the two women watching her closely.

"Honey, are you running from a violent partner?" the older woman asked gently. "'Cause our church has programs to help women who—"

"No," she said with a quick smile, then realized she was, in a way, running from violence. Just not from an immediate family member or romantic connection. "I just… It's complicated."

A knock sounded on the bathroom door, and Evan called, "Isla? You okay in there?"

She tensed and looked down at the phone in her hands again, searching her memory for the repeating pattern she knew was part of her younger brother's number. Their area code was 828, and she tapped that on the keypad screen. Finally, like a gift from heaven, the rest of the number popped into her brain. She entered it quickly, then realized that at this hour of the morning, Daryl would not be awake yet. Shoot, shoot, shoot! A voice mail, then…

"Isla?" *Knock, knock.*

She listened to the line ring, trying to reassure the women who frowned at her dubiously, with a tremulous smile.

"This is D. You know what to do," Daryl's recorded message said.

"Daryl, it's Isla. You need to tell Mom and Dad that—"

The phone was snatched from her hand, and she gasped.

Evan frowned at her, tapped the screen to disconnect the call, then sent the two glowering women a chagrined look. "Sorry for intruding, ladies. My sister went off her meds, and we only just tracked her down here. I'm going to get her to her doctor now, and all will be well."

"What! Evan—"

He tugged her by her arm out of the restroom and picked up a bag sitting on the floor just outside the door. He shoved the bag in her arms. "I bought you clothes and a pair of sandals. Best I could do here. Your food will be ready in a minute, but I think, given your broken promise to me, you'll be waiting in the car."

"Broken promise?" she bristled at his accusation, hating the idea she'd done something uncouth.

"Before we stopped, you promised not to try to escape or call anyone." Evan angled a disappointed glare at her. "Trust is a two-way street, you know. I believed your word was good."

Isla swallowed hard, a prickle of conscience skittering over her skin. "I didn't break my promise…exactly. You asked me not to do anything rash, as I recall. And I was not rash. I knew precisely what I was doing and had planned the move for miles."

He stopped in the middle of the parking lot and faced her, staring with incredulity. "That's your excuse? Really?

Semantics?" He huffed an exasperated-sounding breath, and his jaw tightened. Drilling her with a hard look, he aimed a finger at his battered face. "Does this look like a game to you? Do you not understand how dangerous Gene Gibbs is?"

She squared her shoulders. "Of course I understand! Do you not understand that if my family discovers me missing this morning, the police will be looking for us and your whole plan to hide me from your father will be that much more difficult?"

"I—" His sigh this time was despondent, resigned. He rubbed his face and immediately winced. "Ow! Sheesh."

Isla raised a gentle hand to his cheek. "I really wish you'd see a doctor. You could have broken bones or internal bleeding."

"Maybe later."

She gritted her teeth as she growled. "Why are you so stubborn?"

"I could ask you the same question."

"Me?" She feigned innocence.

With a hand at her back, he propelled her to the rental car and opened the back-seat door. "I have to go back for our food. Promise me you won't bolt or shoot off flares or otherwise draw attention to yourself?"

She tipped her head and sent him a rebellious glare. But then, as she regarded him—bruised, clearly bone-tired and pleading for her cooperation with his dark eyes—something in her melted. Maybe she hadn't forgiven him for his betrayal, maybe she wasn't convinced his plan to avoid Gibbs was their best move, and maybe she needed to keep her guard up to protect her heart from the magnetic pull she still felt around him, but she couldn't deny the sharp pang of worry and respect that sliced through her. He'd risked a lot in defying his father. He'd already suffered a brutal beating because he wanted to protect her.

She dropped her shoulders in resignation. She could give him this battle without surrendering the war. Not to mention, the longer she stood here debating with him, the longer it would take to get food. And her hunger was quickly turning to nausea. Baby wanted food *now*!

"Okay. Uncle." She ignored the back seat he'd offered and climbed in the passenger side up front. "Don't forget to ask for honey for the biscuits." She angled her head and gave him a gentle smile. "Please."

He held her gaze for a beat as if deciding if she had something up her sleeve. "How do you like your coffee?"

"Without coffee, extra tea. No caffeine, remember? Also no refined sugar or artificial sweetener. Just honey."

One dark eyebrow lifted. "Oh, right. I'm tired and just...forgot."

"If they don't have a caffeine-free tea, I'll just drink milk."

He pressed his mouth in a dubious frown. "I'll do my best."

He closed her door, and as he strode back into the restaurant, a gooey feeling spread in her belly as she watched his careful, pained gait. Her heart gave a tug, and she whispered to his retreating back, "I know you will."

Chapter 16

Evan's stomach growled from the savory scent of his sausage biscuit, but when he tried to open his mouth wide enough to take a bite, pain shot from his jaw through his skull. He must have groaned, because Isla shot him one of her worried looks. While he'd been in the restaurant getting their food, she'd donned the sweatsuit and sandals he'd bought her. Her nightgown was balled in the back seat.

"I'm fine," he lied. "I just made a poor choice with this breakfast sandwich, considering—" He waved a finger to his face. "But I thought it would be easier to eat as I drove."

She nibbled a slice of apple and studied him with a crease in her brow. "In truth, you shouldn't be eating while you drive at all. Distracted driving is responsible for—"

"All right!" he said in a tone that came out testier than he'd intended. He pulled onto the shoulder, making sure he was far off the highway, and turned on his emergency flashers. He cut the engine and gave her a level look. "We'll sit here until I'm done eating. Will you pass me a napkin from the bag, please?"

She did, and he set the napkin, then his biscuit, on his lap. He tore off a small piece of the bread and poked it in his mouth. He chewed slowly, trying not to wince as his jaw throbbed. He was pretty sure Leon had broken one of his back teeth.

"Hand me your phone." Isla extended her hand, wiggling her fingers to echo her words.

He barked a wry laugh, which shot lightning through his chest and side, and he pressed a hand over his ribs. "No way," he wheezed through the pain.

She grunted her discontent. "You wouldn't let me finish my call at the restaurant, so now I have to call back on your phone. Earlier, you agreed that my family needs to be warned. Remember?" She took a bite of her own biscuit, and honey dripped off the side onto her leg. Seeing the fallen blob, she scooped it up with her finger and sucked the sticky syrup off.

The action should have been routine, innocent…but it wasn't. Watching her lick the honey from her finger was erotic and mesmerizing. Heat flashed through Evan, and his groan this time was due to a very different sort of anguish. He turned his gaze to the traffic passing on the divided highway, shoving aside the mental images that stirred the hum in his veins.

"Evan?" She nudged him, her hand extended again asking for his cell phone. "Please. It's cruel to let them worry. To let them go unwarned about whatever vile ploy Gibbs has planned to manipulate or hurt them." Her tone softened, trembling with emotion. "They're my family, Evan. If you learned nothing else about me in the short time we were together, it should have been how much my family means to me!"

He cut a glance to her, and his heart quickened when he met her teary blue eyes. "All right. One call."

Her face brightened.

"But—"

Her pink lips bowed in agitation when he added the qualifier.

He leaned carefully to one side so he could dig his phone from his pocket. Even that small movement made his body throb and ache. After retrieving his phone, he took a moment with his eyes closed to wait out the waves of pain. Slow, shallow breath in. Nice and easy exhale. Better, but—

No. No buts. He didn't have time, money or room in his rescue plan to give his injuries any further consideration. He gritted his teeth and returned his attention to his first priority. Isla.

She stared at him with a keen, knowing gaze. "You need a doctor."

"I'm fine."

Isla growled and threw her hands up. "Mule!"

Evan woke the screen on his phone, and when she tried to take the device, he held it out of her reach. "Nope. I'll make the call."

"What? Evan!"

"One, your hands are probably still sticky, and two, I can't risk you telling them where we are and to send the cops after me."

"I promise I won't."

"Oh, do you, Ms. Semantics? I'm not sure I can trust you."

"Ha!" she said, her tone bitter. "That's rich, coming from you."

He pinched the bridge of his nose and shook his head. "I know I have a lot of work to do to earn your forgiveness and regain your trust. But for now, can we at least call a truce?"

She sat back, chagrin softening the hard lines of anger etched on her face. After finger combing her hair from her face and exhaling a slow breath, she nodded.

"The only contact I have for your family besides yours is your mother's. She gave it to me the day of the fire when she invited me for lunch. If you'd rather I called someone else, I'll need their number."

"You can call Mom." Isla's shoulders drooped, and her tone sounded defeated. A strange look crossed her face, as if she'd smelled something rotten.

He noticed she'd stopped eating and pointed to the food on her lap. "Something wrong with that? I thought baby was hungry."

"No, it's…" She pressed a hand over her stomach and leaned her head back, closing her eyes. Without warning, she jerked the passenger door open and lost what little she'd eaten on the side of the road.

He handed her back his napkin to wipe her mouth as she flopped back in her seat again. "Morning sickness?"

"Maybe. Or stress. Or emotions. I told you I feel everything deeply, right? Well, sometimes it's enough to make me sick to my stomach or give me a headache or…" She flipped up a hand. "But in this case, I think it's a little of everything. Heck, knowing this baby is Gene Gibbs's grandchild is enough to make me want to vomit most of the time." She pulled a face. "I really hate thinking I have any of his DNA growing inside me. It's like knowing you have demon spawn inside you. Rosemary's baby or Damien Thorn."

Evan stroked her cheek and tugged lightly on her

earlobe. "Imagine how I feel. The man's my father. I've spent the last several days wishing I could peel off my skin like a snake and be rid of his genes and any connection to him for good."

She angled her head toward him, a smile playing at the corner of her mouth. "That's gotta sting."

"Right? I mean look at me." He tipped his head so she could better see his black eye and purpling cheek. "My own father sicced his bulldog bodyguard on me to send a very clear message. And that message was not a warm-and-fuzzy one."

Sadness washed over her expression. "Oh, Evan... don't do that."

He gave her a genuinely puzzled frown. "Don't do what?"

"Make me feel sorry for you." She closed her eyes again, shaking her head. "Confuse me. Tangle up my emotions any more than they are."

A spark of hope lit inside him. He didn't want her pity, but if her feelings were shifting, getting knotted up, maybe he was making progress toward earning back her trust. Winning back her heart. "Well, no promises there. After keeping you and our baby safe, my number one goal where you're concerned is getting back in your good graces. An amicable relationship would make our joint parenting much smoother."

She snapped a narrow-eyed gaze at him. "Joint parenting?"

"I told you from the start I wanted to be part of the baby's life." He took another careful bite of biscuit and gave her a matter-of-fact stare.

An 18-wheeler whizzed past them, making the rental car shudder and Isla jolt. "Can we move from the side of the road? I feel...vulnerable here."

"Two more bites." He shoved a bigger hunk of bread in his mouth, then a piece of sausage before pulling back onto the highway.

Isla stared out her side window. In a desultory tone, she muttered, "I don't see how it can work. We live on opposite sides of the country."

"I'll move to North Carolina."

"And your mom? You'd leave your sick mother?"

He opened and closed his mouth. A stab of pain pierced his heart. Would his mother even be around after the baby came? He'd failed to secure the funding he needed for her continued treatments. He'd landed himself in financial debt to his criminal father. And the last message he'd had from his mother's doctor was, despite the signs of progress she'd made with the experimental drug treatment, she'd be removed from the study if a second payment wasn't made by Friday.

"Wow," Isla said, giving him a disapproving glare. "Is that really a point of debate for you?"

"What? No, I wouldn't leave her! There are doctors in North Carolina. Or maybe she'll be well by—" He couldn't even finish the sentence, knowing how slim that chance was.

He cut a side-glance to Isla and met a blue gaze full of sympathy and shared heartache. "All of this started because I wanted to help my mom. Do you really think I'd abandon her now? My mom is…"

Her hand moved to his leg, and she squeezed his knee. "I know. I'm just trying to figure out how this could possibly work."

"It will. We'll find a way." He sent her an encouraging smile.

She twisted her mouth, clearly skeptical. "Speaking of mothers, you never called my mother like you promised."

He snorted. "Because you tossed your cookies and distracted me." Evan picked his cell up from his lap and started tapping and swiping with his thumb.

"Not while you're driving!" she scolded, grabbing his wrist.

Evan gritted his back teeth and tucked his phone under his leg. At the next exit, he pulled off and parked at a truck stop. Bringing up his contacts, he called Grace Cameron. When her mother's weary voice came on the line, he said, "I know I'm the last person you wanted to hear from, but I have Isla with me, and she wanted you to know that she's okay."

"Isla is with *you*? Willingly?" Grace said, dismay rife in her tone.

"Well, maybe not exactly *willingly*, but—" Then, realizing how that would sound to a worried parent, he added quickly, "But she's safe, and that's the point. I had to get her out of town, so that my dad—" He stopped short again. How much should he say? He didn't want to cause unnecessary alarm. "Well, it's a long story, but…"

He heard Grace turn to the people in the room with her and pass on the information. Then Isla's father came on the line. "You better not hurt her, damn you!"

"I'd never—"

"Let me talk to her! What's going on?"

Then before he could react, Isla took the phone from him and said, "Mom, it's me. I'm— Oh. Hi, Dad. Yeah." She listened a moment, then said, "I'm fine. It's not like that. I mean, it kinda is but, well, no, I'm not happy about it, but…it's complicated. Dad, Gibbs knows about the baby, and—"

Evan seized her arm with a warning grip, shaking

his head. Isla frowned, but said, "Look, I'll be home as soon as I can, but for now just…" she sighed "Don't call the police and don't let anyone know where we are. I'm fine, but we're trying to avoid Gibbs's goons and…" She cut a look toward Evan. "Yes, we know he's dangerous. You need to be alert too. Let the whole family know to stay vigilant. He could do…anything." After several more assurances that she was unharmed and would call again as soon as she could, Evan made circles with his finger signaling for her to wrap it up.

"I'll be home soon. Can someone feed my animals? Thanks. No, don't call on this number. Just don't. Okay. I love you."

He wedged the phone from her hand and tapped the disconnect icon. "We good?"

She grunted. Nodded. After a beat, she leveled a wary glare at him and pointed at his cell. "Does Gibbs have this phone number?"

He gave her a confused scowl. "Uh, yeah. When I first met him, I—"

And then understanding hit him. He slammed his fist against the steering wheel and muttered a savory curse. After prying the SIM card from the phone, he rolled down his window and tossed the cell phone as far as he could into the grassy median beside the truck stop. Immediately another thought occurred to him. His mom. He grumbled under his breath and climbed out of the car to retrieve the phone.

When he returned to the front seat, Isla gaped at him. "What are you doing? Don't you understand that Gibbs can track you on that phone?"

"Of course I understand. And I know I should have thought of it sooner but, hell…"

"We have to get rid of it! Now."

Growling his frustration, he squeezed the phone and debated. "I can't just get rid of it. This is the only number my mom's doctor has for emergencies. What if something happens to her?"

Isla turned on the seat to face him, her expression far calmer than he was at the moment. "We'll find a store, get a burner cell, call her doctor with the new number. But that phone has to go. It's a beacon Gibbs could be following even now."

Evan jammed his fingers through his hair. "You're right. Of course. I'm mad at myself for not realizing sooner…"

Climbing back out of the car, he dropped the phone on the concrete and smashed it with his heel before carrying the pieces to a trash can. As he resettled behind the steering wheel, he pressed his mouth in a grim line of fury. "I screwed up, and I'm sorry. I was just so focused on getting you out of town and not passing out from pain while I was driving—not that I'm trying to excuse my mistake—but I didn't have a lot of time to make a plan or think things through…"

"Well, it's time to do some thinking." She squared her shoulders with purpose. "We need to know where we're going, think about how Gibbs could find us…" Her gaze sharpened. "Did you use a credit card when you paid for our breakfast?"

Evan groaned. He had.

Chapter 17

"Okay, so no more credit cards going forward," Evan said as he drove away from the truck stop. His glum expression seemed even grimmer because of his bruises. Guilt and regret dug deep lines around his tight mouth and dark eyes.

"Right," Isla said. She gave his thigh a quick squeeze meant to buoy his mood. She hadn't mentioned the credit card to scold him, but they needed to assess the situation and make the necessary adjustments if they were going to stay off Gibbs's radar. "We should also trade this car for another one. It stands to reason that car rental companies have tracking devices in their vehicles for theft prevention and so they can find customers who are stranded with mechanical problems."

Evan nodded. "Well, it did until I disconnected it the other day along with one Gibbs likely planted."

She shivered. "He what?"

"I tried to tell you he'd tracked me, tried to warn you about a lot of stuff when you were blocking my calls and not listening to me." He sent her an accusing look.

She rolled her eyes. "Okay. Point for you."

Instead of gloating, he returned to the business at hand. "So…burner phone."

"Right. And we'll keep the GPS locator turned off. You know…just in case. Besides the fact that it just creeps me to have an inanimate object ask me how I like a business I've just been in." She shuddered. "Also, no ATM machines. That tells your bank where you are."

He cast her a curious side-glance. "How do you know all of this? The average person doesn't keep a list of ways to avoid detection."

Isla lifted a shoulder. "I read a lot. You pick things up. Not just crime novels, like my brother-in-law's, but romance, history, biographies. And…" She gave him a sheepish grin. "Matt and I just had a conversation about his book research into hiding a person a few weeks ago. He says most of it's just a matter of common sense and thinking things through." When Evan frowned, she amended, "I don't say that to be critical. I know this trip was all very impromptu, but…" She paused for emphasis. "Now that we have a chance for a reset, we need to be careful. Chart a new course, literally and figuratively."

Evan leaned up on one hip and fished his wallet out of his back pocket. Tossing it onto Isla's lap, he said, "Check to see how much cash I have."

Isla opened the wallet and checked the bill compartment, fingering through the cash. "It looks like about thirty-four dollars."

He groaned. "That's not even a full tank of gas." His mouth pressed in a hard line. "I assume that financial apps on a phone can be traced the same way a credit card can be?"

"I'd think any financial transaction tied to a computer system that includes personal identifying information, from your name to a phone number or bank account, would count. Yep."

Evan drummed his fingers on the steering wheel. "Then how—" He buzzed his lips. "Well, we've already left bread crumbs this far, so I say I use my bank card at an ATM to withdraw the highest amount I can. I don't know how far it will take us, but we'll have seed money."

She hummed her agreement. "I'd offer money from my account, but I don't have a credit card or ATM card or anything, really, thanks to the abrupt way we left my house. I don't even have my purse."

"If I hadn't had to—"

"Again," she cut in, "not a commentary. Just taking an inventory." She tapped a fingernail on the armrest as she thought. "I could call one of my sisters and ask them to wire money to me. Cait or Emma would be more likely to cooperate than Brody or my parents."

He bobbed a nod. "Okay. Wire it where?"

"I think the truck stop we were at before had a Western Union sign. We could go back there."

"Mmm." Evan angled a curious look at her, his brow deeply creased. "You're being very accommodating and cooperative all of a sudden. Why the change of heart?"

Isla hesitated, realizing the truth of his question. She had done a turnabout. "I don't really know. I mean, I'd much rather be at home, and I do not condone the caveman tactics you used to get me in the car last night, but—" She paused as an uncomfortable twinge pulled low in her belly. She rubbed the spot and tugged the seat belt to put some slack where it cut across her hips. "I don't want to see our baby hurt or used by Gibbs for manipulation of my family. If you think he poses a danger to us, then I want this evasion mission to succeed."

She shifted on the seat as the twinge sharpened. Emma had told her that she'd feel all kinds of weird aches and muscle tweaks throughout her pregnancy as her body changed to accommodate the baby, so she dismissed the dull ache. Her thoughts returned to the crisis at hand. "Speaking of this evasion mission, do you have an end date? An exit strategy? Or am I supposed to run with the baby, hiding from your father, for the rest of my life?"

"Well, not the rest of your life. Surely Gibbs will die before you," he said, casting a wry grin at her.

"That's not funny. I have no intention of running for years to come, so if that's your plan, then you should pull over now and let me out of the car."

Evan cut a quick side-look to her, then seeing her serious expression, he did a double take. "I don't— Do you have a plan?"

She leaned her head back and sighed. "I wish Brody was here. Or Cait. They're much better at planning and organizing than I am." Another sharper pain pulled low in her abdomen. "Or Emma. She could tell me if these pains are normal or not."

He whipped his gaze to her. "Pains? What pains?"

She exhaled through her mouth, her lips pursed. "Just strange little twinges. Probably nothing. Emma said I'd— Oh!" She winced as the throb intensified.

"Should we find an ER?" Evan asked, dividing his attention between his driving and Isla.

After a few cleansing breaths, the ache subsided. Isla

shook her head. "I'm okay. It's not too bad. Could even be something I ate. No need to panic."

His seemed to consider her assurances for a moment, then jerked a nod. "Okay, but tell me if it gets worse."

She hummed noncommittally.

"Promise me, Isla."

She pointed at the highway. "If you will keep your eyes on the road, then, yes, I promise."

He gave a humored snort, then planted his hands on the steering wheel at ten and two o'clock. After locking his gaze forward in an exaggerated manner, he asked, "Like this?"

Isla chuckled. "Works for me."

Evan rolled his eyes, then schooling his face, he said, "So we need cash and a burner phone. What else? Disguises?"

"Well, it's not like we're in witness protection. I wouldn't think we have to go that far. We just don't want Gibbs to be able to track us."

At the next exit, he left the interstate and got back on, going the opposite direction so they could return to the truck stop where she'd seen the Western Union sign.

"We might be able to buy the burner phone at the truck stop too. I can do that while you handle the wire transfer," he said. "And, um…"

Turning toward him, Isla studied Evan's battered profile. His darkening brow was dented in thought, and the midmorning sunlight emphasized the swelling in the masculine contours of his face. Despite his injuries, she still found him one of the most handsome men she'd ever met. She acknowledged the giddy blip in her pulse as she drank in his features. No wonder she'd so easily believed he was her destiny. Her body crackled with a kinetic energy when she was with him. Not only was

Evan physically attractive, she'd seen plenty of evidence that he could be kind and thoughtful. A doubt demon, spawned by her lingering hurt over his betrayal, clambered to the fore.

But he lied to you! You're in this predicament because of his betrayal! the inner voice reminded her, and yet—

The replay of his sins against her didn't hold the same acid sting as they once had. His perfidy still hurt, but... But.

Wasn't he trying to make up for his bad choices now? Was it possible that she could trust him now that he'd seen the error of his ways? She could even understand, if not agree with, his reasons for aligning himself with Gibbs. How far would she go to save her own mother's life?

The answer came in an instant. Sure and true. She'd do whatever it took to protect, defend, heal anyone in her family.

So maybe...

Isla firmed her lips and shook her head. Maybe she was just naive enough to buy into his justifications and excuses. Betrayal and manipulation was never acceptable.

Glancing at his wallet in her lap, curiosity poked at her. She cut one quick glance to Evan and was bitten by a prick of conscience. She couldn't...

Nibbling her lip, she mentally waved away the tug of compunction. *I'm not stealing anything, and if he's sitting right there, I'm not doing anything behind his back.* She pulled out his driver's license and read the fine print. His home address was listed as Portland, Oregon, but he'd already told her that he'd temporarily moved to Seattle, taken leave from work in order to be closer to his mom. *Responsible. Helpful.* Check, check.

He was an organ donor. *Honorable.* Check.

His height—six foot two—looked correct, but his weight seemed a little high. She cast another side-glance at him as he steered the car back off the interstate. "You're not one hundred and ninety pounds."

"Huh?" He shot a glance at her. "Oh. No. That's old. I've lost a bit in recent months."

Since his mother became ill. Stress would do that to a person. Hadn't her mother lost weight in the last two years worrying about all of her children and their various life-threatening crises?

"As long as you're pillaging in there, will you hand me my ATM card?" She did, and he rested it on his leg as he navigated back into the parking area of the truck stop. "Oh, and my satanic-worshipper membership card and my Liars and Cheaters Club ID?"

She flushed hot as she scowled at him. "Very funny."

"Well, wasn't that what you were hoping to find? Something to prove I was a terrible person? Something to substantiate your desire to hold me in contempt no matter how many times I apologize and try to fix things between us?"

"No!" She slapped the bifold wallet closed and handed it to him, his accusation prickling at the back of her neck. "Well, maybe."

He pulled his mouth into a disappointed scowl and heaved a sigh as he cut the engine. "Then I guess it's a good thing I left my Liars and Deceivers Card at home."

"Cheaters," she said with a smug grin. "Earlier you called it Liars and Cheaters. Jeepers. They should kick you out of the club if you can't even get the name right."

Her dry response earned a half smile from him. "I'll meet you back here as soon as I get some cash and the burner."

"And healthy snacks."

"You just had breakfast!"

"The baby wants healthy snacks for later. Baby says please."

He reached across the front seat to brush a knuckle along her cheek. His touch sent a skittering warmth through her veins. "Tell baby I'm on it."

Before following Evan inside the truck stop, Isla took another couple bites of her breakfast, knowing her growing baby needed sustenance, then gathered the trash from their meal. Hands full, she fumbled open the passenger door and headed to the closest trash receptacle. When she neared the overstuffed can, the scent of spoiled garbage caused her stomach to roil, and she nearly lost what was left of her stomach contents.

She hurried away from the trash and hustled inside the truck stop, where the odors of stale grease and overly pine, floor cleaner contributed to her continued nausea. She found Evan in the chip aisle where he was eyeing a bag of spicy tortilla chips. "Please, nothing with a strong scent. Even regular smells are making me queasy today."

He gave her a commiserative look as he exchanged the spicy chips for plain potato chips. "They don't have burner phones. I asked." He waved to the shelf of snacks. "What can I get you and Peanut?"

The nickname caught her off guard, and she hesitated, grinning at him, before studying the contents of the shelves. "It should be healthy. Something like…" She pulled a box of oat bran cereal from the opposite shelf. "This. I can nibble it when needed."

He appraised her choice with a dubious quirk in his brow. "Really?"

Her abdomen cramped again, and she grimaced as she rubbed the painful spot. "Really."

While Evan paid for the snacks and used the ATM to withdraw replacement cash, Isla headed to the restroom. She splashed cool water on her face, then turned to the woman standing next to her at the sink. "Excuse me. Do you have a cell phone I can borrow for a quick call? It's kinda an emergency." The woman hesitated a moment, then seemed to deem Isla no threat and handed her a phone from her back pocket. With the woman watching her, Isla dug in her memory and found a phone number she couldn't recall just hours earlier. Pregnancy-foggy brain? Emma had warned her about that too.

She called Cait and asked her to wire money to the truck stop Western Union office. Cait, of course, had dozens of questions and begged for assurances that Isla was safe and not under duress.

"All's well at this point, but believe me, I'm on guard for deception or misdirection from Evan. If I get a hint that he's—" She caught her breath as a sharper pain gripped her belly. "Oh man. Cait, are you having any weird pains with your pregnancy?"

"Weird how? I've had little muscle twitches. Nothing painful."

Isla groaned, and the woman waiting for her phone to be returned frowned her concern.

"Hey, are you okay?" Cait asked.

The first flutters of concern batted inside her.

"I... Probably. Just a little cramping." She forced a smile for the woman beside her. "So you'll send the money? ASAP? We need to get on the road, get some distance."

"Yeah. Getting on my laptop now. Assuming they allow electronic transfers—'cause I've never done this before, and I'm not sure if they do… You should have the cash in a few minutes."

"You're a jewel, sis. Oh, and I told Dad, but someone will have to feed and clean the pens for my little zoo. Maybe tell Fenn I'll pay her to do it? I don't know how long I'll be gone, so keep an eye on the feed supply. You may have to buy more."

"Yeah, I'll take care of it all, but remember this at Christmas when you're picking my present," Cait said, chuckling.

Despite the tickle of fear and the ache in her belly, Isla grinned at the family joke. Brody had made the comment as a five-year-old when praised for his helpfulness, and the precocious gibe had never been forgotten.

"Thank you," she told the woman as she handed back the phone. Before returning to the car, Isla used the toilet…and found blood spots on her undies.

Her heart rose to her throat, and she battled back tears. "No, no, no!"

Hunched over in pain and pressing a hand low on her stomach, Isla walked back to the rental car as fast as she dared. She tried not to hyperventilate, tried to fight the surge of anxiety that roiled her stomach, but when she climbed in the passenger seat after collecting the money Cait had wired, she met Evan's concerned gaze. Tears bloomed in her eyes. "I think you should take me to a hospital."

Chapter 18

Evan sat at the side of the bed in the ER exam room, holding Isla's free hand while the nurse attached a pulse oximeter and IV port.

"Everything's going to be okay. You'll see," he murmured quietly while stroking her wrist with his thumb. He wasn't sure if he was trying to reassure her…or himself. Ever since Isla had told him about the baby, he'd been on an emotional roller coaster, but knowing that Isla could lose the baby sent a dread to his core that clarified every other feeling he'd had. He wanted this baby. He loved this baby. He'd do whatever he must to protect this baby. Regardless of the wrinkle this baby put in his life, no matter how the baby complicated things with Gibbs, this baby meant the world to him.

The nurse, an older woman with a liberal streak of gray in her brown hair, cast a discerning eye toward him and asked, "And what happened to you? Is your black eye in any way related to her condition?"

"What?" Isla asked at the same time Evan said, "If you're suggesting I hit her or vice versa, the answer is no."

The nurse consulted Isla with a skeptical glance, and Isla shook her head. "Gosh no! He got that black eye from…" She stopped, sighed. "Well, it's unrelated." Now her attention shifted to Evan. "But as long as we're here at an ER anyway, you should—"

He was shaking his head before she could finish the thought.

"—have someone examine you, x-ray your ribs."

"I'm not leaving you."

"Evan, you're in pain," she countered. "I've seen you wince. I know you're trying to be brave and soldier through the hurt, but—"

"I'm not leaving you!" he repeated more firmly.

She huffed, sounding frustrated, "If you're thinking I'll use the opportunity to escape, to call a cab and head back to North Carolina, then—"

"No, I—" He felt the weight of the nurse's stare and realized how Isla's comment must have sounded to the older woman.

Isla must have realized as much too, because she groaned and said, "Oh, uh, poor choice of words. Everything's fine." She scowled at Evan, adding, "Except that he's a stubborn ox." Then turning back to the nurse, she pleaded, "Please take him for a CT scan. Head and chest. He's trying to dismiss his injuries, but he's clearly hurting."

Evan rolled his eyes. "Isla, I don't want to leave you. What about *your* pain? The baby?"

At this point, the nurse intervened. "Sir, if you'll come with me, I'll get you set up in another exam room and put in a request with radiology for some scans…just in case."

"I don't think—"

"I *do* think." The woman's expression and posture brooked no resistance. He got the feeling that if he didn't comply, she'd send for orderlies to enforce compliance. And then he got it. The nurse wanted a chance to talk to Isla alone. He stood slowly, making sure he didn't jostle or strain his sore ribs too much, and followed the nurse to another exam room.

"Please undress and put on the gown on the bed. I'll be back to start your workup in a moment," the nurse said as she left him to brood.

Resigned, Evan toed off his shoes and prayed that Isla wouldn't say anything that got him arrested for kidnapping.

After Isla explained the events of the past couple days, leaving out complicating details that would only raise more questions, the well-meaning nurse seemed satisfied that Evan posed no danger to Isla.

Left alone in the exam room between check-ins from the nurse and the on-call doctor, she realized how much she missed the company and comfort Evan had provided when they'd first arrived in the exam room. The prospect of losing the baby scared her, and his reassurances, no matter how pat or baseless, were soothing. As she reviewed the turbulent past few weeks, she couldn't say that Evan's attentiveness and concern for her and the baby surprised her. She'd recognized his caring and responsible character in the early days of their acquaintance. His obvious devotion to his mother, his graciousness on their date…his generosity during sex.

Her heart tripped, and she watched the numbers monitoring her pulse bump higher for a moment. She took a slow breath and shoved aside thoughts of intimacies with Evan. Raising her blood pressure and heart rate couldn't be good for the baby.

The baby...

Guilt plunged through her as she remembered the words she'd said earlier that morning.

Knowing this baby is Gene Gibbs's grandchild is enough to make me want to vomit. Had she really compared her child to demon spawn?

And the baby heard you, felt your loathing.

A cry of dismay wrenched from her throat as she pressed a hand over her womb. "Oh no! No, darling, I didn't mean it! I'm so sorry. Mommy loves you! Don't give up, *mo leanbh.* Please!"

When a soft knock sounded on the door, she glanced up, hoping it was her doctor, finished with her tests and armed with good news. Instead, Evan slipped in the room and closed the door behind him.

"I'm done with my CT scans and waiting for the radiologist to read them. Mind if I sit with you while we wait?"

She nodded her permission, and to her mortification, she started to sob.

Evan's face blanched, and he rushed to her side. "Isla, what's wrong? Is it the baby? Did you lose—" He snapped his mouth shut, as if afraid speaking the words too soon could jinx the test results.

"No," she said, sniffling and turning her face away. "I'm sorry, Evan. This is all my fault!" Tears leaked down her cheeks, and she dashed them away with her fist.

He rubbed her arm with comforting strokes and wore a puzzled face. "What are you talking about?"

"If I hadn't said those awful things about the baby..." Her voice cracked as another sob choked her.

"What awful things?"

"Earlier today, when I said—" She stopped, then leaned closer to him to whisper, "About hating that our baby had Gibbs's DNA. I compared our sweet child to Damien."

He chuckled softly. "Oh yeah, I remember that."

"It was an awful thing to say!" Her tears and the cold exam room made her nose run, and she sniffed hard, looking around for a tissue.

Without comment, Evan moved to the counter and snagged a couple soft paper towels from the dispenser. As he handed them to her, he said, "I knew you were kidding…exaggerating."

"The baby didn't." She blew her nose and dabbed at her eyes.

Evan frowned. "I don't follow. The baby?"

"The baby heard what I said! She felt the acid emotions I was feeling when I said those things. How could I have hurt my child that way?"

"Hold up…" He rubbed the spot between his eyes with his fingers. "You think the baby, the *embryo*, really, that barely has a heartbeat at this stage much less ears, heard something you said and took offense?" He gave her a wry look as he shook his head and chuckled.

Isla narrowed a glare on him. "I do! What's so funny about that?"

A strangled sound came from his throat, and his face fell as he studied her. "You're serious?"

"Of course I am! Why would I joke about something as important as my baby's life? My baby's feelings?"

He sat back in the chair and massaged his chin, a dent in his brow. "Sweetheart, the baby doesn't have feelings yet."

She folded her arms across her chest and angled her

head as she met his eyes. "Oh yeah? You're sure about that?"

His mouth opened and shut as garbled syllables of hesitation and fumbling spilled out.

"Can you see the air?" she asked. "No. But you can feel it on your skin. You can see the trees sway as the wind stirs. Can you smell a memory? Not directly. But when I smell popcorn, I'm five years old and holding my grandda's hand at the county fair. How do you know when you're happy?"

His mouth flattened, and he dropped his chin toward his chest as he sighed. "Let's not argue the finer points of your beliefs. Not now."

"You feel it in here first—" she tapped her chest and plunged on "—and your heart tells your brain. Our baby's body may not be fully formed, but I believe she can sense things on a very organic level. There are things beyond what we can see or explain in this world, Evan. God. Love. The energy, the force that gives our bodies and all of nature life. That something that weaves through all of earth and sky, light and sound, visible or spiritual, emotional or based in physics. It's that unexplained something that told me you were my future."

His head snapped up, his eyes widening. "What?"

She felt a little hiccup of alarm and mentally replayed what she'd said.

"You believe I'm your future? What does that mean?" He scooted forward, capturing her hand in his again.

Her heart bumped at the wash of hope on his face. "I... Didn't I tell you? I knew we were going to meet that day at Burger Palace. I had a dream about you."

His eyebrows shot higher, and he seemed to be waging a war between skepticism and longing. "What kind of dream?"

She lifted one shoulder. "The same kind everyone has." She nibbled her bottom lip, adding, "It's just that on this occasion, I woke up with a powerful sense about what I'd dreamed. That it was telling me something important. I interpreted it to mean I was going to meet my soulmate. And then I met you, and you were so attractive, and I felt so drawn to you right away. I—"

Even if she hadn't seen Evan's reaction play out in a series of shifting facial expressions, she'd have known how her admission affected him. His surprise, then relief, then joy crashed through her like waves on the shore, lapping at her heart and tearing at the walls she'd put up as if they were no more than a sandcastle.

"No," he said, his tone soft and warm, "you hadn't told me that. Is that really how you feel? You see me as your soulmate?"

She had to glance away. His deep brown eyes pulled at her and muddied her thoughts. "I don't know." Isla exhaled and twisted a hank of hair around her finger. "Usually I can understand what my special sense is telling me, but maybe I was wrong this time. Maybe my interpretation was tainted by what I wanted to happen. I've watched my sisters and Brody marry and find happiness, start families, and I wanted that too. But since my last relationship crashed and burned I've been... wary of dating."

In the silence following her explanation, she could feel Evan forming his opinions, and she braced herself for the inevitable questions about that failed relationship, one she didn't even like to spend a second thought on. She'd moved on from that loser.

Instead, Evan asked, "Your special sense? What are you saying?"

Startled by his question, she flicked a quick glance

at his befuddled expression. "Oh, uh, my family calls it my woo-woo thing. I just…know things before other people. Or can guess what people are thinking when they think they're hiding their feelings. I knew my sister Emma was pregnant with Lexi before anyone else, and figured it out with Cait's pregnancy earlier this month before she realized the truth."

He said nothing, but his eyes held hers. He was listening, trying to follow something that was clearly foreign to his engineer's brain. His desire to understand won him points. Some people were just dismissive of what they couldn't comprehend.

"When we were kids, I knew when my mother had breast cancer before she told us. I could always tell when my parents had been arguing or there was a problem worrying them, even if they pretended nothing was wrong. There'd be a vibration, a hum in the air that I'd feel in my core."

"Can you…read my mind?" The slight quaver in his tone said Evan was uneasy with that notion.

She gave him a wry grin. "Not exactly. Nothing as precise as that, but I picked up on something, I…sensed you were hiding things from me, even from the day you stopped by my house to ask me on our first date."

Compunction swept over his face, and she muttered, "I should have listened to that instinct."

He exhaled slowly, his eyes riveted on her. "Why… didn't you?"

"A bigger part of me *wanted* you to be my soulmate, wanted the dream to be right. I was foolish to ignore what I was feeling, but I'd never had such a tug-of-war, such a conflict of messages from my soul before."

"From your soul? Is that where you think your…" He

paused, then lifting a hand in concession, said, "...your woo-woo thing, for lack of a better term, originates?"

"I don't know what it is, exactly, but I've always been highly tuned to other people's emotions—an empath— and keyed into subtle clues in body language. I listen to and trust my own instincts. I'm usually right about other people, but this was the first time a dream had spoken so loudly to me, shaken me and filled me with such a strong resonance."

Evan slid closer to her again, gently cradling her hand in his, massaging her forearm with calming strokes. Loving caresses. He swallowed hard enough for her to hear him gulp. "So what is your special sense telling you now...about me?"

Isla squeezed her eyes shut, trying to hear a whisper in her core, wanting the same answer for herself. "It's all...jumbled now. Confusing. I don't know what to think. I've never—" A tear dripped from her eyelashes, and when she tried to swipe it away, her hand bumped Evan's, who'd reached up to do the same thing. She blinked and focused her attention on him. The concern in his dark gaze, furrowed forehead and tight lips were echoed in the palpable worry that radiated from him. Worry for her. For them. For their baby.

He's not his father. He knows he messed up. Deep down, he's a good man.

But did that make up for his betrayal? How could she give her heart to him if she didn't know whether she could trust him?

"You've never what?" he asked, prodding her from her ruminations.

Isla fixed her gaze on his. "I've never had trouble like this, figuring out what to feel or believe. My instincts have always been so sharp and strong and clear before. Even as a kid, I just—" she shrugged "—*knew* what I wanted, what to choose."

"Mmm, must have been nice," he said, his voice as low and soothing as the slow stokes of his hand on her arm. "I've spent my whole life making pro-and-con lists and weighing every choice for logic and practicality."

She curled up a corner of her mouth. "Lists. You sound like Cait. And Brody. Our left-brainers."

He grunted. "I did tell you I was an engineer on our date, remember?"

She nodded. "I remember everything about that night." She sobered as she asked, "Do you think we're... *too* different?"

He exhaled, his cheeks puffing out as he lifted a shoulder. "I don't know. I know couples who make it work." He arched a dark eyebrow and wagged a finger between them. "Are you saying you want to make this work?"

She grunted and twisted her mouth to the side. "I'm still here, aren't I?"

Evan blinked and sat back a bit as if mulling what she was saying. "Yeah. You are." With a short, wry laugh, he said, "Honestly, I thought you might try to run while I was getting CT scanned ten ways to Tuesday."

"Honestly... I considered it." When shadows crossed his face, she added, "But I couldn't."

He canted his head slightly, studying her. "Why not? Not that I'm sorry you didn't but..."

"Because I believe you about Gibbs being dangerous. Because... I've come this far, and I figure if you're willing to get beaten up and drive off into the great unknown to keep our baby safe, I can cut you some slack. And as foggy as my crystal ball has been lately, I figured two heads are better than one in sorting things out." She saw the odd look on his face and added quickly. "That was a joke. I don't *actually* have a crystal ball. Or tarot cards or magic beans or any of the things you're wondering right now."

He flipped up a hand and gave her an innocent look. "Did I say anything?"

"You didn't have to. Your face said it for you."

The exam room door opened, and an older man wearing a white lab coat and carrying a clipboard poked his head in the room. "Ms. Cameron?"

Isla nodded and sat up. "That's me."

The man offered his hand to shake. "I'm Dr. Moore. No need to sit up. Stay comfortable. I'm the obstetrics specialist on call for the hospital and was asked to review your lab work."

Evan shook the doctor's hand, as well, asking, "Is the baby okay?"

Dr. Moore nodded and smiled warmly as he motioned to the papers on the clipboard. "I see nothing from the ultrasound or blood test to indicate you are miscarrying."

The relief that flooded Isla left her dizzy, and she lay back on the pillows again, whispering a quick prayer of thanks.

"Then what happened?" Evan asked, putting into words her own question a split second before she could.

"What about the blood spots and cramping?" she asked.

"Not unheard of early in a pregnancy." The doctor gave them a brief medical description involving implantation in the uterus, hormones and how every pregnancy is different.

Isla listened distractedly while her mind wallowed in the reassurance that her baby was okay.

"Your hCG level is high and strong," the doctor said as he consulted the printout on her chart, "but to confirm this, you should have another blood test in a couple days to be sure it remains high."

She zoned back in. "Another test? Does that mean I might still miscarry?"

Dr. Moore raised a hand, motioning for her to stay calm. "Retesting is just a precaution. While there are no guarantees with any pregnancy, ever, I don't think you need to be unduly worried."

"But—" She fell silent when Evan put a calming hand on her wrist and squeezed.

The doctor acknowledged Evan's gesture with a grin and a nod. "Just a precaution. At this point, I see nothing that concerns me, so you—" he made eye contact with Isla and inclined his head toward her "—needn't worry either. I do recommend that you take it easy for the next few days and try to eat well. Healthy foods." He winked at her as he scribbled on the clipboard. "Savor this excuse to prop your feet up and have this guy pamper you." After clicking the pen, he stashed it in his labcoat pocket. "And be sure to follow up with your regular obstetrician and keep up with prenatal screenings."

"I will," Isla promised.

After they assured him they had no further questions about Isla's condition, Isla asked, "I don't suppose you know anything about his CT-scan results?"

Dr. Moore paused as he headed out, and shook his head. "When I give the staff up front your discharge papers, I'll ask what's happening with his tests. Shouldn't be much longer."

Unfortunately, the doctor's assurances proved wrong.

Chapter 19

Six hours passed before the ER staff gave Evan his diagnosis. A string of higher priority emergencies had come into the ER that delayed the shorthanded medical staff from delivering his results—a broken rib, internal contusions throughout his abdomen and a minor orbital fracture, all consistent with having been beaten by Leon. His ribs were taped, but nothing could be done for the contusions or tiny crack near his eye socket. Rest was recommended for Evan, as well, and Isla met his frustrated look with one that said silently she'd see that he followed the doctor's orders. The ER staff physician offered to prescribe painkillers, but Evan declined.

"I need to stay mentally sharp and be able to drive at a moment's notice," he explained when Isla expressed concern over his obvious discomfort.

"Okay," the doctor said, stashing her prescription pad in her lab-coat pocket. "In that case, over-the-counter meds are fine, ice packs for the swelling and…stay out of fistfights in the future, huh?"

"No kidding," he mumbled after the doctor left the room. "Tell Leon that. Sorry, dude, can't get beat up. Doctor's orders."

"You should file a police report. Leon, for assault, Gibbs, for accessory to assault or whatever it would be called," Isla said, scooting off the exam room bed where she'd been resting.

Evan scoffed. "Are you serious? That'd be writing my own obituary. Gibbs would never let that slide."

"So you're just going to let him get away with this?" she asked in dismay, waving toward his bruised face.

Evan sighed. "He'd get away with it even if I filed a complaint."

"What do you mean?"

"He lives outside the town limits. Jurisdiction of the county sheriff."

"And?"

"And he told me he has the sheriff and most of the deputies in his back pocket. You don't run a criminal operation like Gibbs has going without paying the local law enforcement to look the other way. He made sure I knew that when I argued with him over the arson he committed via his hired help."

"You argued with Gibbs over the arson?"

"Of course I did. Did you really think I'd let that go unchallenged? He nearly killed that poor family! Not to mention the destruction of your family's property. I was outraged."

She gave him a wary look. "And what happened when you challenged him on the arson?" Evan didn't answer for a moment, and Isla shuffled closer to him, gently framing his face with her hands. "Tell me. Please?"

"I was put on notice that he could get to my mother anytime he wanted. That he'd known where she lives for years."

A chill ran through Isla. She processed how that had to have hurt him, terrified him, angered him on so many levels. "Oh, Evan."

He blinked hard and rallied, flashing her a strained grin. "Well, it was the catalyst that finally pushed me to look for a way out of my stupid contract with him. I knew I had to get away from him, and somehow protect your family and my mother from the mess I'd made. So…there's that."

He pulled away from her touch and crossed the room to collect his jacket from a chair and gingerly slip his arms in, preparing to leave.

Isla watched him silently, digesting everything she had learned about him in the past several hours.

Once the discharged papers for each of them had been filed, they returned to the rental car and sat for a moment, neither speaking as they stared out the windshield at the sinking sun. Isla was the first to break the quiet. "Now which way?"

"Well, you heard your doctor. You need rest."

"Your doctor told you the same."

He made a dismissive noise with his lips. "Anyway, I say we head to a motel somewhere and get a room."

"You mean quit driving? I thought you were desperate to get us far away from your dad?"

He gave a humorless laugh. "Oh, I am, but I'm not gonna risk our baby's life in the process. If we need to sit still for a couple of days, then I'll find a way to keep us safe while we stay put." Even as he said as much, Isla could see him mentally calculating how he was going to accomplish as much. Giving his head a slight shake—

that he obviously regretted, based on his wince—he cranked the car engine. "Honestly, I need sleep, too, so let's look for a place that won't break our limited bank and regroup there."

"Why don't we just go to that one?" She pointed across the street at a name-brand hotel advertising vacancy.

Evan stared at the hotel a moment before frowning. "Tempting, but no. We've been in this area too long and left too many tracks that could be traced here. We need to relocate at least a little."

Isla mulled that truth. "All right, but for the same reason, I don't want to get back on I-40 and just head west. That, too, would be the obvious choice."

He nodded, then grimaced as he turned to look behind the car as he backed out of the parking space. "You're right, but we can't turn around and go back towards North Carolina either, so…" He twisted his mouth in thought as he navigated the hospital driveway to the road. "Which way?" He drummed his fingers on the steering wheel. "We need proximity to a hospital, in case you started cramping again." He quickly raised a hand to forestall any protest. "I'm not saying you will, but I don't want to tempt fate either. Beyond that it has to be discreet, not right off the road for instance."

"And clean," Isla insisted.

He quirked a grin. "Understood."

"Well," Isla said, "it's five minutes until four p.m.—gosh, those tests took way longer than I thought. Anyway, I say we either head northwest or southeast."

Evan looked at her with a puzzled scowl. "What does the time have to do with the direction you want to go?"

She held her hands up like the hands of a clock. "Minute hand is northwest, and the hour hand is southeast."

Evan reached over and cupped her cheek as he chuckled. "You really do have a unique way of going about things, don't you?"

She shrugged. "Not so unique. The compass is based on the clock, after all."

He opened his mouth, closed it. Raised his eyebrows. "Oh yeah. Okay. Northwest it is. I think Paducah is roughly northwest. Does that sound all right to you?"

She bobbed a nod. "Onward, Captain."

Isla napped in the car as they drove, and a couple hours later, Evan nudged her. "We're at Paducah. Help me look for a good place to stay."

Without a cell phone to do an online search, they relied on the old-fashioned means of finding a motel— driving down the streets of town until they found one that looked suitable. As soon as they were in their room, Evan collapsed on one of the two beds with a groan of exhaustion. "Between Gibbs's late-night summons and driving all night, I've had maybe two hours sleep in the last thirty-six hours."

She climbed on the other bed and lay on her side, facing him. "You've earned a nap. Well done, sir. And thank you."

"Hmm." His mouth twitched in a faint grin.

"What do you want to do about dinner?" she asked. No reply.

"Evan?"

A deep, steady breathing answered her. *Oh well. Let him sleep.*

Isla closed her eyes. Despite her car nap, she was still tired. Emma had told her fatigue during pregnancy was to be expected, but…dang! When she stirred sometime later to the sound of loud snoring, the room was much darker, the sun having set while they dozed. She sat up, her stomach rumbling, and studied Evan. The early stages of nausea were coming on again. The baby wanted food *now*.

"Psst, Evan?" She poked him in the shoulder. Nothing. "Evan?" she said a bit louder. Another poke. If she hadn't heard him snoring, she might have thought he was dead. The man was zonked out with a capital *Z*.

Shaking her head, she sat on the end of his bed and untied and removed his shoes for him. After debating her options—no way did she want to feed the baby food from a hotel vending machine—she peeked out the window to see what restaurants or markets were within view of the hotel. Then her gaze settled on the rental car and she stilled. Something inside her whispered, "Go."

She turned back toward Evan, biting down on her bottom lip before digging carefully in his pocket for the car key. She folded the duvet over him as a cover, then tiptoed to the door.

Evan woke suddenly as a sharp pain shot through his chest. He rolled from his side—the side with the cracked rib and obviously the source of his pain—and stared groggily at the ceiling for a moment before he realized the dark hotel room was not the same one he'd woken to for the past several weeks. Clarity elbowed its way through the fog of sleep, and he struggled to sit up, his breath catching as the movement caused fresh ripples of agony to grip his chest. His muscles had stiffened as he slept, and for a moment, he regretted having turned down the offer of prescription-strength pain management from the ER doctor. He rubbed his eyes and glanced at the other bed. It was empty.

"Isla?" Holding his side, he eased off the bed and stumbled to the bathroom to look for her. When had he taken off his shoes? He didn't remember doing that. But then he didn't remember much since he'd flopped on the bed God-knows-how-long ago. He tapped on the closed bathroom door. "Isla? You all right?"

When he got no reply, he glanced down and realized no light was coming from the bathroom through the crack at the floor. He pushed on the door and it swung open to an empty tile-lined room. Panic flashed through him like hot water dumped on his head. "Isla?"

He darted back out to the bedroom, sweeping his gaze over both beds, the chairs, the floor. Darting to the window, he checked the parking lot. Their parking space was empty.

His heart sank. Isla was gone.

Isla juggled the numerous bags of merchandise and groceries she'd acquired on her trip out, in what her mother called a lazy-man's load, coming in from the car. She knocked on the hotel room door with her elbow. "Evan? Open up. My hands are full."

Evan's face was whey colored when he yanked open the door. Knocking her load of bags aside, he hauled her into an embrace muttering, "Oh, thank God! Jeez, Isla. I don't know whether to kiss you or strangle you."

"Oof," she wheezed as he squeezed her close. She let the bags she held drop to the ground as she raised her arms to gain some breathing space between them. "How about neither? I'd rather you help me get these supplies inside."

When he finally allowed her to back out of his arms, she caught the flicker of fear in his eyes, and her stomach swooped. Her insides quivered as she absorbed the depths of his distress, noticed the grooves of worry lining his face. "My gosh, Evan! You really are upset."

He barked a harsh laugh. "Ya think? I woke up to an empty room, the car gone and no note saying where you'd gone—"

She winced. "Oops. My bad. I should have left—"

"While somewhere out there," he continued over her, "a homicidal megalomaniac is hunting you so he can lock you in his basement until your baby comes or cut the baby out to transplant in a surrogate or—"

"He wants to do *what*?" she asked, her voice going a little shrill. "That's not a thing!"

Evan scowled and waved her off. "I don't know. I made that up. But he definitely has twisted designs on our baby, and you should not have gone off on your own! If anything had happened to you—" He plowed his hand through his hair and groaned. "God, Isla, I had no way to know if he'd found us and kidnapped you or if you'd—" He clamped his mouth shut, and the muscles in his cheeks flexed as he gritted his back teeth.

Isla narrowed her eyes, suspicion creeping over her. "Or if I'd what? Ditched you? Is that what you thought? After I'd promised you earlier today that I was sticking by you through this—this…whatever this is?"

His chest heaved as he gulped shallow breaths and clutched his ribs. "Can you blame me? It looked pretty much that way from my vantage point."

She set her jaw and lifted her chin. "Yes, I can blame you! Trust is a two-way street, Evan. How is this going to work if you don't trust me?"

His shoulders slumped. "I—I don't know. When I found you gone I…flipped out, I guess. I blamed myself for not being more alert, for not protecting you, for not—"

Isla couldn't say why she kissed him then, but she did. She rose on her toes, capturing the back of his head to draw him closer, and silenced him as her mouth slanted over his. His body stilled for a heartbeat, and then his hands were framing her face, holding her near as he returned her kiss with a tender, lingering passion.

For a moment, she was lost. Her soul sang and her blood hummed as she surrendered to the kiss. More than just a tender moment, the kiss drew her into a sense of comfort, like a homecoming. *Your soulmate.* The whisper in her heart insisted, drowning out the voice in her head that still flashed caution.

Finally, as her stomach grumbled loudly that the baby must be fed, she stepped back from Evan and rested her forehead against his. "We have to have mutual trust. If I can try to rebuild my trust in you, can't you grant me the same faith?"

He sighed and nodded. "Of course. I'm sorry. I—" He glanced down at the bags at her feet. "What is all this anyway?"

"Food. A burner phone. Clothes and toiletries for both of us. Over-the-counter painkiller for you. Vitamins for me."

He bent to lift the bags, then winced and pressed a hand to his ribs.

She waved him inside. "I've got this. You're supposed to be resting."

"You are too," he said, his tone mildly scolding. "Speaking of, how do you feel?"

"Much better after getting some sleep, but starving. Find the bag with the bananas, please, before I start gnawing on the furniture."

The next morning, they shared a breakfast of low-sugar granola bars, fresh fruit and milk, and studied the paper map she'd bought, simply because it could be spread out on the bed and viewed easily by both of them.

"I'm kinda shocked the store even had a paper map. Did you find it in the antiques section?" Evan teased as he settled beside her on one of the beds, their backs propped against the headboard with pillows.

"Yep," she returned playfully as she munched a banana. "Right next to the phone books and VHS tapes." When he grew quiet, staring at the new phone, she knew immediately where his mind had gone. "Call her. It's safe now with the burner."

He twisted his mouth. "It's pretty early on the West Coast still. If she's sleeping, I don't want to wake her."

She reached for his leg and patted his thigh. "You're a good son."

He snorted. "Because I don't call before six a.m.?"

"Because you've devoted your life to helping her, loving her, protecting her. And you've put your life on hold these past weeks, trying to save hers."

His shoulders drooped. "For all the good it did. I ended up putting you at risk. Maybe even putting Mom in more danger because of—" He stopped abruptly and swung his legs off the bed, his face awash with some horrible realization.

He grumbled a curse as he stood to pace stiffly, scrubbing a hand on his unshaven face. "We have to go to Seattle. I have to protect my mom if Gibbs decides to send Leon or some other goon after her to flush us from the bushes."

"You think your father would hurt a dying woman to get at us?" Isla's stomach swooped in dismay, but a sick sense told her Gibbs was not beyond such despicable measures.

"He's threatened as much. I wouldn't put it past him."

He cursed. "Getting back to protect her had been my focus before—" He waved his hands, vaguely indicating all that had transpired over the past days.

"But...what if, despite our precautions, he's tracking us, and we lead the danger to her? Should we keep our distance to—" Evan shook his head with certainty, so she didn't bother finishing.

"He can find her with or without following us. If he does, in fact, already know where her house is, it'd be easy enough, given satellite maps and all the information available on the internet these days." He smacked a fist into his opposite palm. "Given our delays and sidetracking, he could already be ahead of us. Hell, he could have flown there and be sitting at her bedside now, with a gun to her head!"

Isla could feel the waves of terror rolling off him, and she hurried across the room to block his pacing. "Evan, don't take your mind there. Negative thoughts are counterproductive. Not only that, it's not good for the baby to be bathed in bad energy."

For the briefest moment, he seemed to be prepared to dismiss her assertion as hokum. That he didn't, that he visibly and palpably reined in that impulse impressed her, touched her. He was trying to understand and accept her beliefs and realities. But he was still a ball of jitters, of worry for his mother and eagerness to act.

"Take a cleansing breath. Fill your body with it and then exhale slowly. Push out all the bad vibes and clear your mind." She demonstrated. "Then with your next breath—"

Evan sighed and sidestepped her. "I'm sorry, Isla. But we don't have time to meditate or whatever it is you want me to do. We need to pack up and go."

Isla gathered in her composure. She'd have to share

her patience with Evan. Touching his arm lightly, she blocked his agitated pacing again. "Call her first. Reassure yourself she is all right."

A beat passed before her words, her calm seemed to sink in. Evan finally exhaled and gave a nod of agreement. While he talked to his mother—for most of the call reassuring *her* that he was all right—Isla began packing her new clothes in the backpack that was among her purchases. She noticed that Evan didn't say anything about Isla being with him, about her pregnancy, about fleeing North Carolina to avoid Gibbs. He also said nothing about their imminent arrival. His only warning to her was to be alert and watchful for danger herself.

When he disconnected the call, he seemed to know the questions in her mind. "No point worrying her more than I have. We don't know if and when we'll get there. And, honestly, I'm saving the you're-going-to-be-a-grandmother news until I can see her reaction in person. Holding her grandbaby was one of the few bucket-list things she's expressed to me. Until now, I didn't think it was something I could make happen." His smile was melancholy, and Isla swore she felt the baby kick inside her, even though, according to everything she'd read, it was way too soon to be feeling movement.

Or maybe it was just her own eagerness to meet the woman who had raised Evan, who would love and spoil their baby one day—because she had a flash of certainty that Tracy Murray *would* check her wish for a grandbaby off her life list. She just prayed that opportunity was more than a fleeting moment. Finding the resources to help Tracy get the medical care she needed pounded through her blood with an urgent drumbeat.

Isla paused in her packing and glanced at Evan,

who'd started collecting their food items into a bag. When had she made the shift to making Evan's priorities her own? Of course she'd always wanted Tracy to get well, but now the need, the mission to secure the treatments to facilitate her healing burned in her core with a fiery passion. Like it did in Evan's. The connection between them was growing stronger, even before she knew what to do with it. She'd put her heart out too fast before and been crushed. She'd use more caution this time. Evan may have mended some fences with her, but she still needed some unnameable assurance, the balm that would satisfy her wounded soul of his unconditional allegiance.

The acetaminophen Isla had bought helped his pain. Minimally. But something was better than nothing. And sitting in the car, even reclined while Isla took a turn driving, was only making his body stiff. Potholes were torture. He gritted his teeth, biting back the groans of misery each time they bounced over one, jarring his ribs. He tried to sleep, tried not to dwell on how long it was taking to drive across the endless wheatfields and cornfields of Western Kansas. Tried not to replay the markedly weaker sound of his mother's voice. Without a second payment made to the medical facility where she'd started the experimental treatment, the progress she'd seen in the first two weeks of the trial were already slipping away.

But there had been progress initially, his mother had said. And that gave him hope. If they could get her back in the program, did she have a real chance of... being cured? Did he dare to believe in something as miraculous as that? A lightness filled his chest for a few precious seconds before reality burst the bubble.

Without the money to get her back in the new treatment program—

As if sensing where his thoughts were, Isla reached over and squeezed his shoulder. "Stay positive. Anxiety and pessimism don't help your mom. We'll figure something out. Together."

He snapped his gaze to hers. "Together?"

Her brow puckered slightly. "Well, yeah. I'm here, aren't I? Why wouldn't I help you solve whatever crisis you faced? She is my child's grandmother, after all. That's worth a lot." Her returned smile of confidence buoyed him. Maybe there was something to this woo-woo–connection thing she claimed she'd predicted in a dream. Or maybe it was just that Isla was good to her marrow. Good for him, good for their baby, good for a world that needed more kind and positive people.

He exhaled and forced a smile to his lips, discovering just the act of pretending to be happier, more optimistic did lift his mood some. Maybe Isla was onto something with her talk of spirituality and emotional energy and unseen connections.

After a bathroom break and driver swap near the Colorado border, Isla angled her body toward him and said, "Tell me more about your childhood, your mother." She reached over and kneaded the knots in his neck and shoulders. Her touch was bliss, and he relaxed his grip on the steering wheel as he sank into the happy memories of holidays past, school programs that his mother never missed and meals at a kitchen table—never in front of a screen—where they planned for his future. He told her all of it, his smile returning with relish as he shared stories of mischief, summer jobs and a pet goldfish named Fido when they couldn't afford a dog.

Isla regaled him with more history of the Cameron

family, her collection of strays through the years that included an injured turtle, wild turkey eggs that she hatched using a heating pad, and numerous kittens and foster dogs.

"My last two foster dogs didn't mix well with the chickens and Doodle-doo, so for now I'm taking a hiatus from that. I think Brody and Anya mentioned they were thinking of getting a dog though..." She looked thoughtful. "I should tell them about the beagle mix Nancy is looking to place."

"Nancy?" he asked.

"Oh, sorry. Just thinking out loud."

"You do that a lot, don't you?" He reached over to squeeze her leg, his chest warming as he considered all he was learning about her.

"Talk to myself?" she asked, chuckling. "I guess."

"No, I meant thinking of others. You seem to always be looking for ways to help others, solve problems for your family, ease other people's pain."

"I—" She flushed a little. "I hope that's true. I mean, isn't that what we're all supposed to do?"

"True. Not everyone is as good at it as you are though. Did you ever consider becoming a social worker? Not that there isn't merit to nutritional science," he amended quickly.

Her red-gold eyebrows dipped. "I couldn't do social work. As an empath, I'd soak up all the pain and emotional upheaval as if it were my own and be in a constant state of distress with migraines and ulcers and, whew!" She shook her head. "Like the level of burnout mental health counselors suffer, on steroids. I wouldn't last a month." She chuckled wryly. "See, I am selfish after all."

"Or self-aware and wise to protect your health. So

as an empath, you feel others' emotions, huh? How does that work?"

"I really don't know how it happens or why, just that it happens, and generally only with strong emotion. Good or bad."

Another thought came to him, and he buzzed his lips with regret. "Dang it, you're missing class because of me, because of this trip. Aren't you?"

She rolled her eyes. "So, what else is new?" With a shrug she said, "I guess I'll drop the class and take it again next fall." With a lopsided grin, she leaned her head back on the seat and let her hand rest on his thigh. "Although then, I'll have a new baby to think about. Huh. I swear, if I ever finish grad school, it will be a miracle."

Evan thought about his job at the paper mill, about the two-month family leave without pay he'd taken, which would be expiring in a few days. Would he have a job when this mess was over? He couldn't expect his boss to wait for him to return with no end date in sight.

"Evan?" Isla's voice called him out of his reverie. "You went somewhere dark again, didn't you?"

He snorted in amazement and lifted her hand from his leg to kiss. "Isla darling, your mood radar is going to take some getting used to."

But it would be a task he'd relish.

Chapter 20

By taking turns driving and sleeping, Evan and Isla made good time traveling cross-country. By the time they reached Boise, Idaho, however, they decided they both needed a good meal and a good sleep. They found an inexpensive motel and had dinner at a restaurant, where Isla loaded up on vegetables and milk. When they finished eating and were walking back to the car, Isla placed a hand on her abdomen and sighed contentedly. "Peanut enjoyed that, I think."

"Peanut did, huh? And did Mommy?" Evan asked with a lopsided grin.

Isla returned a smile. "Mommy likes hearing you say Mommy." She blinked, as she shook her head in joy and wonder, repeating, "Mommy. I'm a mommy."

Evan pulled back his shoulders and with a playful wink said, "You're welcome."

She snorted and play-punched his arm. "Dork."

While she waited for Evan to fumble the key fob

from his pocket and unlock the rental car, a faint mewling sound reached her, layered under the ruckus of traffic on the street, music from someone's radio and chatter of birds gathering in a nearby tree for the evening. Isla turned, scanning the parking lot, trying to zero in on the exact location the sound was coming from. The tiny cry came again, and her heart twisted. She hadn't imagined it.

"Something wrong?" Evan asked when she didn't get in the passenger door he'd opened for her.

"I hear something." Her attention still focused on pinning down the source of the cry, she handed him the to-go box, with the remnants of his fried fish dinner and her slice of cherry pie for later.

"What kind of something?"

Without answering—she needed quiet to hear the weak sound better—she headed across the parking lot toward the neighboring Jack in the Box fast-food joint.

"Isla?" She heard Evan's steps behind her as she quickened her pace, drawn to the back of the fast-food parking lot near a wooded area. She went toward the trees and tall grass, then stopped when she realized the pitiful sounds were now behind her. Coming from the large dumpster behind the Jack in the Box.

Her gut pitched—first, realizing that something that shouldn't be in that trash bin was and, again, when the rancid scent of the refuse triggered her pregnancy-sensitive sense of smell.

"What are you doing?" Evan asked as he caught up to her.

She reached the trash bin and stood on tiptoe, trying to peek inside. "Dang it, I'm not tall enough. And I think to get whatever's in there out, I'm going to have to climb inside."

He barked a laugh. "You're what?" He tugged her arm. "I don't think so. You're pregnant. You are not going to go climbing in God-knows-what kind of garbage to have a look around."

"Are you volunteering, with your broken ribs?" she asked, facing him with an expression that said her way was the only logical choice.

"I'm saying, let's go back to the motel and get some sleep. It could just be crickets or an owl in the woods or—"

At that moment, Evan fell silent as the mewling became louder, changed tone and clarified in identity. The strident and terrified cry of a kitten.

Isla's chest squeezed so hard she could barely catch her next breath. "Either give me a boost in or go get the car and pull it up close enough that I can climb on it and jump into the dumpster from the hood."

He shot her a look that said she was out of her mind.

She returned a look that said she was not leaving without rescuing the kitten. For a moment, they simply stared at each other in a silent battle of wills. But as the kitten's whines continued to echo around them, she watched Evan's determination chip slowly away. The pitiful cries clearly burrowed through his sense of practicality.

Finally he let his shoulders drop and he heaved a sigh. "I'll be right back with the car. Don't try to climb without me here to spot you. Will you give me that much?"

She flashed a bright smile. "I promise."

Once Evan had the rental car parked alongside the large trash bin, he waved her away, saying, "Broken rib or not, I won't stand here and do nothing while my pregnant girlfriend climbs in a garbage can. I'll go in."

The term *girlfriend* sent a ripple of something warm and sweet through her. Or maybe it was just his offer to do the literally dirty work in her place. Either way, she felt another chip of the wall she'd erected after his betrayal fall away.

Evan climbed onto the hood of the sedan and peered into the garbage bin, his nose wrinkling at whatever he saw—or smelled—there. Then, as if mustering his will, he firmed his mouth and exhaled heavily. He eased himself over the side, wincing with the effort, and she heard a grunt of disgust as he disappeared from view.

Maybe she wasn't climbing in the dumpster, but she wanted to see what was happening. Isla climbed on the car and moved to the side of the trash bin to follow his progress. The scared gray kitten had stopped crying, apparently startled by Evan's arrival, and was struggling to dig through the waste packaging and rotting food away from its rescuer. "Oh, that poor baby!"

Evan's head snapped up, his gaze locking with hers. "What the— Isla, you're not coming in here! You promised—"

"I'm not coming in, but I can watch. Oh, get it!" she cried when the kitten made another panicked attempt to climb the metal wall of the dumpster. She gasped, realizing the further cause of the kitten's distress. "Oh, Evan, that bag is wrapped around its neck!"

Evan fumbled forward through the piles of muck and snagged the tiny gray fur ball. Predictably, the kitten struggled and, claws out, flailed for purchase to launch an escape.

"Ow! Jeez, stop that, damn it!" Evan grumbled, almost losing his footing in the refuse as he attempted to subdue the wiggling body booby-trapped with fishing hooks long enough to remove the plastic grocery bag.

Isla held her breath as Evan lost his grip on the kitten, then recaptured it, only to go through another round of writhing and scratching. Somehow he managed to get the bag off the kitten's head.

She held out her hands. "Give the baby to me."

"Gladly." He waded closer, nearly losing his hold once more before managing to pass the kitten to Isla. She tried to grasp the kitten's scruff and found the pitiful thing was terribly emaciated and likely dehydrated. Condition dire. Fragile. Her heart broke all over. The kitten instinctively went still as she held it by the scruff, and she cooed softly to the trembling creature as she drew it close to her body, pressing it snugly against her chest, all four legs tucked in so that it felt secure. "Easy, baby. You're okay. I'm gonna help you," she crooned.

The squeaking meows the kitten made tugged at her, while a fury for the cruelty that landed a kitten in a plastic bag in a dumpster seethed in her blood. "What kind of sorry jerk does this to an innocent animal?"

"You think someone put it in here?"

She angled her head as she looked at Evan. "Look at it. Do you really think it climbed in there by itself? That it would have gotten that bag around its head on its own?"

Evan scowled as if just realizing the truth of what she was suggesting. Then muttered a dark curse word. He struggled back through the knee-deep trash to the side of the bin and stood contemplating the climb back out for a minute before heaving himself over the side to the car hood. He shouted in pain, and the kitten startled at the loud noise.

Isla pressed the gray kitten closer, held it tighter, whispered more soothing words to the tiny cat.

Once Evan was back on the ground, he reached up

to hold Isla's elbow, stabilizing her as she scuttled off the car. With his arm around his ribs, Evan stared at her, cradling the kitten and asked, "Now what do we do with it?"

She smiled as if the answer should be obvious. "I think I'll call him Jack."

Two hours later, after they'd purchased a cartload of cat supplies, bathed and defleaed the kitten, and given the ravenous baby food and water, Isla walked into the bedroom of the motel room, having taken her own shower, and found Evan fast asleep on one of the beds. The exhausted kitten was curled in a ball on his chest with Evan's hand splayed protectively against Jack's back.

Isla blinked as tears of affection bloomed in her eyes, and her chest ached with tenderness for both Evan and Jack. Evan had put up a futile argument against keeping the kitten. He'd wanted to take it to an animal rescue. But Isla responded simply with "Why? We've already rescued him. He's mine now."

Seeing her determination and attachment to Jack, he'd wisely conceded. Now, standing in that motel room, miles from home, a dangerous man hunting her and her unborn child, Isla knew she couldn't blame pregnancy hormones for the rush of love that swamped her. The sweet and pure emotions that surged in her as she reflected on the past days, traveling with Evan, were a deeper and truer expression of what she'd started feeling for him before he betrayed her. She might have been in lust with him before, a feeling sprinkled with the pixie dust of a dream that he was her soulmate. But seeing Evan in action, living out his promise to protect her, cherish her, trust her—and be trustworthy—he'd sneaked past her defenses and rooted himself in her heart. He was proving to be all the things she'd originally believed about him.

Dabbing at her damp eyes, Isla crawled up on the bed next to Evan and Jack. She stroked one finger on the kitten's small head, and the sacked-out kitten emitted a contented thrum. Tucking herself close to Evan, she rested her hand on his arm and quickly drifted toward sleep. If she'd been a cat, she, too, would have been purring.

Chapter 21

The next morning, they set out on the last stretch of their journey with Jack curled on Isla's lap while Evan drove.

"Have you let your mom know we're coming yet?" she asked as she stroked the kitten's now-clean fur. Once spiffed up, Jack proved to have three white paws and a white belly and bib.

In answer to her question, Evan gave a side-look and a shake of his head. "I guess I'm waiting to make sure nothing happens to us before we get there. I still feel like Gibbs is breathing down our necks, even all these miles away."

She hummed her agreement. "I find myself looking over my shoulder or checking the car mirrors a lot too." She sighed, then asked quietly, "Are we going to be doing that for the rest of our lives?"

Evan didn't answer right away, but his expression said he hated the idea of needing to be constantly vigilant, never shaking the threat Gibbs posed, always having danger lurking in the shadows. "Maybe not forever, but…"

…for the foreseeable future. He didn't finish the sentence, but he didn't have to.

They fell silent again, each stewing over what that would mean going forward, how they'd cope, until Isla asked, "Is your mother going to be okay with me bringing Jack to her house?"

The dimple appeared again, and he lifted her hand from his leg to kiss her palm. "She's going to love you. And Jack."

Evan finally let his mother know they were coming when they entered the outskirts of the city and were making their approach to his childhood home. His mother's home-health nurse met them at the front door and told them his mother was in her bedroom.

"Evan? Is that you?" a thin voice called from the back of the house.

Isla handed Jack to the nurse, who was already cooing over the kitten, and asked her to watch Jack until after they'd greeted Tracy. Then Evan led her through the small but homey bungalow to meet his mother.

Isla swallowed the gasp that swelled in her throat when she saw the too-thin woman with sparse hair and dark, sunken eyes. Her heart broke for Evan's mother… and Evan. Clearly the illness had taken a tremendous toll on Tracy, and Isla could only imagine how she'd feel seeing a family member fade away, growing more gaunt every day.

The instant Tracy met Isla's gaze, though, her eyes lit with delight, and a smile brightened her pale face. She stretched her arms toward Isla. "Oh my goodness! Is this Isla? Come in, dear. I'm so pleased to meet you!"

Isla returned a bright greeting and clasped Tracy's hands. The woman's grasp was surprisingly firm, and a sensation of purest love and joy filled Isla from head to toe. Her heart thumped harder as she acknowledged the whisper of spiritual recognition. Her soul knew Tracy, loved Tracy, needed Tracy. *Of course.* If the fates still believed that Evan was her soulmate, then Tracy was destined to be family. Or maybe it was her child's soul recognizing their family bond with Evan's mother.

Isla squeezed Tracy's hand gently. "The pleasure is mine. Evan has told me so much about you and the loving childhood you gave him."

Evan's mother spared a warm glance for her son. "That's sweet of him. I wish I could say he'd told me all about you too. But I only learned you were a couple a few days ago when he called to say you were on the road together and had a new phone number."

Isla's grin faltered. "He said we were a couple?" She cut a quizzical look toward him and scowled. "I'm afraid he's misled you. Our relationship is…not that straightforward. In fact, it's rather complicated."

Evan sighed as he took a seat beside the bed. "And in light of the complicated nature of things, I decided to keep explanations simple." He bent to kiss his mother's cheek. "No deception intended."

"How complicated can it be?" Tracy asked. "Either you're a couple or you're not."

Isla moved to a chair on the other side of Tracy's bed. "How much time do you have?"

Tracy spread her hands. "Got nothing else to do all evening."

Evan exhaled through tight lips, making a buzzing sound with his mouth. "I hadn't planned to get into the weeds so soon, but…" He glanced at Isla. "You okay with telling her all of it now?"

"Isn't that kinda why we came—" she reached over and touched Tracy's arm lightly "—besides the opportunity for us to meet?"

"And check up on me. Make sure I'm following doctor's orders." Tracy sent her son a knowing look. "I've told you, you don't have to hover. Live your life. Don't sit around waiting for me to die." She gave a wry, sad laugh. "I do enough of that for both of us."

Evan's back stiffened. "That's not funny, Mom. And I haven't written you off yet. There's still hope we can get you back in the medical trial—"

"No," Tracy's tone was firm. She shook her head to echo her words. "I won't have you bankrupting yourself and swimming in debt because of me. That is not the legacy I want to leave."

"Mom, I can't—"

"You have a much happier legacy already," Isla blurted, hoping to redirect the unpleasant and unproductive conversation.

Both Tracy and Evan turned their eyes to her.

Isla took a breath, covered her belly with one hand and smiled as she said, "You're a grandmother. I'm having Evan's baby."

Tracy blinked, staring at Isla blankly for a moment as if mentally replaying her announcement. "I…am?" Her expression brightened, and she looked to Evan for confirmation.

Evan raised both hands and waggled them. "Surprise."

"Oh!" Tears filled Tracy's eyes. "Oh my—" She hiccuped a half laugh, half sob as she lifted a hand to her mouth. "That's wonderful!" She sobered a bit, then dividing a look between Isla and Evan, said, "Oh. So that's one layer of complicated, hmm? Can I assume there's more?"

Isla chewed her bottom lip for a moment as she nodded. When Evan flapped a hand, inviting her to make the explanations, she pressed Tracy's frail hand between hers and leveled a steady gaze on Evan's mother. "The most troubling layer involves Evan's father."

She felt Tracy jolt, her hand gripping Isla's. "What?"

Tracy's gaze darted to Evan. "What did you do? I told you not to wake that sleeping giant! Gene is dangerous!"

Evan firmed his mouth and turned to look out the window for a moment before sighing. "I thought I could handle anything he threw at me. Being forewarned and all that…" He returned his focus to his mother, his eyes unrepentant. "And to me, the risk was worth it, if it meant you could get in the trial."

Tracy's eyes narrowed, her nose wrinkling in disgust. "Are you saying the money you sent as the down payment on the trial came from Gene?"

Evan scrubbed a hand over his face. "Mom, the experimental treatment was working. Isn't that the important thing?"

"Not if it means we're somehow indebted to Gene Gibbs, it isn't!" Tracy settled back, pressing deeper into her pillows, as if she could create more distance between her and the idea of any connection to Gibbs.

Isla shared the other woman's revulsion but kept silent about the more frightening details of the situation, waiting for Evan to confess the full truth. If he couldn't be completely honest with his mother, how could she expect to have any level of trust with him going forward? He claimed to be sorry for his choices and resolved to be forthcoming and loyal in all ways going forward. So, here was a chance to prove himself.

Isla's pulse was fluttering in her ears, and she held her breath. Held Evan's gaze. She refused to even raise an eyebrow to prod him. He had to find the courage and motivation within himself. His actions had to be organic and true, not coerced.

Evan stood and paced across the small bedroom, then back to the chair by the bed. "Mom, just… Everything I did was with the best intentions. I was desperate to get you the trial treatment and—"

"Evan—" Tracy's already pale face grew a shade whiter "—what did you do?"

Shame filled Evan's face, and Isla's chest ached in sympathy, despite her continued anger over his actions. He'd put her family and Cameron Glen in real jeopardy, and she was still working on forgiving him for that.

"I made a deal to help him with…" He faltered, then said, "A business deal."

Isla flinched despite her best effort to remain stoic and give no encouragement or judgment as he told his story to Tracy.

Tracy's clearly noticed Isla's reaction, because her attention shifted to her. "Isla? What isn't he saying?"

She shook her head. "It's not for me to explain."

Raising her chin along with her gaze, she silently indicated that Evan once again had the floor. He cleared his throat, and angling his body toward his mother, he said, "I betrayed Isla's trust and put her and her family in harm's way. We're here because Gibbs threatened to kidnap Isla and use our baby's life as leverage to steal her family's homestead."

Saying the words, seeing his mother's expression of dismay and disappointment, reliving the awful truth of how far he'd sunk, good intentions or not, roiled Evan's gut, and he had to swallow several times to keep the bile down his throat. He sent a guilty glance to Isla, measuring her response to his confession. She remained surprisingly calm, though her expression reflected her continued hurt and anger. "I am doing my level best to make amends to Isla for all the wrongs I've done her, but you should know, she's not here willingly."

His mother's brow furrowed. "What does that mean? You brought her here by force?"

He rubbed sweaty palms on the legs of his jeans and grimaced. "Kinda."

"Not *kinda*. Absolutely," Isla countered, then after frowning, she met his mother's eyes and amended, "At least, at first. After some discussion and compromise, I saw the wisdom of getting far away from Gibbs, until another solution to neutralize him can be found. And…" She patted his mother's hand and smiled warmly. "I wanted to meet you. You are the baby's grandmother, after all. And none of this mess is your doing."

Tracy shook her head in dismay as she turned back to Evan. "I tried to warn you that Gene was no good, that he was selfish and had no moral conscience."

"You did. But he also has millions of dollars and owes a huge debt to you. I thought I could make him see reason."

Tracy groaned. "He'd have to be reasonable for that to happen."

"Yeah, well, he may not be reasonable, but he is dangerous and…he's likely on his way here, as we speak."

Tracy's pale face grew even whiter. "Here?"

Evan nodded grimly. "He pegged my weak spots pretty easily and threatened you as well as Isla. I brought Isla here because I needed to protect you both."

* * *

One afternoon the next week, after the home-health nurse left, Tracy napped with Jack—whom she was besotted with—beside her. Evan slept in the chair next to her bed, his hand resting on top of his mother's. Isla's heart swelled painfully knowing how difficult it was for Evan to see his mother fading, weakening. She left them to have time alone together and busied herself puttering around the house. A little cleaning. A little reading. A little flipping through photo albums. She had just wandered into the kitchen to begin browsing the contents of the pantry, with a mind toward starting dinner, when a movement out the window over the sink caught her attention. Even before she reached the window to glance out, a tingling premonition raced down her spine.

She'd opened her mouth to call a warning to Evan when the back door burst open, the wood around the slide lock splintering. Isla screamed. A barrel-chested man in dress pants and a high-end windbreaker strode boldly in, and she stumbled backward, putting as much distance as she could between herself and the intruder. She'd never met Gene Gibbs, but she knew instantly that's who he was. The tall and beefy man with a crew cut that marched in behind him, a handgun at the ready, she assumed to be Leon.

"Hello, Isla," Gibbs said, his thin lips curved in a smugly satisfied grin. "And how are you and my grandchild?"

She quaked from the inside out, and her voice stuck in her throat. Shaking her head and holding her palm toward him, she eased backward. "D-don't— Get o-out!"

"But we just got here." Gibbs advanced on her slowly, his eyes narrowed and disturbingly intense.

When she ran up against the counter, she began inching sideways. Her instinct screamed for her to flee, but Gibbs was between her and the door to the hall, the back room where Evan and Tracy were. Tracy, who was as helpless as a newborn, an obvious pawn for the horrible man to manipulate Evan. And herself, she realized. Because Isla had come to love Tracy as well. The warm and wise woman had so quickly become a second mother to her, and Isla knew she had to do everything she could to protect Tracy.

Keep Gibbs occupied. He's here for you, for the control of the baby. Use that to protect Evan and Tracy.

"I know why you're here. I...I—" she rasped.

He chuckled mildly. "Of course you do. I'd think that was patently obvious." He glanced over his shoulder to Leon, and with a hitch of his head toward the butcher block of knives on the counter, Gibbs growled, "Get rid of those, then search the house."

Isla's blood chilled. If Gibbs was getting rid of potential defensive weapons, he had violence planned for Evan, Tracy and her. Within seconds, Leon was back from chucking the knives outside and strode toward the hall door with purpose.

At that moment, Evan appeared from the back, wielding a baseball bat like a cudgel. Rage stained his cheeks red, and through gritted teeth, he snarled, "Get the hell away from her!"

Gibbs faced Evan now and gave an irritated scoff. "How cute. Look, Leon. He thinks he can stop a bullet with that bat."

The man's expression darkened, and like an icy wind sweeping through the room, Isla felt his evil intent wash through her, chilling her to her marrow. "Evan, no! Run!"

When Leon aimed the gun at Evan, Isla spent no

time analyzing or planning. She just…acted. Grabbing the closest thing to her hand, she flung Tracy's ceramic tea mug at Leon's head. Hit him. Next, in rapid fire, she lobbed the sugar bowl. The bottle of dish soap.

Leon swung a scowl toward her, shifting the gun her direction. "Cut it out!"

The distraction proved enough to give Evan a split second to lunge forward and swing the bat in a downward arc at Leon. The thug dodged, receiving only a glancing blow.

Terror froze Isla lungs, her breath stuck in her chest as she watched Leon turn the weapon on Evan again. Evan shoved Leon's gun hand up, just as the thug fired. Plaster rained down from the ceiling as the two men grappled for control of the gun, the bat.

Help him! her brain screamed. Jolted into action again, she scrambled for more ammunition. She opened the cabinet beside her and snatched out a soup can. Flung it with all her strength, beaning the muscled man in the head.

Squaring his shoulders, Gibbs moved toward her, his teeth bared. "Stop it!"

She grabbed another can—and another—which she fired at Gibbs, then at Leon, until her supply of missiles was depleted. As she scuttled to the next cabinet and flung it open, Gibbs surged forward and seized her wrist. As she twisted and fought to free herself from his grip, he snaked an arm around her waist and hauled her against his thick chest and rounded belly. She immediately recognized the hard lump against her shoulder blade as another weapon, likely another handgun, hidden beneath Gibbs's jacket.

His breath was hot in her ear as he hissed, "Don't make

me hurt you—" then pitching his voice lower "—not before I get what I came for, anyway."

And then something clicked. Maybe it was being pressed roughly against Gibbs, his nose and glare inches from her face. Maybe it was just the truth behind his warning. Or maybe it was some manifestation of her special sense. But she knew. If Gibbs needed her alive, needed the baby unharmed for his twisted scheme, she was Evan and Tracy's best chance to survive. If she could get free from Gibbs—

"Gene, no!" Tracy's voice, with surprising force, sounded from the other side of the room.

Isla felt the ripple of recognition and surprise that flowed through Gibbs in counterpoint to her own dread. He turned, yanking Isla with him as he faced his former lover. A grunt vibrated in his chest before he said, "Hello, Tracy. Damn! You look like hell."

Clinging to the doorframe for support, Tracy hiked her chin up. "And you belong in hell. Why are you doing this to us? What happened to you?"

The distraction of his mother's arrival meant Evan lost ground in his hand-to-hand battle with Leon. With Leon's muscled arm around his throat from behind, Evan shot his mother an anxious glance. "Mom…go!" he croaked from the choke hold.

Gibbs chuffed a laugh. "Blame your son, Tracy. He came looking for me. Not the other way around."

"Obviously." Tracy's eyes lit with fury. "Since you abandoned your family and never looked back, like the selfish pig you are."

Gibbs's grip on Isla tightened, a sure sign Tracy's comment had struck a nerve. "I never signed up for a kid or commitment. You knew that." He shifted his posture, throwing Isla off balance. She stumbled and had to grab her captor's arm to stay upright, as he said, "I don't do family. Never have, never will."

From her peripheral vision, she saw Leon snap a sharp look at Gibbs, his thin lips frowning. She turned and focused on Leon, studying him closer, and Tracy's reply, another gasping warning from Evan both became muffled background noise.

Thin lips...thick chest...

A tingle of intuition nipped at her nape, but a louder voice, the one rooted in the danger surrounding her, shouted, *Now!*

Seizing the disruption of Tracy's arrival, Isla raised one foot and, just as her brother had taught her, slammed it backward into Gibbs's kneecap as hard as she could. As he reacted to that painful surprise, she went limp, making herself a deadweight in the man's arms. Gibbs lost his grasp on her, as she'd hoped, and she scuttled on her hands and knees in a modified crawl out of his reach. Yanking the legs of one kitchen chair, she toppled the chair into his path.

Isla heard commotion as she scrambled to her feet and darted toward the hall door. As she reached Tracy, Isla positioned herself squarely between Evan's mother and the twin threats in the kitchen. Arms splayed to make herself as big of a shield as possible, she surveyed the new dynamic. Evan had managed to wrest free of Leon's suffocating arm and once again had the thug's arm and weapon shoved toward the ceiling.

"I called 9-1-1 before I came out," Tracy whispered to Isla. Evan's mother moved her grip from the doorframe to Isla's arm. "If we can just stall until they arrive..."

Isla angled her head to answer Tracy, to tell the woman to hide herself, to flee the danger. But another gunshot reverberated in the tiny kitchen. Tracy's gasp of horror echoed in Isla's ears as she pivoted, checking on Evan. Instead of Evan, Leon clutched his arm, glaring coldly at Gibbs. "You hit me, you son of a bitch!"

"You got in the way." Gibbs still held his gun aimed at Evan, and as the older man squeezed the trigger again, both Leon and Evan dived for the floor.

Leon spared Gibbs an annoyed look, and Evan used that brief moment to attack Leon from behind, using his full weight to hold Leon down. Gibbs strolled closer to the grappling men and picked up the baseball bat. Isla had taken two steps forward, determined to block any blows Gibbs intended to land with the club, when he opened the back door and flung the bat outside. Again eliminating potential defensive weapons. She swallowed hard and backed up to Tracy again, knowing things could get ugly—uglier—quickly.

"You need to go to the back room, Tracy. Stay safe," Isla said, giving Evan's mother only a fleeting glance while she monitored the quickly evolving situation with the men.

But Evan's mother shook her head. "I'm probably the only one here who can negotiate with Gene." Her grip tightened on Isla's elbow. "You get safe. Protect yourself and my grandbaby. Please!"

"The baby is the reason he won't hurt me. He needs the baby as his bargaining chip with my family, and therefore, he needs me unharmed as well."

Tracy's gaze shifted, filling with fear, just before Gibbs seized Isla's other arm and spun her around. But rather than Isla, Gibbs's target turned out to be Tracy. He jerked Isla out of his way and pressed his gun to Tracy's temple. "It appears killing you now would be a mercy. Save you the final weeks of suffering from your…*disease*." He said the word with a sneer, and his haughty disdain fueled Isla's ire.

Isla forced her way between Gibbs's weapon and the frail woman, puffing her chest in anger and defiance. "Stay away from her, you bastard! She has nothing to do with your fight with me and my family. Let her walk away from this. Please!"

Gibbs grinned, clearly satisfied by something in her argument. "Oh, but she does have a part to play, Isla dear, because clearly you care for her more than I expected and wouldn't want to see her in agony."

Isla's pulse hammered so hard she could feel the pulse throughout her body, heard it thudding in her ears. The grunts of Evan and Leon still wrestling for the upper hand and control of the gun faded in the background as Gibbs reached for his inside jacket pocket and pulled out several folded papers. He flashed a legal document in front of her. "You can make all of this go away, and I'll spare Tracy and your boyfriend…if you sign this."

Chapter 22

Isla didn't need to see the contents of the document. "No."

"But you haven't even read it yet. The terms are very generous. I assume full custody of your baby, my grandchild, along with your inherited share of Cameron Glen, and in exchange, I let these two live," he said, his reasonable tone in direct conflict with the highly unreasonable terms he laid out. "You will have visitation rights with the baby, of course."

If the situation weren't so dire, she'd have laughed in his face. "Not a chance. You will *never* have custody of my child or ownership of even one square inch of Cameron Glen."

Evan gave a grunt of pain, and she cut a side-glance toward him. Her heart wrenched, seeing Evan now below Leon, his arm twisted in at an awkward angle. Leon bent low to growl something into Evan's ear before pressing the handgun to the back of Evan's head.

"Leon!" Gibbs barked. "Hold your fire."

The beefy man gave Gibbs a puzzled look. "What?"

"Ms. Cameron is being as stubborn as her father. So we'll move to plan B." He unfolded a different set of folded papers. "Bring him to the table." Gibbs nodded toward Evan.

A prickle of premonition and alarm chased through Isla.

"Isla, don't sign anything!" Evan said, his voice strangled.

"Gene, please listen to me." Tracy held a hand out in a beseeching manner, and Isla's heart broke for the woman, whose feeling of betrayal by someone she'd once cared for enough to have a child with them was a palpable sting in Isla's heart as well. She'd experienced that feeling with Evan just a few weeks earlier. But the difference between Evan and his father, Isla saw in the starkest clarity now, was that Evan was doing everything he could, moving mountains, risking his life to make amends for his mistake and to take care of her and their baby. The love that surged through her in the wake of this perspicuity brought tears to Isla's eyes. She *loved* Evan. Deeply. This rush of pure emotion, on top of the assault of so many other feelings she was soaking up from the other players in this standoff, was making her dizzy, making her head throb. She struggled to clear her brain and focus her resources on navigating this horrid situation.

"For the sake of what we once had," Tracy said, "put the guns away and let's talk about this ra—"

Gibbs shoved Tracy, cutting her off midword.

Isla gasped in horror at the same time Evan snarled, "You son of a bitch! Don't touch her!"

Ignoring them both, Gibbs sneered at Tracy as he

leaned closer to his ex. "Anything you think we had was all in your imagination, Tracy. And I won't have you interfering with this matter again."

Shaking off her shock at Gibbs's treatment of a sick woman, Isla tried to push past the older man to comfort and protect Tracy from further abuse. Her attempt was met with an impeding arm and a shove that sent her stumbling. She saved herself from a fall only by catching hold of the table's edge.

"What persuasion are you talking about, Gene? Please don't hurt Isla or Evan!" Tracy begged.

Gene cut a glance at Leon. "How many bullets do we have between us?"

Leon arched an eyebrow, replying, "Enough to turn the three of them into Swiss cheese, one nonlethal hole at a time."

Gibbs scowled at Leon, snarling, "Are you a complete moron? Didn't I tell you my grandchild is not to be endangered? That baby being born is my legal tie to her family and is more valuable to me than these two." He waved his gun from Evan to Tracy. Then, his voice dropping in timbre, he added, "Or *you*, for that matter. Don't screw this up, bonehead."

Isla bristled at Gibbs's vicious words for Leon, before puzzling over her strange reaction. The hate and rage that filled her were wholly uncharacteristic of her and felt like poison in her soul. She was still shuddering and sick with the vitriol when she saw Leon's face and realized she was absorbing the fury and disgust rolling like heat waves from Gibbs's thug.

Leon hated Gibbs? That was part of it but not the whole picture. She sensed something else there, too, but didn't have time to process that or weed out Leon's feelings from the thick stew of other emotions in the room, because the dynamic was still changing.

"But so Ms. Cameron doesn't get any ideas of being immune in this situation…" Gibbs grabbed her hand so fast she had no time to react before he twisted her pinky back until it snapped.

Isla screamed in agony and crumpled on the floor cradling her hand to her chest.

Through the fog of her pain, she heard Tracy's gasp of horror, Evan's angry shouts. Isla fought waves of nausea as her finger throbbed and her head spun. She refused to pass out, had to stay cognizant of the changing dynamic.

Gibbs seized her arm and hoisted her from the floor, slamming her into a chair opposite the one where Leon had put Evan. The older man then rounded the table to loom over Evan. He slapped a paper in front of him. "Your turn to play."

He unfolded the last set of papers in his hand, and shoved them close to Evan's nose. "Look familiar? This is the agreement you signed…*and broke* a few weeks ago. The one that says you still owe me the fifty thousand dollars I advanced you." He nodded to Leon, and with the butt of his gun, Leon dealt Evan a blow to the back of his head that made Evan's eyes roll back. Evan blinked hard, staying conscious, but Leon was able to wrest Evan's hand onto the table and pin it there. Ready and vulnerable to a new form of attack.

"Evan!" Tracy sobbed.

"Please don't hurt him," Isla pleaded, her head spinning as Tracy's panic, her pain and Evan's bombarded her like physical blows. She tried to filter out the cascade of outside emotions pelting her in order to think, plan, respond. Could she sign the damn document in order to save Evan and Tracy? She swallowed hard as bile rose in her throat.

"Debt paid," Gibbs told Evan as he ripped the document in three pieces and let it litter the floor.

The same surprise that spun through Isla flashed on Evan's face. "I don't understand."

Gibbs slid the other pages toward him. "I have a new offer for you."

An oily suspicion puddled in Isla's gut, and coupled with searing pain in her broken finger, she had to swallow several times to keep from vomiting. Where were the police Tracy had called? *Please hurry!*

"*This* reframes our previous deal." Gibbs tapped the paper in front of Evan, then braced his arms on the table as he glowered. "It claims you as my son and offers you the full amount of cash you requested before, to get Tracy her medical treatments. No repayment required."

Evan's chin jerked up, his expression both shocked and hopeful. But what was more curious to Isla was the dark frown, the—was it jealousy?—that furrowed Leon's stern face. The thug's feet shifted, and as his jaw tightened, he narrowed a suspicious look on Gibbs.

"In exchange, you grant me what Ms. Cameron so unwisely refused—full custody of your child, effective immediately. As the baby's father, you should have as much say in the child's future as the mother. Don't you agree?"

Evan told Gibbs in bitter terms what he thought of Gibbs's proposal, adding, "You're asking me to sell you my baby. That's insulting!"

"Is it?" Gibbs blinked innocently. "But you haven't heard the best part. If you *don't* sign, right here, right now, your mother will die." He gave Tracy a sneering look. "And not the slow painful death of disease, but with a bullet to her head."

The room seemed to spin, and Isla caught the edge of the table. She saw the desperate look Evan shot his mother and moaned. She had to signal Evan somehow, tell him to just hold out a little longer, to stall, and the police would arrive. *Please, God, let the police get here soon!*

"Your choice." Gibbs straightened, spreading his hands as if making a reasonable offer. He placed a pen in front of Evan. "Free money to save your mother or she dies now. The choice seems rather clear."

Evan put his hand on the pen, and Isla's blood ran cold.

"Evan, no! He's talking about stealing our baby!" Gibbs backhanded her, and she tasted blood but persisted. "Don't sign it. There's got to be another way!"

"Evan darling," Tracy said, tears falling freely, "If I die, so be it. But you can't let him have your child!"

Gibbs turned an angry glare on Tracy. "Stay out of this!" Then turning back to Evan, he said, "Isla has nine more fingers if you need more convincing."

Evan shuddered and curled his fingers around the pen. He met Isla's eyes with a look that asked for forgiveness.

"Evan, no! Just…give it more thought… Wait!"

Gibbs grabbed her hand and grasped another finger. "Sign it! Now!"

Isla shot Tracy a pleading look, silently begging her to help stall.

"Leon?" Gibbs said, still holding Isla's finger bent back at a threatening angle.

The henchman slammed the butt of his gun into Evan's nose. "Sign it!"

"No!" The anguished mother's love that rang in Tracy's voice as she staggered forward, throwing herself against Leon in an attempt to help Evan, ripped through Isla like jagged glass. Leon shook the frail woman off and knocked her callously to the floor. Pointed his gun at her.

"You ready to sign?" Gibbs's grin gloated as Leon stepped closer to Tracy and pressed the pistol to the frail woman's head.

Isla's mouth dried, and her gut swooped. She couldn't betray her family, couldn't give up her child, couldn't sign anything that would give Gibbs even a toehold in Cameron Glen. But neither could she stand by and let Gibbs torture Evan or kill Tracy. "Wait. If I sign, will you let them go?"

Gibbs released her hand and plucked another pen from his pocket. "Now, this is getting interesting."

Her hand shook as she took the pen. She had no intention of signing, but if she could make Gibbs think she was, could she bluff until the cops got there? "M-maybe we can negotiate?"

Gibbs divided a look between her and Evan. "Son, if she signs first, the money for your mother goes away."

The panicked expression on Evan's face sliced through Isla. "Evan, no! Please trust me!"

Instead, he picked up the pen and scribbled his name at the bottom of the document in front of him.

Her breath froze in her lungs. What had he done? He'd caved to Gibbs, given that monster a legal claim to their baby...for money.

Evan refused to meet her eyes as if knowing he'd betrayed her. Again.

Chapter 23

Evan's nose throbbed, and he could feel the well of blood there. Leon had likely broken it. But a greater pain sliced through Evan's chest, hearing Isla's gasp of dismay replay in his head. He deserved every bit of her ill will.

As he let the pen fall to the table, Isla's whole body seemed to wilt in defeat. Her tears flowed unchecked down her cheeks, and a light seemed to go out inside her. He'd done that to her. He may have saved his mother, but he'd killed Isla's spirit, her love for him.

"Good boy," Gibbs crooned, as he picked the document up from the table, folded it and stuck it in the inside pocket of the jacket he wore.

Evan prayed that with good lawyers, Isla and her family could fight whatever terms had been spelled out in the agreement he'd signed. Courts gave preference to mothers in custody fights, didn't they? The sour bite of guilt—a flavor he'd tasted too much lately—sat on his tongue.

"I gave you what you wanted," Evan said darkly, softly, raising his gaze to Gibbs's. "Now leave."

Gibbs straightened his back and smiled smugly. "Of course. We're finished here." He seized Isla's arm, dragging her to her feet. "But Ms. Cameron is coming with us. We have to ensure she doesn't try to get rid of the baby to spite me."

"What? Hell no! She stays h—" As Evan shoved to his feet, Leon struck him from behind. Evan stumbled, and as he caught his balance, he twisted around to face his attacker.

"Ready for me to plug 'im, boss?" Leon asked, jamming his gun under Evan's chin.

Gibbs shrugged. "Your choice. I have what I want." He patted his chest pocket. "Just make it clean and see that it can't be traced back to me."

"Gene, it's not too late to correct this," his mother said, her voice thick with tears. "Leave Isla with us. Leave us *all* unharmed, and—" she hesitated "—and we'll tell the police I called to stand down."

Gibbs's attention snapped to Tracy, anger boiling in his eyes. "You what?"

Tracy squared her thin shoulders. "Did you really think I'd let you storm into my home and not call the cops?"

Tracy's announcement clearly left Leon feeling antsy as well. Evan saw the debate that played out in the other man's face as he weighed his choices. Covering up a murder took time…

"I warned you long ago not to betray me, Tracy. I warned you what would happen." Gibbs's eyes narrowed. "Leon, I believe my ex took an unfortunate fall when she got out of bed, and she broke her neck. See to that."

"No! Don't touch her!" Fresh adrenaline spiked in Evan's blood, and he grabbed at Leon trying to stop him.

Leon flung Evan off and stalked across the kitchen to the doorway where his mother had crumpled on the floor, her gaze defiant.

"Leon, wait! You don't have to do what he says just because he's your father!" Isla blurted.

Evan glanced at Isla in surprise. What did she know?

Leon stopped and sent Isla a puzzled look before continuing across the kitchen and yanking Tracy up by an arm.

"Deep down, you know he'll never give you what you want. You've tried to make him happy, to make him proud all your life, haven't you? That's why you still do his dirty work for him," Isla said in a rush. "But he doesn't care about you. The way he treats you and insults you is proof of that. He has no respect for you or your relationship to him!"

Gibbs yanked Isla's arm, spinning her around to face him and shouting, "Shut up! Leon is none of your business."

Isla drew back from the hostility towering over her, but continued, "He's using you, Leon. He'll let you go down, take the fall for him, before he—"

Gibbs grabbed her chin, pinching so hard her mouth was forced open, squeezed in his vise grip.

Nudged by fury, Evan took a step toward Gibbs, until Leon swung his gun first toward Evan, then angled it toward Tracy. "Choose wisely, pal. Take another step, and the old lady gets a bullet in her brain."

Evan hesitated.

Please trust me! Isla had begged.

Evan only needed a second to realize he had to have faith in whatever Isla had started. Maybe she was onto something, had sensed something with her special intuition. Raising both hands, Evan said calmly, "If you're his son, too, then we're brothers. I don't know what happened to your mother, how he treated her, but my mother deserves to live. She's good. Kind. Loving. Everything *he* never was for me. And, I'm guessing, never was for you either."

Clearly this approach had caught Leon off guard. He furrowed his brow and glanced once to Gibbs as his expression darkened.

"Don't listen to this crap, you idiot! Kill Evan and the old woman and let's get out of here!" Gibbs roared.

"You've seen how he's treated me," Evan said, ignoring Gibbs's tirade, "how he's had me beaten, how he used me for financial gain, asking me to manipulate Isla, only to twist the existence of his grandchild to make himself more profit."

Flinging Isla away, Gibbs reached again for his handgun and aimed it at Evan. "Shut the hell up!"

When Gibbs fired, the cabinet behind Evan splintered.

"You see?" Evan said quickly, his heart racing as Gibbs stomped closer, knowing the next shot could hit its mark. "He doesn't love me or that grandbaby. Or you." When Leon flinched, Evan pushed further. "Are you even in his will? How has he repaid you for all you've done?"

Leon released Tracy and aimed at Evan with both hands. "Shut the hell up! You don't know nothin' about me!"

"Leon!"

The henchman gave Gibbs a quick glance.

"Why isn't Tracy dead yet? Don't turn soft on me now, just because I didn't play ball with you as a boy." Gibbs's tone was condescending and cruel as he glared at Leon, pivoting his gun toward his henchman. "For God's sake! Finish them off, or I'll shoot you in your tiny balls and let you bleed out!"

Movement called Evan's attention briefly to Isla as she inched toward Gibbs, her intention to stop Gibbs clear.

"Isla, be care—" Evan started as Gibbs swung quickly back toward him, leveled his pistol in Evan's direction and squeezed the trigger.

Evan jerked. But when Gibbs's expression of confusion, then irritation, registered, he exhaled. His father's gun had jammed.

Cursing, Gibbs quickly dropped the magazine and racked the slide several times, working to clear the problem.

Isla sidled between Leon's gun and Evan, and Evan's heart stilled. "Isla, no…"

"Search your heart, Leon. You know the truth," she said. "I saw your hurt, felt your hatred for how Gibbs belittles you. You owe him nothing!"

A distant wail of sirens wafted in through the still-open back door. Growling his frustration, Gibbs shoved his magazine back in place and racked his pistol again. "What are you waiting for, you dumb bastard? Kill them!"

"If we're dispensable to him," Evan shouted in a rush, trying to pull Isla behind him, "then you know you are too. He only thinks of himself!"

The next few seconds were elastic. Terrifying. Confusing.

Gibbs raised his pistol.

Isla shoved Evan aside, yelling, "No!"

Twin gun blasts ricocheted in the small kitchen.

His mother's scream echoed in Evan's ears.

As Evan stumbled from Isla's shove, he grabbed her arm, pulling her down with him. He landed on the floor, and the wind whooshed from his lungs. As he rolled to his back, scanning the room to assess the threat, Gibbs roared in pain.

Clutching his bleeding arm, Gibbs snarled at Leon. "You worthless idiot! You hit me!"

Leon sneered. "You got in the way."

With a feral rage contorting his face, Gibbs aimed his gun at Leon.

But Leon was faster. He fired once, killing Gibbs with a bullet in his forehead.

Beside Evan, Isla gasped.

As Gibbs crumpled, Leon blinked as if waking from a trance and frowned at his boss's body, sprawled on the floor.

Tracy moaned and began sobbing, and Isla crawled to her, wrapping Evan's mother in a comforting embrace.

When Leon shifted his dark glare to Evan, the henchman's gun arm dropped to his side as he seemed to process the turn of events. Then, as if sobering, he took aim again at Evan. "How did you know all that about me?"

"He didn't," Isla said. "I did. And I knew you deserved better than the father life gave you."

The sirens wailed louder, and Leon yanked his gaze to the back door. Then, with a panicked glance toward Gibbs, he wiped his gun with his shirt and crouched to shove the gun in Evan's hand. "I was never here."

Then Leon bolted out the door, and the kitchen fell silent.

* * *

The hour grew late before the police finished interviewing them all, forensics completed their evidence collection, and all three of them received appropriate medical care at the emergency room. Isla's finger had been dislocated, not broken. Evan had a broken nose and more contusions. Tracy had some bruising and elevated blood pressure. But they were alive, and Evan was deeply thankful for that mercy.

Through it all, Isla had been solicitous toward Tracy's every need, but concerningly distant with him. Evan knew it had to do with his signing the damn papers Gibbs had shoved in front of him. He'd tried to explain his choice, but something always seemed to interrupt them. News from a police officer that Leon had been arrested a few blocks from the Murrays' house, the arrival of the ambulance, questions from the responding officers. He'd tried to rip up the document he'd signed, but the lead forensic investigator had stopped him. The blood-splattered documents were evidence.

A longtime neighbor of the Murrays had offered them a guest room until the grisly scene in the kitchen could be cleaned and repaired. Isla had chosen to go to a motel, taking Jack, whom she'd found hiding under Tracy's bed after the commotion had died down. When Evan had offered to stay with her, she'd sent him away. "Be with your mother. I'll be fine."

What she'd been, the next morning when he went to the hotel to talk to her, was gone.

He had no way to call her, since she had no cell phone. He had the burner they'd bought. But at least he knew where she was headed. Home. North Carolina. Cameron Glen.

He reconciled himself to waiting until she'd gotten

back to her house and her cell phone before calling her. He told himself her leaving made sense. After the traumatic events they'd experienced, of course she wanted to be surrounded by her loved ones, what was familiar, what she cherished. He just wished he could be sure he was still on her cherished list—or if he'd ever been.

He had his answer all too soon. Two days after leaving Seattle, Isla was home. She and Jack had flown home with an airline ticket her parents purchased online for her.

"I'm guessing by the way you left town without saying anything that you're mad at me," he said when he finally reached her. "Because I signed Gibbs's offer."

He heard a hum of agreement. "Not so much mad as…deeply disappointed. And resigned."

"Resigned how?"

"I thought we'd put the issue of trust behind us, but when you chose Gibbs's money over trusting me—"

"No! It's not like that!"

"Isn't it, Evan?"

"I—"

"Be honest with yourself if not with me. You had your hand on that pen, thinking about signing from the minute he offered unconditional money for your mother's treatments. Even before you heard the catch."

His heart tripped, remembering how hope had leaped in his chest when Gibbs dangled that damn money as bait.

"And it was a big catch," Isla continued. "Our baby. You sold that horrid man custody rights to our baby, and nothing you can say now will ever change that for me. I'm finished with you, Evan. Don't call again."

Her tone was heartbreaking, largely because it was so resolved.

"Isla, wait. You can't just write me off. We're having a baby together. What about—"

"My lawyer will be in touch." And the line had gone silent.

Seven months after her return from Seattle, Isla found Gene Gibbs's lawyer standing on her front porch when she returned from a prenatal checkup. She flashed back to the day in October when the attorney had approached her in her backyard and later pressured her parents to sell Cameron Glen.

Her stomach roiled, and as she lumbered awkwardly with her rounded belly toward the house, she called out, "Cameron Glen is still not for sale. You can leave now, Mr. Mellinger."

Ignoring her request, he produced a folded sheaf of papers and held them out toward her. "I think you'll want to hear what I came to say."

"Unlikely." She folded her arms over her chest.

"Do you remember Evan Murray signing a document shortly before his father, Gene Gibbs's—" he paused, waggling a hand as if searching for a word "—*demise.*"

Ice sluiced through her. Surely the horrid agreement that Evan had signed couldn't be valid. She took a step back as if the papers were a snake that could bite her.

Since returning to Cameron Glen, she had thrown herself into anything that could help distract her from the pain of Evan's choice. He'd demonstrated his lack of faith in her, had broken his promise to keep their child away from Gibbs, had shown where his heart truly lay. Not with her. Not with the baby's best interests. Not with protecting Cameron Glen.

Now everything she'd been trying to forget rushed

forward again. "I—I do, but…you can't mean to try to enforce— Gibbs is dead!"

"Be that as it may, Evan Murray did sign it. The probate courts have decided it is legally binding."

"This is a nightmare," she rasped, her knees buckling. She sank onto a porch step, trying not to panic.

"Have you read the document?" Mellinger asked.

She gave him a dirty look. "There was hardly time. Gibbs wasn't in a patient mood that night, and then the police took the signed copy as evidence." Something in the lawyer's expression stopped her, made her heart clench. "Wait. Why? What does it say? He told us it gave him custody of my baby, but if he's dead he can't—"

Mellinger raised a hand, a wry, lopsided smile tugging his lips. "That's the crux of the agreement, yes. But in drafting the agreement for Mr. Gibbs, I included language that Gibbs either overlooked or gave no significance. Language that has a great deal of significance in light of his death."

Isla's mouth dried. "Meaning?"

Mellinger came down the steps toward her, again offering the document to her. "Gibbs had no will, despite my encouragement for him to have one. He saw no reason, since he had never acknowledged any heirs."

"But Leon—"

"Yes, and Gibbs dangled that fruit in front of Leon his whole life. That poor boy chased acceptance and acknowledgment for years."

Despite the cruel thug's treatment of Evan, her heart broke for him.

"So, with his death, Gene's estate went to probate court, and I presented this proof—" he flapped the proffered document again "—that Gene acknowledged Evan and Evan's child with you as blood relatives."

Isla's pulse slowed as she played the scenario forward. "Are you saying—"

"I presented this information to Evan Murray last week, and he refused the inheritance. He's signed it all over to your child for the baby's care and future needs."

Even though she was sitting, Isla grabbed the stair railing to steady herself as the world tipped dizzily. "I don't…understand. Evan—"

"Passed on eleven million dollars so that your baby will be provided for."

Isla blinked, numb with shock. "B-but I don't want Gibbs's money. It's ill-gotten. Tainted."

"Oh, the illegally obtained funds have already been reclaimed by the authorities. What's left is clean."

He motioned to the space next to her on the step. "May I sit with you? I can explain all the particulars."

She nodded absently. Her thoughts were on the West Coast. With Evan. With Tracy. Did Evan's refusal of the money mean his mother had died and the money was no longer needed for her treatments? The last update she'd had on Tracy had been a couple months ago when she'd sent Evan sonogram images and a pregnancy update. Had his mother taken a turn for the worse?

"—and I inserted language here to cover the fiduciary responsibility—" Mellinger fell silent when Isla grasped his arm. "Ms. Cameron, are you all right?"

"When you saw Evan last week, when he signed away the money—" she drilled a hard look on the lawyer, her grip tightening "—did he mention his mother? Is she…? How is…?"

The man's face fell. "Ms. Murray was in a back bedroom during our meeting. She's quite ill, I'm afraid."

"I—I know." Isla swallowed hard, both relieved Tracy was alive and confused by Evan's decision. "Then why didn't Evan keep the money from Gibbs for her medical treatments?"

Mr. Mellinger lifted one shoulder. "I don't know. You'll have to ask him that question."

Isla exhaled a slow breath then hoisted herself to her feet. "I intend to."

On a rainy day in May, Evan had his mind on his mother's most recent MRI results—no tumor growth, but no improvement after the last round of chemotherapy either—as he arrived from work to the tiny apartment he shared with his mother. He'd found the new job in Seattle—one not exactly in his field of expertise but which paid some bills—and had sold his mother's house in a last-ditch effort to pay medical expenses. He refused to give up hope of getting her back in the medical trial, but hadn't figured out how...yet.

His head was down, his view hindered by his umbrella, as he approached the front door of the apartment, when he heard a familiar voice say, "Hello, Evan. Can we talk?"

He snapped his attention to Isla's face, and he almost dropped the stack of files he'd brought home from the office—paper copies since he and his mother couldn't afford Wi-Fi. "Isla!"

His gaze dropped to her round belly—his baby, their baby—and his heart swelled. Though she'd kept him apprised of her condition, the baby's health and progress toward her due date, the emails, received at his office, had been short and all business.

"You sold your mother's house." A statement, delivered in sympathetic tones. "I'm sorry."

He shrugged, pretending it didn't matter. "We needed the funds more than we needed sentimentality."

The look she gave him said she saw through his response, understood the difficulty of letting his childhood home and refuge leave the family. Of course she understood. Her family had fought hard to protect their home from Gibbs.

"I— Come in. Get out of this weather. My mom will be so glad to see you!"

"And you?" she asked.

He stilled. She had to ask? "Of course. I—" A flash of lightning and crack of thunder interrupted and hurried them inside.

Once their umbrellas were put away and coats hung up to dry out, he showed her to the living room. She refused his offer of a warm drink.

"Mom is probably asleep. She...naps a lot these days. I—" He paused, seeing the grief that crossed her face at the mention of his mother's fading condition. Clearing his throat, he added, "I'll just check on her, then..."

He slipped quietly to his mother's room, found her asleep and closed her door before returning to the front of the apartment where Isla waited. He took the chair across from her, venturing, "I'm guessing this visit means you've heard from Gibbs's lawyer."

She bobbed her head once in affirmation. "Why did you refuse the money? It could have paid for Tracy's treatments."

He slumped back in his chair and rubbed a hand on his rain-dampened face. "Couple reasons. I've promised you and our child that I would take care of you. That inheritance was my best chance to do that."

Isla scooted to the edge of the couch, leaning toward him. "But Tracy needs the money now for treatments!"

"She hated the idea of using Gibbs's money for her expenses as much as I did. My foolish fixation on getting Gibbs's money for her care is what hurt you. I put you in danger. I broke faith with you. I made so many mistakes because my vision was skewed by the dim hope of saving my mom." He sat forward, spreading both hands in appeal. "I know you've heard me say it too many times, but I am sorry."

"Dim hope? I thought you said that for the brief time Tracy was taking the experimental medicine, she was improving."

He nodded. "She was."

"So there was *real* hope." The hope she spoke of glimmered in her eyes, as well, and Evan's heart tugged. After everything he'd put her through, Isla still cared about his mother. "Evan, why did you sign that contract when Gibbs—" Her voice broke, and she fell silent.

He exhaled, glancing away when guilt pinged through him. "I shouldn't have. I should have trusted you. But I thought—"

She said nothing, waiting for him to finish. He got up to pace, knowing he owed her an explanation. "A couple of reasons. I know it looked like I did it for the money, but that's not true. When you asked about negotiating with Gibbs, when it looked like it had become a case of who'd break first to save the other from torture…" He faced her, met her blue gaze. "I signed so you wouldn't have to. I knew how guilty you'd feel, how it would tear you apart, how you'd feel you'd betrayed your family. I couldn't let you suffer through that, even if it looked like I'd been swayed by his money."

She drew a shaky breath, tears pooling in her eyes. "Evan…"

"But I should have trusted you when you asked me to.

I didn't know Mom had called the police, and I should have realized…"

She ducked her head, then bent awkwardly to dig in her purse to extract a thick envelope. "Here." She handed him the packet without saying more, and he knitted his brow in query. "What's this?"

"You'll see. Open it."

He slid his finger under the flap, tearing the envelope open, while a variety of possibilities whizzed through his brain. Was she suing him for full custody of their child after everything that had happened? Serving him with a restraining order? His pulse thumped a little harder as those possibilities, as unimaginable and painful as they were to consider, presented themselves. Taking a deep breath, he removed the paper inside and unfolded it.

The first thing that caught his attention, before reading the hand written letter, was the banker's check, made out to him, for exactly the amount of money he'd told her his mother's medical-trial expenses were predicted to be. He stared numbly at the multiple zeros in the sum. Blinked. Held the check closer to make sure his vision wasn't blurring or causing him to see double.

Raising his stupefied gaze to Isla, he shook his head. "I don't understand. Gibbs's estate was supposed to be held in trust for our baby's care. That's how his lawyer and I arranged it."

She nodded. "I know. It is."

"Then how— Where did you get this much money?" She opened her mouth to speak, and he stopped her. "Never mind that, it's—" He shoved the check toward her. "I can't take this."

Isla frowned. "Of course you can. And you will! Your mother needs to be in that medical trial!"

"Isla, I…" Gratitude tightened his vocal cords, and he had to pause and clear his throat before he could speak again. "*Thank you.* Truly, but…" He tried again to hand the envelope back to her. "I can't. It's way too much to ask of you. I could never repay—"

"No repayment necessary." She struggled to her feet and wrapped both of her hands around his, pushing the check back toward him. "Take it."

He eyed her, still dubious about accepting the money. "Where did this come from?"

She hooked her arms around his waist, their baby nestled between them as she leaned back a bit to gaze up at him. "I sold most of my share of Cameron Glen."

He jolted. Stared at her, not believing his ears. Replayed her words as if he'd missed something. "Um. What?"

A smile like sunshine lit her face. "Well, the whole family was involved, really. The business with Gibbs motivated my dad to do some creative accounting and real estate deals. All legal, I promise."

Evan narrowed a curious look on her as he led her back to the couch to sit. "Go on."

"Well, he started by dividing the property up into tracts, like a checkerboard. He then sold each of his five kids, for the bargain price of one dollar each, one eighth of the plots in random order, keeping one eighth each for himself and Mom and one eighth in Nanna's name. This way, with each family member's holdings being scattershot blocks of land across the property, a developer would have to convince all of the family to sell in order to obtain a tract large enough to build anything."

Evan dragged a hand down his cheek and chuckled. "Brilliant."

"Then each of my siblings sold me a small fraction

of their holdings for a dollar, so that I owned closer to one fifth of the property," she continued. "Which I then sold partly to Anya's parents and partly to Matt's ex-wife, Jessica, keeping just a small chunk of land, where my goat pen is, for myself, so I still have a stake in the land."

Evan released her, dumbstruck. "Hang on. So…you really sold your share? Outside the family?"

"Most of my shares, yes. But Anya's parents and Jessica are extended family. And we trust them completely not to do anything foolish with their shares. They'll pass their shares back to any children Anya and Brody have and to Matt's children, respectively, down the road. The family heritage will continue in exchange for a share as co-owners of the rental income and Christmas tree sales."

"But…why would you give up so much of something you love so deeply?" he asked, stunned by her generosity.

"A couple of reasons," she said, echoing the preamble to his earlier explanation. She scooted closer to him on the couch and flattened her hands against his chest. "First, because I want our child to have his paternal grandmother around to love and dote on her for many, many years to come."

Evan's heart squeezed painfully, touched to the core by the sentiment.

"And second—" she leaned in to give him a soft kiss "—because, as much as I love Cameron Glen, I love you more. Call it a wedding gift from me to you."

His eyes widened, and adrenaline shot electricity through him. "What?"

"If you'll still have me?"

"Of course! Yes!" He laughed with joy and relief,

even as tears filled his eyes. He swept her into a hug, her round pregnancy-belly keeping him from crushing her as close as he wanted. "I... Oh my God, Isla. Of course!" He kissed her long and hard and only raised his head when he needed air. "You have made me the happiest man in the world. I love you, Isla Cameron. So much."

She tipped her head to one side and tugged her lips into an impish grin. "I know."

Epilogue

Fourteen months later

"**H**appy birthday to youuu!" the Cameron clan finished singing to the two youngest members of the family.

Nanna, seated across from the babies, added, *"Co-la-breith sona, m'eudail!"* To each of her great-grandchildren.

"Wait! Get a picture of the cakes before they destroy them!" Cait shouted to her husband as two identical mess cakes were placed in front of the cousins celebrating their shared first birthdays.

A year earlier, on a hectic and joyful July afternoon, both Cait and Isla had given birth to daughters. The girls, Erin Grace Harkney and Tracy Flora Murray, were more like fraternal twins than cousins, preferring each other's company to that of any of the numerous doting adults in their lives.

"Got it!" Evan called as he snapped a photo of the

small birthday cakes his mother-in-law slid onto her granddaughters' high chairs.

Erin and CeeCee, as baby Tracy was often called, gave their respective cakes puzzled looks before Erin face-planted in hers for a taste. Seeing her cousin's wide grin, CeeCee scooped a handful of her cake and offered it to Erin. "Mo'?"

"You try it, darling," CeeCee's namesake said, guiding her granddaughter's messy hand to her mouth. After tasting the cake, CeeCee's eyes lit, and with an excited squeal, she face-planted in her cake as well.

Isla groaned, even as she laughed. "Oh well. There go my hopes of convincing our daughter refined sugar is not all it's cracked up to be."

"Everything in moderation," Tracy said diplomatically, and Isla noted the shine of pride and love that glowed in her mother-in-law's eyes as she gazed at her first grandchild.

Having been allowed back in the medical trial, based on the progress she'd shown before, even with limited treatment, Tracy's health had improved enough for her to travel to North Carolina for the joint birthday celebration. Her tumor was not gone, but she'd made significant strides toward recovery. Her blood work had improved, her appetite was back, and she grew stronger every day. Her doctors were amazed and, based on the dramatic remission of other patients in the trial, they were optimistic Tracy, too, would fully recover in time.

"Can we cut the big cake now?" Daryl asked. "I'm starved."

"You just ate one of Mom's huge lunch spreads! How can you be hungry?" Emma asked.

Daryl, who topped six feet two inches now, shrugged. "I'm still growing."

"You should see him after football practice," Grace added. "It's unreal how much that young man can eat!"

"I remember those days," Matt said, giving his grown son, Eric, a nudge.

"Still there," Eric muttered, swiping a finger through his half sister's mess cake and licking it from his finger.

Isla sliced the family cake and slapped Daryl's hand away when he reached for the first slice. "Back off. First piece goes to the pregnant lady." She turned and handed the plate to Anya, who was nine months pregnant and due any day.

Anya waved her off with a weak smile as she rubbed her back. "No, thank you. I'm not feeling so well. Let D have it."

Brody squatted next to the chair where his wife sat. "Honey, what's wrong?"

"No need to panic. Just more false labor pains, but I— Ooo." She winced and held her belly, breathing through the contraction. "I'm fine. Eat cake."

"Wouldn't it be funny if Anya had her baby today too?" seven-year-old Lexi chirped. "Then all three babies would have the same birthday!"

Brody laughed awkwardly. "Yeah. What are the odds of that?"

"I can calculate that for you if you want. It's simple math," Daryl said around a large bite of cake.

"Simple for you maybe, Mr. Brainiac," Fenn said.

"Hey, you're smart too," Emma told her daughter. "I mean, who's going to start at Duke next month? Have I told you today how proud I am of you?"

Fenn grinned. "You have. Thanks, Mom."

Isla cut more slices of cake, doling them out to the family while keeping an eye on her daughter's antics.

CeeCee and Erin were now smearing each other with icing and giggling.

"Um, Brody?" Anya said, her tone sounding strange. "I don't think Daryl needs to calculate those odds. I'd say they're good. Real good."

The whole family quieted and looked to Anya, who wore a startled expression.

Brody set his cake aside. "Anya?"

"My water just broke."

Mild chaos ensued as the family hustled Anya to Brody's truck and Fenn raced to Brody's house for Anya's prepacked suitcase.

Cait and Isla exchanged humored looks as most of the family departed for the hospital.

"I guess the party's over," Cait said.

Tracy chuckled as she stroked her granddaughter's hair. "But the fun and memories have just begun."

* * * * *

#2243 CHASING A COLTON KILLER
The Coltons of New York
by Deborah Fletcher Mello
Stella Maxwell is one story away from Pulitzer gold, but when she becomes the prime suspect in the murder of her ex-boyfriend, those aspirations are put on hold. FBI agent Brennan Colton suspects Stella might be guilty of something, but it isn't murder. Between his concern for Stella's well-being and the notorious Landmark Killer taunting them, Brennan never anticipates fighting for his heart.

#2244 MISSING IN TEXAS
by Karen Whiddon
It's been four brutal years for Jake Cassin, who finally locates the daughter who's been missing all that time. But his little girl is abducted before he can even meet her. Despite his reservations and an unwanted stirring of attraction, he must work with Edie Beswick, her adoptive mother, who is just as frantic as he is. How can they stay rational on this desperate search when they have everything to lose?

#2245 A FIREFIGHTER'S HIDDEN TRUTH
Sierra's Web • by Tara Taylor Quinn
When Luke Dennison wakes up in the hospital with amnesia, he doesn't know why a beautiful woman is glaring down at him. He soon learns he is a firefighter, a father and someone wants them both dead. After engaging the experts of Sierra's Web, Luke and Shelby are whisked into protective custody. Could this proximity bring them to a greater understanding of each other...or finally separate them forever?

#2246 TEXAS LAW: SERIAL MANHUNT
Texas Law • by Jennifer D. Bokal
For more than twenty years, Sage Sauter has been keeping a secret—her daughter's biological father is Dr. Michael O'Brien. Michael has never forgotten about his first love, Sage. So when Sage's daughter shows up at his hospital—presumably after being attacked by a serial killer—he offers to help. Sage knows that Michael's the best forensic pathologist around, but she's terrified that he'll discover her secret if he gets involved with a very deadly investigation.

Get 3 FREE REWARDS!

We'll send you 2 FREE Books plus a FREE Mystery Gift.

FREE Value Over **$20**

Both the **Harlequin Intrigue®** and **Harlequin® Romantic Suspense** series feature compelling novels filled with heart-racing action-packed romance that will keep you on the edge of your seat.

YES! Please send me 2 FREE novels from the Harlequin Intrigue or Harlequin Romantic Suspense series and my FREE gift (gift is worth about $10 retail). After receiving them, if I don't wish to receive any more books, I can return the shipping statement marked "cancel." If I don't cancel, I will receive 6 brand-new Harlequin Intrigue Larger-Print books every month and be billed just $6.49 each in the U.S. or $6.99 each in Canada, a savings of at least 13% off the cover price, or 4 brand-new Harlequin Romantic Suspense books every month and be billed just $5.49 each in the U.S. or $6.24 each in Canada, a savings of at least 12% off the cover price. It's quite a bargain! Shipping and handling is just 50¢ per book in the U.S. and $1.25 per book in Canada.* I understand that accepting the 2 free books and gift places me under no obligation to buy anything. I can always return a shipment and cancel at any time by calling the number below. The free books and gift are mine to keep no matter what I decide.

Choose one: ☐ **Harlequin Intrigue Larger-Print** (199/399 BPA GRMX)   ☐ **Harlequin Romantic Suspense** (240/340 BPA GRMX)   ☐ **Or Try Both!** (199/399 & 240/340 BPA GRQD)

Name (please print)

Address _____ Apt. #

City _____ State/Province _____ Zip/Postal Code

Email: Please check this box ☐ if you would like to receive newsletters and promotional emails from Harlequin Enterprises ULC and its affiliates. You can unsubscribe anytime.

Mail to the **Harlequin Reader Service:**
IN U.S.A.: P.O. Box 1341, Buffalo, NY 14240-8531
IN CANADA: P.O. Box 603, Fort Erie, Ontario L2A 5X3

Want to try 2 free books from another series? Call 1-800-873-8635 or visit www.ReaderService.com.

HARLEQUIN
PLUS

Try the best multimedia subscription service for romance readers like you!

Read, Watch and Play.

Experience the easiest way to get the romance content you crave.

Start your **FREE TRIAL** at
<u>www.harlequinplus.com/freetrial</u>.